D0064586

DISCARDED

The discovery of an immortal dog
with miracle healing powers upends the world.

The Dog of Jesus

Michael P. Sakowski

Baltimore Books

Dog of Jesus

The characters and events in this book are fictitious. Any similarity to real persons, living or dead is coincidental and not intended by the author.

ISBN: 978-1-939103-00-0

Printed in Kaohsiung, Taiwan.

FIRST EDITION by Baltimore Books.

Visit us at www.baltimorebooks.us

To God and Pilar, for their inspiration,
And to my mother Rita, whose faith sustained her.

To all those who have lost loved ones needlessly,
And to my wife, who inspired me to finish.

Contents

1 A Miracle 1

2 The Old Sailor's Tale 5

3 Raising the Dead 11

4 A Fiesta 23

5 A Stranger's Body is Found 35

6 Can a Man Stop the Wind? 41

7 Pilar and Alita 45

8 Healing Souls Selling Vegetables 53

9 Time Shapes Everyone's Life 61

10 Santo is Shot!! 73

11 The Tragedy at Chamizal Park 79

12 Mr. Big Takes Notice of Santo 91

13 Jesus is Born Again 97

14 Aunt Maria and a Strange American 103

15 A Miracle at University Hospital! 117

16 The Chosen One Speaks 129

17 The Revolution Begins 135

18 The Purification of Juarez 141

19 The World Comes to Pueblo del Cielo 151

20 The Vatican Takes Notice 169

21 Pilar's First Kiss 183

22 The Spear of Christ is Found 201

23 The Research on Santo Begins 213

24 A Meteor Message From God? 229

25 Science Attempts to Decode Santo 241

26 The Mark of the Three-One God? 249

27 Hell at Hopkins Campus 265

28 The World Seeks Santo 279

29 Santo Returns Home 297

Afterword 323

A Few Notes About Carolina Dogs 325

About the Author 327

Chapter 1

A Miracle

The dust blows dry through Pueblo del Cielo and spits against the white mission walls at the end of its only street. A boy leads a curly-tailed dog by a rope through swirls of dust toward the old two-towered mission. The boy opens the mission door amidst a big blow of wind and the sound of breaking glass is heard from within.

"Jesus," the padre says in the Spanish, "Close the door!"

"Si, Padre." The boy obliges, and stands hat-in-hand, waiting, as the padre picks up the broken glass from a candleholder overturned by the wind. A shard of glass finds its mark and blood spurts from the padre's finger. The boy drops the dog's rope and rushes to help clean up the glass.

"I'm sorry, Father."

"For nothing, Jesus. It's not your fault. The wind is just angry today."

"I think the old sailor is dying, Father." He asked me to come for you. He wants the absolution. He asked me to take his dog away."

"The church is no place for a dog, my son. Especially now, with Rosa being ill here, as you can plainly see." The padre motions with his opened hand and extended arm toward a pew.

Jesus sees a young girl lying on the pew; her mother huddled over her praying. The girl is shaking with fever.

"Father, please," the woman cries, "ask God to spare my Rosa. I'm a sinner, let him take me."

The padre approaches the woman, pats gently on her shoulder and comforts her before turning back to Jesus. "Come. Let us get the dog outside. Where is he?"

They search and find the dog. He has run to the altar and is pointing, his eyes locked on a large crucifix above. The boy grabs the dog's leash and pulls, and the dog sits back on his hindquarters and raises his paws and strokes at the air.

"What is he doing?" asks the padre.

"I don't know," Jesus says quickly with an air of guilt. He pulls the rope leash hard and knocks the dog off balance, but the dog rears back up and assumes the same begging pose.

"Ai-eee," says the padre, making the sign of the cross. "This dog loves the saints."

"Maybe that is why Sailor named him Santo. Sailor said I should keep him and not bring him back. Is it okay to keep him?"

"Yes, my boy, if that is what the sailor wishes."

"FATHER!" the woman screams. "Help!"

The woman's daughter has arched her back and is convulsing. Her eyes are rolled back in her head and only the white shows as she shakes violently.

"PLEASE, GOD, not my Rosa! Don't take my Rosa from me!"

The padre kneels beside the girl and grasps her hands between his and prays.

"Not my Rosa," the woman sobs.

Jesus gravitates toward the convulsing girl, afraid, but simultaneously fascinated by the prospect of seeing death up close. Seconds pass, and the girl suddenly goes limp as all movement ceases.

"No, God, no!" the woman sobs.

The priest takes her hand and molds it with his and the girl's, and continues to pray. The mother's sobs slowly fadc, until all that is heard is the muffled wail of the wind and spitting sand. Suddenly, the padre hears a wet lapping sound and raises his head. The dogging is licking the young girl's face, covering it with slobber. He pushes the dog away.

"Jesus! Take your dog!"

The girl is still, a sleeping angel. Tears streak the priest's face as he gently wipes the dog slobber from her cheek with his handkerchief. The mother whines in stifled agony. The padre checks for a pulse and finds none, then bends over the young girl and places his ear against her chest. He sighs and lifts his head, then gently straightens the girl's curled fingers and folds her arms over her chest in a cross. He crosses himself and whispers a brief prayer before turning back to the mother.

"Her suffering is over now," says the padre, and the woman sobs louder.

The girl's eyes suddenly open.

"Don't cry, Mama. It's alright."

The woman screams and faints. The priest crosses himself again and looks up to heaven. He places his hand on the girl's perspiring brow and feels that the fever is gone. He wipes her dry, and the dog tries to lick her again.

"Jesus, get this dog out of here!" he starts to say angrily, but bursts into tears and laughter. “It’s a miracle! A miracle! Thank you, Lord.” He bends and tries to revive the mother, who is still on the floor.

“What about the old sailor? Can you come see him now?”

“Yes. Yes, Jesus, tell him I am coming and that I will soon be there. Tell him not to die just yet.” The padre laughs through tears as he helps the mother from the floor.

Rosa sits up in the pew and looks around the church, then rises to help her shocked mother. She shows no sign of weakness or ill health. She and the padre seat her mother on the pew and her mother stares at Rosa in disbelief with a face of mixed horror and happiness. Joy finally overcomes all fear and the mother grabs her daughter and hugs her tightly to her chest, weeping.

The padre hugs them both laughing, crying: “Jesucristo! Jesucristo! A miracle!”

Chapter 2

The Old Sailor's Tale

The old sailor lived high on the cliff road outside of the village. It was a humble mud brick home, with carefully managed gardens that made him largely independent of the village. He kept to himself and tended his small area.

The villagers would see him walking the hills or tending his gardens, but like most old men, he was largely invisible and there was not much curiosity about his background. It was said that he came from Spain, and Jesus, the young boy who had come for the priest, was his only apparent local friend.

Never once did he receive a visitor in all the many years in which he had lived there. He did not attend church, but was friendly to all who took occasion to say hello in passing. Neither was there any sign of the cross in his home or on his property. He never swore and consumed no meat, and his sustenance was due to his own gardening efforts.

He sold some vegetables in the town, and they were always delicious. Some even claimed that they had curative powers, having recovered from illnesses shortly after consuming them. The small money he made from his sales efforts allowed him to buy bread and wine from the local merchants, so in this way he was an economic asset to the village.

The young padre walked quickly with Jesus, who had come to meet him, and was throwing a stick for his new pet. While walking, he removed the handkerchief that he had wrapped around his cut hand. To his amazement the cut was gone. No sign whatsoever remained of it. He started to think that perhaps in the excitement of Rosa dying he had imagined it, but the bloodstained handkerchief gave witness to his memory.

He shook his head in disbelief and recalled how Rosa had seemingly come back to life. He had been so sure she was gone. He was young, but as the only priest in the village, he had witnessed several passings already, and he recognized the death rattle, the lifeless eyes, and the final end of all respiration. It was truly a day of miracles. How else could he explain it? The Holy Spirit and miracle of the Christ had descended upon them and blessed all those there.

Was that why the dog, stood up and prayed before the crucifixion? He wondered while he walked.

They were near the sailor's house, and Father Santiago was glad, because his thighs burned from the steep climb up the north road. It was too steep for the old sailor, he thought. Maybe his heart couldn't take it any longer.

Jesus ran ahead and opened the gate for the padre, and stood by it patiently waiting with Santo. The padre smiled at Jesus and walked through the gate and under the trellis of roses beyond it, then paused, admiring the old sailor's gardens. The earth was rich and dark, unlike any near the village. The sailor had carried it by the basketful on his back from the forest on the far side of the mountains. It took him years to acquire it all.

The gardens were very fruitful because of the rich earth and the abundant water supply, which came from a mountain spring in the side of a nearby cliff. The sailor had made his own cement and made a small aqueduct to carry the spring water to his garden where it was gently distributed in just the right trickle to keep the plants perfectly watered automatically. Any vegetable one might imagine could be found there in various quantities throughout the year.

"Very inventive," Santiago said to Jesus, pointing to the aqueduct, and then he turned and gently opened the door to the cottage and they walked inside.

The old sailor lay in bed, his skin dark and leathery, so much so that he appeared more to be made of wood than of flesh and bone. His hair was thick and as white as snow, and his eyes, which opened when he heard the door close, shone a brilliant blue in the sunlight that slanted through the cottage window illuminating his face.

He smiled, and his teeth were white in the sun, unusual for such an old man. Most of the local villagers had poor teeth due to a lack of care and a diet high in carbohydrates. But the old man ate no animals and the many plants he chewed kept his teeth polished and his gums sound.

Suddenly, he saw Jesus and he shouted: "Get out! Jesus, take the dog away. He is your dog now. I gave him to you and you must not bring him here. Take him outside!"

"Jesus, take the dog outside, please," said the padre.

The boy looked sad, but obeyed without question. "I will be outside, if you need me. Goodbye, Sailor."

"Goodbye, Jesus. You have been a good friend, and you are a good boy. I am sorry I scolded you. We will meet in the clouds one day. Farewell."

The door closed behind Jesus and the old sailor turned to the padre and smiled.

"A fine boy. He will live a very long time, but I hope not as long as me." The sailor laughed ruefully. "Do you know where I am from, Father? From Zaragoza...from Spain...a long time ago. Did you know that I once had a young and beautiful wife and three beautiful children? No, of course, you could not know. That was many years ago, and they are all gone."

He looked up at the padre, who had pulled a chair up to the bed, and tears streaked down his leathery face. "You see, I didn't know...I didn't know the secret then. It was later, only later that I found out, and it was too late then.

"Too late," he said sobbing. "Too late to save them. And later, it did not matter. Later, I found the evil that was concealed in the good. I learned my burden and my task, and it has been this way with me all these years. Will you hear my confession?"

"Yes, of course," said Padre Santiago.

"And you must promise, when I tell you," the sailor said, grasping the padre's robe and arm very tightly, "you must promise to protect the boy!"

"Yes, I promise. But protect him from what?"

"I swear by the Virgin, Padre, that what I am about to tell you is all true. I knew the saint you are named after. I knew him long ago, in Zaragoza. I met him in the flesh and spoke with him. I helped build the first chapel to Our Lady there...many, many years ago."

"You mean you dreamed of Saint James? You met him in a dream?"

"No, Padre. I was there. I knew him in real life. It was from him that I got the dog, in the year A.D. 40 of Our Lord. But he didn't know...he only told me how he came to have the dog. He didn't know the secret. He didn't know the pain," the old sailor said crying. "If he had known he wouldn't have done that to me. I wouldn't have accepted the dog from him. It was my blessing...my curse. You will explain and instruct Jesus, and protect him. You must promise me, because I love the boy, like my own son."

"I will do so," promised the padre.

The padre closed the front door of the cottage behind him and blessed the house with holy water, praying in Latin. He looked up at the sky and crossed himself in the sign of the cross, then kissed his crucifix and whispered: "Christ has mercy."

Jesus was curled up under the tree next to the garden sleeping with his dog. Santo lifted his head and wagged his tail as the padre approached. Santiago knelt on one knee and took the dog's head in his hands and looked into his eyes. He saw his own reflection in the clear blue eyes of the dog. There was no sign of cataracts or excessive age.

Then he picked up the dog's paws one at a time and examined the pads on the dog's feet. The dog appeared to be no more than a few years old. His teeth were clean, and without tartar; his breath was fresh and smelled from mint plants. And then he remembered.

Santiago remembered seeing an old sailor in Sonora as a child, some twenty years ago, and seeing a dog walking with the old sailor, who was very old, even then. A sailor was an unusual sight in his town. Was it the same sailor? But even if it were, he never thought for a second that this was the same dog.

Surely, it had to be a descendent of that dog. The story he had just been told by the old sailor from Zaragoza couldn't possibly be true.

Jesus felt Santo's tail thumping his leg and awoke and looked at the padre.

"Is Sailor gone?"

"No, Jesus, he is sleeping. He wants to be left alone now."

The padre rubbed his hand thoughtfully over Jesus' head.

"Jesus, it has been a hardship for your aunt to take care of you and your cousins. How would you and Santo like to stay with me at the mission? Your aunt will not take kindly to another mouth to feed, but you and Santo are welcome to live with me. You can have your own room to sleep in with your own bed."

"My own room? Can Santo sleep with me?"

"Yes, my son."

"Then I would like that very much!"

Chapter 3

Raising the Dead

Thirteen-year-old Pilar laughed and threw the stick for Santo to fetch. She loved throwing the stick for him, and Santo never tired of chasing it. He would bite hard on the stick and swing it side to side like he was trying to shake the life out of it as he ran back each time.

Jesus sat on the same bench in the sun on which the old sailor used to sit, smiling happily as he watched his young granddaughter playing.

A deep rumble like the distant sound of cannon echoed up the mountain, and he looked for clouds but saw none.

Pilar reminded him very much of her mother, who was taken from them so tragically by the terrorist bombers. It seemed like yesterday that her parents had left their youngest child with him to care for, as they finally returned to Spain for a long-dreamed-of vacation. If only they had not gone to Madrid. The image of his son and daughter-in-law waving goodbye at the gate flashed into his mind, he with baby Pilar in his arms, lifting her tiny hand in his to wave back at them.

It was a very happy parting. How could he have known that it would be the last time he would see them alive? His eyes clouded with tears before he could brush the image away. What was the word they used to describe their twisted mission of Allah? Jihad: the struggle to improve oneself; to fight for God.

Jesus had fought his own personal jihad for most of his life, ever since Sailor had given him Santo. To walk and run and play everyday with a gift of love directly from the Christ was both a blessing and a burden, and Jesus had battled the passions of youth, ever trying to improve his soul. Padre Santiago had helped him along the journey, but even he was at a loss to explain the miracle of Santo.

Many years ago, when Jesus was still a young man, Santiago had traveled to Spain, where he searched the old manuscripts, until he finally found the story, a legend of a remarkable dog that had followed Christ (along with some other dogs) through the streets of Jerusalem and outside the city to Golgotha and the crucifixion site.

He was just a stray, but somehow felt the love of Christ and was compelled to follow him. When the Son of God was stabbed with a spear, Santo was the dog nearest the base of the cross. He licked the salty blood of Christ as it dripped to the ground. A guard tried to chase him away, and in frustration, stabbed him with the shaft of the same spear that had pierced the body of Christ. The dog was hurt badly, and did not run away.

Neither did he die. He shared the last moments of the life of Christ, as he lay wounded near the base of the cross. The Apostle James, took care of the dog out of mercy, and years later took him along to Caesarea Augusta in Spain. James left the dog in the sailor's care when he went on a mission to Palestine, where Herodes Agrippa martyred him.

It later became a local legend that any sick person that the dog befriended had their illnesses cured. That was the only mention of the dog that Santiago could find in the ancient manuscripts of the local church. Why James had left the dog with the sailor was unknown. He had probably expected to return soon, never guessing that he would be murdered.

Santiago asked some local historians but none had ever heard of the legendary dog. The trail of the dog ended long ago, and there was no hint of its fate.

"Grandfather, come and play with us!" yelled Pilar. She was chasing Santo, who was teasing her, refusing to yield the stick. Each time he would pretend to put it down for her to throw, but then he would snatch it back up and run before she could get to it. Finally, she tired of chasing him, and walked back toward the cottage, and Santo ran behind her, prodding her with the stick.

"No, you've teased me enough. I won't throw anymore," she laughed.

A trail of dust was coming up the cliff road towards the cottage. Pilar saw Padre Santiago at its head and waived and ran to greet him.

Santiago's face was pinched with worry, and Pilar knew there was something wrong, even though he forced a smile when he saw her. The smile melted quickly, and he called out as he approached the cottage:

"Jesus, come quickly! We are needed!"

Jesus was half-asleep, dreaming of his son and daughter-in-law Maria; dreaming of happier times, from before the bombers took them. Pilar reminded him so much of them both. Whenever he looked at her, he saw both their faces molded as one into her face.

"JESUS!"

Jesus jumped awake, and saw Santiago coming through the gate.

"A great tragedy has befallen us. Come quickly, and bring Santo. We are needed."

"A tragedy?" whispered Jesus as he rose, wiping the drool of sleep from his left cheek. He said no more and fetched a leash for Santo from inside the cottage, and then, emerging from the door, he called the dog and attached the leash quickly and they were off towards the village with Pilar closely following, tugging at Santiago's robe.

"What? What is a tragedy, Padre?"

The three and the dog went off down the mountain, almost at a run. In the distance, Jesus saw a cloud of dust and smoke from the village below them.

The first wisps of smoke wafted over them as they approached the edge of the village.

"I smell bread," spoke Pilar.

"Yes," whispered Santiago.

They turned the corner onto Mission Street and soft cries and whimpering came from ahead. The bakery was mostly gone, and in its place was a crumbled pile of bricks and log beams, which spilled out into the street. A small crowd of people were carrying bricks out of the ruins and gently piling them along the street.

Several women were sobbing, watching as the men frantically dug through the twisted mess of bricks and debris.

One man pulled out a doll and gently dusted it off and one of the women watching screamed and cried uncontrollably.

Santiago went to her and tried to solace her. "There, there, Rosa, pray with me, have faith."

"Oh, Father, why? How could God let this happen?"

Jesus handed the leash to Pilar and helped the men digging,

while Pilar studied the scene, trying to figure out what had happened. It looked like a bomb had gone off. Rugs, furniture, and pictures from the baker's upstairs apartment were now in amongst the debris on the first floor.

The walls seemed to have just dissolved, and thousands of pieces of shattered clay roof tiles were sprinkled everywhere. Santo had sniffed out a freshly baked loaf of bread that had escaped the damage, and he lay down on a pile of bricks gnawing it as he held it trapped between his paws.

A leathery old woman with rounded shoulders stooped to pet Santo.

"He doesn't mind a little dust on his food." Her withered fingers, bent like a claw, scratched gently on Santo's head, and Pilar noticed a ring of warts that lined the web of the old woman's thumb and index finger.

"You are Maria's daughter. You look just like your mother did at your age. She used to like our ensaimadas after church on Sundays. Her eyes were big and soft, just like your eyes. And your dog, looks just like the old sailor's dog from so many years ago, when my Rosa was almost as young as you are."

The old woman pointed to her daughter, who was being consoled by Father Santiago. Then she looked up from petting Santo, and the scarf slid back from her head. Her eyes were smoky gray and cloudy, and the lines in her forehead were deep and sharp.

"It was the oven," she said emptily. "We thought it was a blessing when we finally saved enough money to buy it. No more dirty coal to shovel, and so easy to start. The man from the city...he had just changed the gas bottles outside. His truck is still there," she said, jerking her head towards a truck half-buried in bricks beside the partially collapsed building.

Rosa screamed: "Mi nieta!"

Pilar turned and saw the white stocking of her best friend's foot exposed by the careful digging of Jesus and the other men. She turned empty and cold, and started to shiver. Whispers passed the word to the small crowd in the street and their voices died away. The clinking of bricks thrown aside by the rescuers grew more frantic, and each tossed brick now echoed from storefronts on the far side of the silent street, doubling the cadence.

"Please, God, no," Pilar prayed silently to herself. "This is not what I wanted or meant!" She remembered when her adopted little sister, Alita, first lost her appetite. Then later, her eyes became tinged with yellow. The doctor man from the city said Alita had an illness in her stomach, which would only get worse.

There was nothing they could do, and it could be become very painful. Pilar had prayed with all her might, many times over around her rosary. Even to her namesake, the Lady of the Pillar, she had prayed fervently. On some nights, her grandfather had to pry the rosary from her hands as she slept, having prayed herself to sleep. She prayed for Alita to not have to suffer, because Alita could never tolerate a bellyache.

Surely, when you pray, you should not have to be so precise. God must understand. This was not the answer to her prayers. But no one knew what she had prayed, for she had not mentioned the stomach illness to her grandfather. Pilar had faith, and she was sure that God would cure little Alita.

The men had cleared the debris away from Alita, and she lay very still and gray, covered with brick dust and flour. Jesus tried to revive her. He was the nearest thing to a doctor that the village had, and many professed that he had healing powers. He placed his mouth over Alita's and breathed into her and her chest expanded and fell, but there was no motion in her body.

Father Santiago left Rosa with her mother. He took Santo from Pilar and knelt down beside Alita and prayed. Then he opened one of her eyes with two fingers while Jesus continued trying to breathe life back into the tiny frail body. Santiago closed Alita's eyelids and looked knowingly at Jesus, who gave a very slight nod of his head.

The padre continued praying and turned his back towards the onlookers, while he maneuvered Santo in front of him. He made the sign of the cross over Alita and released slack in Santo's leash, never stopping his prayers. Santo sniffed at the tiny girl and licked the flour dust from a small portion of her bare arm, while Jesus kept rhythmically breathing into her lungs.

Rosa sobbed quietly in her mother's arms while the old woman patted her on the back, and Pilar thought how nice it must be to have a mother. When she was younger and Grandfather used to leave the village on short trips of faith with Father Santiago, she had stayed at Rosa's house. Back then, Alita was still an infant, and an orphan like Pilar. Alita's mother had been taken by the fever and her father drank himself to death, so Rosa raised her as her own.

Many times Rosa would draw Pilar towards her as she rocked Alita to sleep, and rock them both together, while telling stories about Pilar's mother who had been killed by the jihadists when Pilar was too young to remember her. Those stories were the closest thing that Pilar had to memories of her mother.

Pilar imagined that she saw movement from the tip of the white stocking. It looked as though Alita's toes tried to curl and then relaxed. She stared at the foot as if hypnotized; praying so hard, trying to will it back to life. Suddenly, the foot twitched and Pilar jumped. Her neck hairs rose in a chill as the leg to which the foot was attached moved, and Jesus sprang back in surprise as Alita awoke with a start.

"Blessed be God!" shouted Santiago as he made the sign of the cross over Alita. "Blessed be his son and our savior, Jesus Christ."

"Minieta!" cried Rosa. "Oh..." Rosa tried to stand, to run to her granddaughter, but her knees buckled beneath her, and her mother and two bystanders helped her to her feet.

Tears streaked the dusty face of Jesus as he cradled the small girl's head in his left hand, and she stared up at him, like a child awaking from a brief nap. Before he could stop her, she sat straight up and looked at Pilar and smiled as if nothing had happened.

"Hello, Pilar," she said cheerily.

Pilar stood wide-eyed and startled, initially unable to speak, but finally managed to whisper: "Alita." And then a broad smile grew on her face and washed her fear away.

Alita stood up and walked carefully across the rubble and broken bricks to both of her grandmothers and they hugged her joyously.

"Christ has mercy," said Santiago in a whisper.

Jesus joined with the other men who had formed a line and were passing bricks and debris through the staggered remnants of the bakery to the street outside as they picked their way through the remains of what was once the sidewall of the bakery.

An arm appeared, and then a hand, which was grasping a second hand.

"It's the gasman," one rescue worker said. "He was standing by his truck when it happened." Then he lowered his voice and whispered: "That's Carlos's hand that he is holding. They were shaking hands when it happened."

In silence they quickly and carefully removed the pile of debris from the two men, but they were both dead, their eyes half-open and covered with dust. Carlos's mouth was agape, as if he were mouthing words. Their faces were expressionless and showed no signs of trauma, but their bodies were severely twisted and deformed from the great weight of the wall.

"Poor Rosa and little Alita," one man said. This is a black day. God help us."

"He always does," said Santiago, as he approached with Santo. "Pray for his mercy."

The men removed the rest of the debris, and gently pulled the bodies from the rubble into the side street of the bakery. Their hands had to be pulled apart as they were tightly clenched together.

"They were friends in death," one man said, as he made the sign of the cross.

"Yes," said Santiago as he knelt to pray over them. "They travel together to meet our lord."

The men turned and went back through the collapsed wall of the bakery and began shoring up the standing remnants, leaving Santiago to pray over the bodies. Inside, Rosa and her mother were hugging and kissing Alita, wiping her face clean and brushing the dust from her hair. She seemed unfazed by the incident and strangely calm.

"I'm okay, Mama, really. Where is Poppa?" she said innocently.

Rosa's face froze as her mind cleared. "Carlos?" she whispered.

Two men installing a support below a dangling floor that was in danger of falling stopped their work and looked towards Rosa. One shook his head grimly and thumbed his hand towards the outside of the bakery. Rosa looked through the hole in the collapsed wall and saw Santiago hunched over two bodies praying, administering the last rites of the church.

She pulled Alita to her chest and clutched her tightly and began to sob. Her mother stood beside her and patted her back and steadied her as she started to swoon.

"God help us," Rosa cried. "What will we do now? What will become of us?"

Pilar stepped toward them and put her arms around Rosa and Alita. She felt so cold and empty and just a little bit guilty for not having prayed for the others. All she had thought of, selfishly, was the fate of her little sister. She had momentarily forgotten any others.

In a little while Rosa was cried out, and she opened her eyes and wiped away her tears with her apron. She looked up, and saw Padre Santiago coming slowly towards her with Santo at his side. A look of solemn compassion covered his face and he smiled very gently as he stroked Alita's head.

"Christ has mercy," he said softly.

Rosa started to cry again, and Santiago stepped aside. Behind him, and walking through the hole in the wall, was Carlos. Carlos looked up through the floor to the rafters of the roof and shook his head.

"What a mess," he said. "This is going to take a lot of fixing."

Rosa yelled. "Carlos!"

One of the two men working on the vertical support column grabbed the sleeve of the other. "Sacred Mother!" he whispered.

"Ghosts," said the second man. "I saw you dead!" he said as

the gasman emerged through the hole in the wall from the street. "You were dead."

"No," Jesus said, as he stepped towards them from the street. "They were just unconscious."

"Dead," said the first man quietly. "I know dead when I see it." A look of fear was on his face, but Jesus calmed him quietly.

"They were just in shock," said Jesus. "The wall had knocked the breath out of them."

The first man looked in disbelief to Santiago and pointed to the gasman: "His leg was broken."

"No, no. As you can plainly see, he is walking."

"I saw the bone."

"No," said Santiago. "No, the lord has delivered his mercy here to us all today."

"Blessed be God," said Jesus, making the sign of the cross.

"Let us pray," said Santiago, and they all bowed their heads and joined in together as Santiago recited the Lord's Prayer.

Rosa's mother felt something licking her hand as she prayed, and she looked down and saw Santo. She bent to pet him and looked into his blue eyes. "You look just like Sailor's dog," she said smiling, and went back to praying.

Chapter 4

A Fiesta

Word quickly spread to the onlookers in the street of the good news, and shopkeepers declared a fiesta. The café owner across the street promptly brought out a large spread of moles, various mixtures of peppers and nuts over turkey and rice, and cold beer was soon flowing with other iced drinks. Someone tied a chain of lanterns across the street, and another shop owner brought speakers to her storefront and began playing Duranguense music.

Father Santiago took Rosa in one hand and Alita in the other and climbed up the small pile of bricks that were the rubble from the previous front of the bakery, and as they became visible to the crowd in the street, everyone cheered.

"Friends! We have all witnessed the mercy of our lord this day. Our children, almost taken from us, are all alive and well." He made the sign of the cross and blessed the crowd, and they all bowed their heads and crossed themselves. "Tomorrow, we shall begin a novena to show thanks, but let us rejoice this day."

The crowd cheered again, and someone turned the music louder. Some pickup trucks arrived from nearby villages, rescue workers who now found themselves at a happy gathering. Most stayed, but a few left to bring back even more partiers.

Rosa cried with tears of joy and hugged Carlos. He smiled and picked up Alita and held her high on his shoulder and they waived to the dancing crowd. Some cheered, and threw their hats in the air. Then Carlos grabbed the gasman's hand and raised both their clasped hands in the air, and another cheer went through the crowd. Then they all three walked down the hill of rubble and crossed the street through the crowd as well-wishers thronged them and patted them all on their backs. In a place where the land did not give up its fruits easily, they were all grateful for good news.

Rosa hugged her mother, who wiped the tears from Rosa's face, and soon Santiago and Jesus joined them.

"Mama," said Rosa, "your eyes look so blue! I have never seen them so pretty."

"I am happy, filled to the brim with joy."

"Father, look at her, she is beautiful."

"Yes," said Santiago, "she is. Her eyes are bright."

"As blue as the Mexican sky," said Jesus, waving his arm above his head. "A mother's joy lights her face. Isabel, if I were an older man I think I would chase you."

"If you were older, why would I want you? Old men are all the same. They have eyes bigger than their appetites, and they can never finish what they start."

"Not Grandfather, he always cleans his plate. Sometimes he licks it clean," said Pilar.

They all laughed but Santiago, who frowned abruptly, and said: "Bless her innocence."

He took Pilar by the hand and led her down the rubble pile, and Jesus and Rosa followed them. Isabel stayed behind and watched the two men shoring-up the second story floor joists. A dresser had fallen from her bedroom above and was staggered across a pile of bricks and ceiling tiles in front of her, its mirror cracked from the fall. She walked dreamily toward it, and thoughtlessly wiped her hand across its dust-covered surface. She drew a sharp breath as she saw her reflection in the mirror.

Gone, were the cataract clouds from her eyes, and her white hair had turned to a beautiful silvery sheen. In her excitement, she hadn't noticed the sharp focus of her eyes and the new clarity of her vision. The face staring back at her was one from some forgotten previous decade.

She raised her hands to her cheeks and they felt plump and soft and they had color in them for the first time in years, and the backs of her hands had no wrinkles and showed no melanin speckles. She traced the web of her right hand between the thumb and forefinger and saw that the ring of warts was gone and it felt meaty and supple, and she stretched out her fingers in front of her and they were straight and without any pain.

From across the room, she heard the whispers of the two men working and the one was voicing his concerns to the other.

"I know a ghost when I see one. Carlos was dead, and his leg was broken. I saw the bone."

"Then what?" said the other man. "If it is as you say, we have witnessed a great miracle, no?" The man crossed himself and went on working.

"Yes," said the first man. "But such things never happen in this day and age. How do we know it is not the work of Satan? Why did the bakery blow up in the first place? Just to give God a chance to perform a miracle? Why would he not just prevent it from blowing up to begin with?"

"It is a mystery. God works in mysterious ways," said the second man.

Isabel's mind raced back across half a lifetime to the day her daughter, Rosario, had the fever and was convulsing while lying on the pew in the church. Every detail stood sharp in her memory and she remembered old Sailor's dog, and how he licked Rosa's face. Then she touched her own hand, which felt tingly warm where the dog of Jesus had licked her.

She remembered the blue of the dog's eyes and the faint smell of mint and her memories, both recent, and those from the distant past, connected. Then she looked back in the mirror and smiled at her reflection, and it smiled back at her with lips that were no longer thin and pale and dry. She made the sign of the cross and bowed her head and said a secret prayer, a thank you, to God.

The crowd had grown, and people from the surrounding villages were still arriving, many bringing food, tables and chairs. Isabel wandered through the congested street, which had become a crowded dance floor. The sun was low on the mountains and the air had cooled, and she felt more at home in the town than she had in a very long time, perhaps since before her husband had passed.

Everyone was smiling and children ran in groups through the crowd, boys teasing girls with whatever they could find to annoy them. Carlos and Rosa were dancing and smiling, happier than she had seen them in years. On the far side of the street she finally found her great granddaughter, Alita, who was arm-in-arm with Pilar, laughing and swaying to the music.

"Look at us!" said Pilar, upon seeing Isabel. "Bisabuela, come and dance with us."

Isabel joined hands with them and they danced in a circle,

three children in a careless celebration of life. After awhile they tired and turned to a nearby table and got plates of food and ate. Alita looked at Pilar and laughed as she piled her plate high for a second time and stuffed food in her mouth.

"Alita, you will never eat all that!" cried Pilar. But Alita just laughed impishly, as she worked through the pile of food on her plate.

"Not so fast," said Isabel. "Eat more slowly, or you will get sick." She bent down to Alita and saw that her color was good and without jaundice. The whites of her eyes lacked the yellow tinge of yesterday and the irises were big soft-brown discs. "Is your belly hurting?"

"No," replied Alita.

"That's good," said Isabel. She kissed her on the forehead, and then she turned to look for Father Santiago. Further up the street, she saw a group of children playing at the fountain, and she could see the heads and shoulders of Jesus and Santiago as they moved amongst the children. She wove her way through the crowd, up the street toward them.

At the fountain, the last rays of the sun were lighting the water that spilled from the top tier fountain bowl through several small spillways before it splashed into the main fountain below. The reflected rays of the sun bounced off the streams, and danced across the faces of Jesus and Santiago, making them glow brightly in the reduced light of dusk.

Santiago was holding a small child in his arms. A queue of several families had formed at the fountain, people from the more remote farms who had come to Pueblo del Cielo on word of the tragedy, and who had experienced a rebirth of their faith. "I baptize thee in the name of the Father, and of the Son, and of the Holy Spirit," recited Santiago as he made the sign of the cross on the child's forehead and let the blessed water of the fountain wash over the child's head.

Isabel stepped into the shelter of a closed shop's doorway and watched in silence. She replayed in her mind a series of events that occurred during the previous forty-five years. Innocent events, that now seemed to take on a whole new meaning. The many times that Father Santiago and Jesus would take short journeys to surrounding towns, sometimes as often as once a month. They were always together, Father Santiago, Jesus, and...a dog, always inseparable when they ventured out beyond the town.

She waited, thinking silently, watching Santiago and Jesus as if they were strangers, seeing them in a whole new light. Finally, the last of those to be baptized, received their blessings and left, and Father Santiago turned and began to walk towards the church at the far end of the street. Isabel called out softly: "Father, may I speak with you?"

Santiago turned, still not able to recognize the woman in the shadows, but he smiled and said: "Of course, I am easy, Daughter." He walked towards her, while drying his hands on his robe.

"My granddaughter seems to be cured, Father, but I don't understand and I am afraid. Is it a miracle? How can it be?"

Santiago placed the voice, paused, and then replied. "What is a miracle, Isabel?"

"I always thought a miracle is performed by Christ."

"That is true," said Santiago. "Saint Augustine said that the miracles performed by our lord Jesus Christ are divine works that teach us to rise above visible things, to understand what God is. A miracle is a sign, that this world order is superseded by another higher power.

"Do you agree?"

"Father...the dog. Is it the same dog...the one that belonged to the old sailor?"

"How could it be? That was so many years, ago?" replied Santiago.

Jesus walked up to them with Santo, and stood listening in silence as Santo sniffed at Isabel's dress. She stooped in the doorway, gently patting Santo's head.

"He is just a mongrel. There is nothing special about him at first glance," Isabel said thoughtfully. "He looks like a million other mongrels from around the world; the short hair, the curled tail, like a Pariah."

"He is a very plain dog," Jesus added quickly.

"Yes, except for his eyes. They are a very strange, luminescent pale blue, like the sky seeded with light."

"That may be from his diet. He never eats meat," said Jesus.

"Perhaps that explains his breath," Isabel said, as she tried to open Santo's mouth. He licked her nose and she laughed. "He always smells of mint. His teeth are very clean, too."

"From chewing our native bushes," said Santiago. "He likes to chew things."

"And lick them, too. He was licking my Rosa's face that day, so many years ago, Father, in the church. Remember? We thought she had died."

Santiago and Jesus both were silent, and their faces blank.

"He licked my hand several times this day, Father. See?" Isabel stood up and extended her hand from the doorway for their inspection. "See how straight my fingers are, and how easily I move them without any pain. And the string of warts that I have had on this hand for twenty years is gone, as are the wrinkles. How would you explain that, Father?"

Santiago took Isabel's hand and examined it as carefully as a doctor. He rubbed the skin and tested its elasticity by pulling a fold outward from the back of her hand, and he watched it snap back quickly into place. "Your hands look young," he finally said.

"How do you explain all this, Father?" Isabel said, as she stepped from the shadowed recess of the doorway into full view in the street.

Santiago smiled, and touched his palm to Isabel's face.

"Christ is great."

"Isabel, you are a beautiful woman," Jesus sighed.

"A very long time ago, before either of you were born and when I was just a little girl, the sailor, who even then was old, told some of us children from the village a fairy tale about a remarkable dog that had been blessed by Christ with the gift of eternal life. It was just a story to entertain us, but I remember clearly that he said the dog was very plain and could be any mongrel, just like the dog that he himself owned at the time. Just like this dog."

She paused, and looked at Santo, thinking, and then finally looked Santiago in the eyes.

"Father, is this that dog of Christ?"

Santiago smiled and patted her cheek gently, and looked down at Santo.

"You have been greatly blessed by our Lord, Isabel. First, when he spared Rosario's life from the fever. Then again today, when he spared her husband and granddaughter from what appeared to be sure death. And then still again, by his blessing you with rejuvenated health and vitality.

"There is no doubt that you have been restored to a vitality that you have not known in years. Now, you would have me tell you whether some fairy tale told to you a lifetime ago by an old sailor is true? What if it were?"

"Then I would want to know why you and Jesus have kept this a secret all these years, when you could have helped many sick people. You should have told others!"

"Isabel," said Jesus sternly, "Do not speak to Father that way. You do not know—"

Santiago raised his hand and smiled gently. "I wonder, Isabel, how much of the fairy tale the sailor, told you. Did he tell you what became of the dog of Christ? Did he mention the consequences or burdens of such a legendary dog? Can you imagine the hysteria of the masses; the enthralled throngs of people all wanting to be cured?

"Or did his story mention how evil forces in power would fight to gain control of such a blessed creature? For I doubt that young children could comprehend the power of evil, and perhaps that part of the fairytale the old sailor thought not to mention.

"For if this dog, were that legendary dog of the Christ, then I would hate to think of the possible chaos and grief that might befall our poor village. Nothing here would remain the same, as believers from all over the world would descend on Pueblo del Cielo like a horde of locusts from the sky. And beyond the believers, there would also be the forces of evil that would come to decry any such miracle of Christ. For as always, they want no belief in a loving God, or in his son who was sent as an act of love to free us from our sins. They would do anything to destroy and discredit anyone who made such a claim as to having such a blessed creature."

Isabel looked back and forth from Santiago to Jesus, and then back down at Santo.

"You know," continued Santiago, "a slow miracle is just as effective as a fast miracle.

"An old sailor, driven from his homeland of Spain by hysteria and evil powers, might have made a new home here. He might have lived a very long time, making many journeys of mercy to all the surrounding countryside, encouraging people to meet and pet his dog, especially sick people…all those crippled, wounded, or afflicted with disease. In the course of decades, he might have helped many thousands of people with no one ever being the wiser.

"Such would be the wisdom of a very old man, who had lived for many generations, guarding a blessing that was his burden, and his faith. Such a man, living all alone and asking for nothing from anyone, would be a very great man indeed, I think. He might also tire of living eventually, even though he knew that he could forestall his own death. At that point, he might finally unburden himself and make a gift of his dog to a young and innocent boy who had befriended him, and whom he loved as a son. Being wise, the old sailor might also want the boy to have someone to help guide him in guarding the blessing left by Christ, so that it would continue to help many souls.

"Did he tell you that part of the fairy tale, Isabel?"

Tears filled Isabel's eyes and streaked down her face as she crossed herself and smiled warmly. "No, Father. He did not tell me that part of the story. You are right. I was too young to have understood. Forgive me."

She reached out and hugged Father Santiago and Jesus, and the three of them kneeled down around Santo and prayed.

"Father! Father Santiago!" The cry arrived ahead of the runner coming up the street, and the trio finished their recital of the Lord's Prayer and stood up as the breathless runner pushed his way past the fountain to where they stood. "They need you, Father. We found another body at the bakery."

"Who?" said Santiago.

"We don't know," said the runner. "A stranger."

Chapter 5

A Stranger's Body is Found

The runner led the way back down the crowded street. He was young and still excited by his first glimpse of death, so close and real and unexpected.

"It was a shock, Father. We had no idea there was anyone else in the building. I was helping to remove and stack the bricks, saving them to be used again. I lifted a brick and saw some hair, and then after I took away more bricks I saw a face. At first, I thought it was a young man, because the hair was pulled back tight on her head, but then I saw, it was a woman. None of us know her."

When they arrived at the shell of what was once the bakery, the entire site was transformed from what it had been several hours before. The chaos and phantasmagoric imagery was replaced with order. Most of the debris had all been removed from the interior, and a chest-high wall had been made of the bricks across the front, and down the adjacent street. Inside, furniture had been arranged as best as possible, and many new vertical braces supported the second story floor and the remnants of the exterior walls. Men on the roof were tying bright blue plastic tarpaulins across the top of the structure.

The runner led Father Santiago past the stacks of bricks,

through the hole in the shored-up side street wall of the bakery, and finally, through a collapsed wall at the rear of the remaining structure. Isabel and Jesus followed in single file, and Santo trailed behind them on his leash.

There was almost nothing left of the building that had formerly joined the bakery at its rear. The roof was entirely gone, as were both its sidewalls. The wall opposite the shared bakery wall had been blown into the next building beyond. In the center of the small building, which measured about twenty by forty feet, the long side being the rear of the bakery, was a long wooden work bench, and on it could be seen a dust-covered body. It was dressed in women's clothes, a simple cotton dress with a red and yellow pattern. Someone had respectfully placed clean linen over the face of the body and the woman's arms were lying neatly at her sides. She was shoeless, and portions of her clothes were burned.

Santiago gently took the woman's arms and crossed them across her chest as he began to pray.

Isabel carefully lifted the linen across the woman's face and sighed. "Hesser!" She crossed herself, and mumbled an unintelligible blessing. "Hesser Amatallah," she whispered. "She rented this space from me last month. She was an artist, here on vacation to practice her oils."

Jesus was examining some scraps of papers lying in the dust. He picked up one and touched his finger to it and then touched his finger to his tongue. "Where are the paintings? Where are the canvases? Are there any sketches or frames lying around? I doubt that we will find any." He tried to walk closer, but Santo wouldn't budge. Jesus pulled on the leash and Santo growled.

"What is wrong with you?" asked Jesus. He tried again, but

Santo refused him, so he tied the leash to a vertical post and approached the body. "Destiny, servant of god," he growled. He thrust the piece of paper in his hand towards Isabel and pointed to some writing on it and read it aloud: "For garden use only."

Isabel raised one eyebrow in puzzlement and stared at Jesus who was red with rage.

"Call the SSP, and tell them we have a suspected terrorist's body. Those papers are the remnants of bags that contained potassium nitrate."

Isabel stared blankly at Jesus.

"Just do it! Call them now. Go!"

She turned quickly, and went away without another word. She had never seen Jesus angry in all the many years since he was a small boy in the village.

Jesus crumpled the remnants of the fertilizer bag in his clenched fist and walked over next to Santiago who was administering the last rites to the woman on the table. He looked down at the woman, his body involuntarily shaking from a rush of adrenalin.

"Even in death, she is beautiful," Jesus said softly. "Almond eyes and full lips, and such a long and feminine neck. If she were alive I would break that pretty neck. Do you think the last rites of the church buy us absolution?"

Santiago paused his whispered prayers. "Of course. How can you even ask me that?"

"Then stop your prayers, Father. Let her soul go straight to hell, where she belongs. She is one of them, a jihadist, just like those who stole my son and daughter-in-law from me. Just like those who have killed so many innocent children in the name of Allah. Let her go to hell. An eternity of fire is too easy for her and her kind. There must be some special section of hell for animals like her."

"Judge not, lest you be judged, my son. You have to let go of hate. In all these years that have passed, and after seeing the miracles of Christ you still haven't learned to forgive. Bring Santo here, and let the lord decide her fate."

Jesus turned round and untied Santo and tried to lead him to the girl, but it was no use. Santo bucked and growled and refused to advance any further jerking wildly on the leash, so he tied him back up to the post, and then went back to Santiago.

"Santo knows," snarled Jesus. "Why should we forgive those who are the murderers of children? When will God extract his vengeance? How long must we wait to see justice done on this earth to all their kind? I tell you, if I could, I would gladly kill them all. I would sacrifice my immortal soul without one moment's hesitation."

Santiago raised his hand and signed the cross and began to pray again, but Jesus grabbed his arm and squeezed hard. "Let her go, she doesn't deserve your prayers."

"Somewhere," said Santiago softly, "a mother will cry when she finds that she has lost this child. Do you think that this girl's mother will suffer less than you did when your son was taken from you?"

"Yes, I do. Because her mother is probably like her and is just another murderer."

"And if she is not? How do you not know that her mother did nothing wrong, and raised her daughter with all the love and care that she had to give? Then she is just like you and will cry and ask why this tragedy had to happen. Such is the trial of evil, Jesus. It tempts you to embrace it, but what then? You would be just like them, your mind diseased with hatred, wanting only revenge. We can only leave them to God. He will judge them all.

"We will talk more about this later, when I confess you."

Santiago removed Jesus' grip from his arm and began his prayers again.

"At least only her mother will cry now, and not the mothers of many. Perhaps God caused the explosion, after all. Who can say?" He turned away and walked back to Santo, who was struggling to pull free of his leash. "Eh, you sense it too, my friend, no?"

Jesus untied Santo from the pole and the dog bolted and ran out into the street, disappearing into the crowd of partiers. "Santo!" Jesus shouted, with no response. He whistled loudly several times, and then finally waded into the throng in pursuit.

There was much excitement in the village in the days following the explosion. The secretariat of public security identified the young woman who was killed as a member of a known Al Qaeda cell. For several weeks, federal police went door to door interviewing the people of the village and searching for clues as to what the final target had been for the potassium nitrate, but to no avail.

It was theorized that the potassium nitrate had spontaneously combusted when it reacted with something in the storage area, especially since it was stacked against the rear wall of the bakery, which was next to the bakery ovens and sometimes got very hot. The increased temperature would have made it more susceptible to combustion. The debris field patterns proved that the center of the explosion was just behind the rear wall of the bakery.

Isabel testified that the young woman, Hesser Amatallah, had originally arrived with her boyfriend, and that she had seen no suspicious behavior during the several weeks of her tenancy.

Several other locals said they had seen people carrying bags in at night on several occasions, but no one thought anything unusual about it at the time. One man said he thought it was just bags of flour to be used by the bakery.

All the questioning with so few answers left Jesus, more than anyone in the village, in an agitated state. He questioned the police at every possible opportunity and monitored the progress of the investigation, and when it led nowhere, he was more frustrated than the police. He didn't want to accept a dead end. Santiago counseled him and bid him to pray for relief from his frustrations, but the old memories of his son, and the loss of his loved ones were ignited and wouldn't let go of him.

Jesus didn't see it that way, but his behavior had certainly changed, and Santiago tried to reason with him during each of his frequent visits to Jesus' house, where they frequently talked while Jesus attended the gardens that he had inherited from the old sailor.

Chapter 6

Can a Man Stop the Wind?

"Jesus," Santiago said softly, "how many miracles must you see before your faith is complete?"

"It is not a matter of faith or a lack of it," returned Jesus, as he expertly worked a hoe along a row of spinach plants. "You tell me to leave things to God, and I do, but maybe God wants me to be more proactive. Of all the places in Mexico to store explosives, why should those killers of children have chosen Pueblo del Cielo? Why here?"

"Our isolation," answered Santiago. "This is a perfect place to avoid traffic cameras and the police. No one would search here. Except for the rare tourist just passing through, no one comes here but we locals. It is not surprising."

"I disagree. What are the odds that Muslim extremists should just happen to impact my life again, after I had spent over a decade ridding myself of their memories, cleansing my mind of the hatred I felt for them. You know very well how much I have studied the Koran through the years, trying to divine why they twist the laws of God and man.

"One must know his enemy, to recognize that he is the enemy. To be sure, I have, as you always told me, left them to God. But now

God brings them here, back to me in our peaceful little village. Surely, it was not without purpose, and I must somehow divine his will. I must not turn my ear away if I am being called."

"Called to do what?"

"I don't know...perhaps to connect the dots, to recognize what others might have missed."

"And you see?"

"Nothing. But I am vigilant. I am searching, Father, and I pray for revelation. Jesus reached down and plucked a large green bell pepper from one of the plants and held it up for inspection. "These peppers grow very well as God designed them, but how many of them would survive if I let weeds and vines infest the garden?" He reached down and jerked a small vine from the base of the pepper plant and tore it to shreds.

"There is anger on your face, Jesus. I think perhaps Santo senses the hatred in you and that is why he seeks more the company of Pilar in these days."

"It is not anger, but frustration that I feel. Who does God's work upon this earth but men? Yet we search and seek his guidance, only to be left wondering what to do next. Somewhere out there, the killers of children are planning more attacks, and I must do what I can to stop them."

"It sounds laudable, an altruistic effort to save innocent lives, but I worry for you. The mind can fool you into believing your motives are unselfish, when in fact there is a hidden agenda. I fear your old hatred is not yet vanquished."

Jesus paused in thought for several seconds, and then looked Santiago in the eyes and smiled warmly.

"I do not pretend to be a saint, my friend. I admit the old anger rose quickly in me when I realized that murderers had invaded our village. Suddenly, it was as if no time had passed and they were here to murder my family again. I wanted to kill them all. In all these years, what have I done to fight them? Perhaps this is a chance sent from God to set the record straight."

"I fear not," said Santiago. "The work we have done all these years with Santo has been the work of Christ…works of love and compassion. I fear it is not God calling you now, but instead an internal need for revenge."

"I cannot deny that I have asked myself the same question recently. Sometimes frustration with my inability to effect positive change leads to anger. It is troublesome."

"That is good." Santiago smiled. "It makes me less worried, to know that you worry."

Jesus huddled over a bean plant. He pulled out an exceptionally deep-rooted vine with a groan and held it out for Santiago to inspect, before snapping the root in half and tossing it out of the garden. "Sometimes I feel sad for the weeds…for they are innocent in their growth. They crave the light and water and just want to live in my garden, but there are too many to transplant elsewhere, and even if I could, they would not grow in the barren, dry soil of the surrounding plateau. The wind blows them here, and they take root, only to be destroyed, because of the harm that they do. In their own environment, where they might grow freely, they could be beautiful.

"I am sorry," Jesus said ruefully as he bent and pulled out another weed. "If I could stop the seeds, there would be no need to weed."

"Blame the wind," lamented Santiago. "If our plateau were not so barren, there would be trees to block its path. Then the seeds would not come here. The wind grows strong on the arid plain. You must stop the wind."

"No man can do that," Jesus said emptily.

Chapter 7

Pilar and Alita

The two years following the explosion saw many changes in the world, but Pueblo del Cielo remained the same. The brief excitement that attended the bakery explosion faded with the departure of the national police, and soon all was as it had been in the quiet, dusty little village. People talked about the weather more than anything else.

The village population was shrinking, as the land seemed to get thirstier every year from a continued lack of rain. The water table continued to drop and some wells had gone dry, which made irrigation impractical in many areas. The mountain streams that formerly graced the nearby countryside were now a distant memory, and some families who had lived there for generations finally gave up and moved away.

Pilar, having grown taller, was on her way to becoming a beautiful young woman and she exhibited an emotional and mental maturity that was beyond her years. She was like an older sister who had assumed the role of a missing mother for Alita. Grandmothers Rosa and Isabel were wonderful, but they were so much older and serious, carrying the weight of the world on their shoulders. They saw the danger in any adventure and were quick to point it out. But with Pilar, Alita could run and jump and play, without having to listen to a constant chorus of cautions as when with her grandparents. Pilar was protective of Alita, but she was still too young to see life as a gambit of dangers, waiting to pounce upon the unwary individual, and together they explored the rocky heights above the village, where they often would lie watching the clouds, or searching the plateau below them for dust devils. Santo would usually accompany them for he was sure to be rewarded by Pilar, who would tirelessly throw the stick for him.

Pilar cradled Santo's head in her hands and gazed deeply into his pale sky blue eyes. The white iridescence that ringed the pupils, seemed to sparkle, throwing shafts of light outward across the iris, like thin white spokes on a wheel. Laced between them, were more spokes that folded back on themselves and mirrored the blue of the Mexican sky. Some days they seemed to change with the passing of clouds, and other times, when the sky was painted with cirrus, the spokes blurred together in brush strokes. Like a kaleidoscope, they never seemed to repeat.

Santo panted, and his tongue dripped to whiffs of dust below him on the ground, while his tail thumped bigger dust clouds behind him. Pilar had more colors than Jesus, he thought. All around her was a many-colored halo, and her hands, so soft on his snout, were much more gentle then the calloused hands of Jesus. He liked that she threw the stick more than Jesus, whose colors had gone mostly to red since the explosion.

"Come on, Santo," Alita said eagerly. "I will throw for you." Santo liked Alita, too. Her colors were brighter now, since they had gone so faint at the bakery.

"No, let him rest awhile," said Pilar. "He is getting too hot. I think he would chase the stick until he died, if we would keep throwing it."

Alita ran and jumped, kicking her legs like a colt with too much energy. She ran up to Pilar, who was sitting on a rock by Santo, and bent down and hugged her around the waist, and then tickled her till she let go of Santo, laughing, and as soon as he was free, Alita threw the stick hard. It sailed into the tall brown grass further down the hillside, and Santo bounded off after it.

Pilar scolded her, but then quickly laughed, and they hugged one another laughing, as they watched Santo searching in the tall grass for the stick.

"Look at you," said Pilar, as she looked down at Alita, who was rosy-faced from exertion, but clear-eyed and healthy-looking. "You are feeling fine?"

"Yes." Alita smiled. "I am perfect."

"Have you ever wondered...what happened to your body, and why you suddenly got well again?"

"No. It was just a passing thing, part of growing up, I guess"

"Grandfather says it was a gift of love from the Savior. Did you feel anything special or different after the bakery exploded?" asked Pilar.

Alita's eyes narrowed as she thought carefully. "No, nothing. I was just going to go upstairs. There was a big noise and a thump, and the next thing I knew, people were all around me. When I looked at all the damage, I felt very lucky to have not been hurt."

Pilar brushed the hair back from Alita's face and remembered the horror of that day when they dug her from beneath the rubble. "Yes," she said. "It was all very strange, and I still wonder about it. Did God hear me, and answer my prayer. I want to believe he did."

Something poked Pilar on her leg, and she looked down to see Santo gnawing on the stick, anxious for it to be thrown again. They both laughed and bent down to pet him before ascending to their favorite rock where an old mesquite tree gave small shade and the dry breeze from the plateau blew steadily upward during the day. This was where they spent many hours together talking about the world beyond the village. Here one could see for many miles, and thoughts could not be confined to a small place.

The far off horizon was rimmed by blue mountains and Alita promised to travel there and beyond one day, to seek work in the maquiladoras. She was adventurous and seemed driven by a wanderlust that was non-existent in Pilar.

Pilar gained nobility from her surroundings and she relished their trips to Mesquite Rock. It calmed her and filled her soul; the clean dry smell of the air tinged by the sweetness of mesquite and an occasional cooking smell, wafted from the village far below. Here she could ponder the teachings of Father Santiago and dream about better days in the village and what her parents must have been like.

She could see the speck that was her grandfather working in his garden on the adjacent ridge far across the high plateau. Her whole life was stretched out below her, and as far as she believed, her whole future. But their high perch always seemed to agitate Alita and caused her to lament their confinement in Pueblo del Cielo. She was like a goldfish at the edge of its bowl, looking out wide-eyed and curious and contemplating escape.

They stayed until moonrise, and then started back down to home. By the time they reached the village the moon was just rising over Mission Street and the dry fountain of the plaza cast a long, silent shadow in front of them.

Alita turned and looked up to kiss Pilar goodnight as they arrived at the bakery, and her face became lit by moonlight.

"It's a new day in China," she said quietly.

"Yes," returned Pilar, "they are already working." She kissed Alita on the cheek and sent her running up the outside stairs to her home above the bakery. Grandmother Rosa was sitting on her wicker rocker on the porch at the top of the stairs enjoying the evening cool. She waived silently, and Pilar continued up the street toward the mission.

The mission seemed to lean forward into the moonlight, looming white out of the darkness behind it. Its reflected light lit the whole end of the street to a lunar twilight. She could see Father Santiago through the open door, kneeling and praying in front of a group of flickering red glass candleholders. Santo ran to the door and looked in and then ran back to her when she kept walking. Santo took the lead, and both their shadows ran long in front of them as they passed the mission and took the north road up the plateau to home.

The evening air rolled down as a cool breeze from the mountains, and rustled through the brown grass and bushes in whispers, which ran and faded across the lower plain where they ended in timid silence, not bold enough to venture past the village edge. Out on the open plain the wind was braver and spoke louder to passersby, keeping them company on their journeys.

Pilar loved the wind, and she loved living on the hill with Grandfather where the wind was often loud and rambunctious and sang for many hours at a time during the change of seasons. Grandfather Jesus said that he could hear God in the wind, but she had not yet heard him, although she had tried very hard to do so. So far, all that she had heard had been the wind in its many voices.

The picket fence surrounding the house enclosed etiquette of order that was distinct from the random chaos of all outside it. Even in the moonlight the ordered rows and islands of growth in the garden bespoke discipline and routine and a complete lack of randomness. Pilar saw beauty in its reliability, as well as safety and comfort. Near the gate, under the rose trellis, a red light winked on and off in the darkness, and as she got closer she saw the silhouette of a man, and realized that Grandfather was smoking his pipe in the yard watching her return, and it comforted her.

"You saw me coming?" Pilar said softly.

"Since before dark," Jesus said, and at the sound of his voice, Santo became happier than he already was and started weaving back and forth excitedly in front of the gate, waiting for someone to open it. "I saw you and Alita up on the rocks."

He pointed his arm across the plateau.

"I saw you in the garden," Pilar returned. She thought it interesting that they were both watching one another with neither knowing the other was watching. "How did you know it was me?"

"Three specks on a hill, one speck kept moving away from the other two, and then returning. I knew it had to be you and Alita throwing the stick for Santo."

"Oh, very good," Pilar said, as she mused to herself that the observant eyes of her grandfather had been watching over them the whole time.

"Tomorrow," Jesus said, as he opened the gate, "I have a surprise for you. Father Santiago and I are going to take a trip, and we want you to come with us. Would you like that?"

"Yes!" Pilar swooned. Finally she was being invited to go with her grandfather and Father Santiago. "Where are we going?"

"Wherever God leads us," Jesus said. "But for certain, it will be some place new to you."

Chapter 8

Healing Souls Selling Vegetables

Pilar awoke to the sound of a truck door, and looked out her window from bed. The sun was not yet up, but Jesus and Father Santiago already had the mission's pickup truck loaded with crates and baskets of vegetables from Jesus' garden, and were tying them down. She jumped from bed and dressed quickly and then ate the breakfast that Jesus had already left prepared for her on the kitchen table.

In twenty minutes, they were bouncing along the road north, with her and Santo on the back of the truck, nestled between baskets of bell peppers and string beans and tomatoes and squash. Santo looked more excited than Pilar, but he couldn't be, because this was the first time that Grandfather had ever taken her with him on a trip with the father.

Pilar had often wondered, about the places that Grandfather had gone, and what it was like beyond the mountains at places like Carcachita and Mata Ortiz and beyond. Riding along the northbound road, she watched the countryside turn greener as they drove through a long valley bounded by mountains on either side. By mid-day they had rolled into Mata Ortiz where they sold some vegetables at the square right off the back of the truck to the first people who walked by.

They paused for lunch and Grandfather took her to visit the old train station where she marveled at the long parallel tracks that went far into the distance, disappearing between the distant mountains. Pilar had still never seen a train in real life. She wondered what it must be like to sit on a train and look out the window, watching the scenery fly past.

These things stimulated her imagination like never before, and she suddenly, for the first time in her life, felt the wanderlust that so often plagued Alita. To travel north without stopping by train, perhaps even into America. What must that be like? Who were the glorious people who had such lives?

Those thoughts captured Pilar's imagination and stayed with her as they drove further north to Casa Grandes, but they were soon erased by the excitement of the biggest town that she had ever seen. The church of San Antonio de Padua was more than twice as big as the little mission of Pueblo del Cielo, and as she stood in front of it counting the tiers of the steeples, she felt an awe that was new to her; that of architectural beauty and aesthetic pleasure.

Father Santiago was working a small crowd in the park plaza next to the church, selling vegetables and handing out prayer cards with pictures of the Savior, while Jesus walked alertly through the group observing. He spotted a woman bent with age and hobbling along with a cane whose eyes were clouded by cataracts and he made a point of greeting her and introducing her to Santo. Her face seemed to brighten and she smiled broadly while petting Santo.

By the time Pilar came back from observing the church, most of the remaining vegetables had been sold. Her grandfather brought Santo to her and they sat on the park Gazebo while Santiago finished selling the last of the produce. The old woman with the cane came by, barely hunched and with a very slight limp, and she smiled and said hello to Jesus.

"Is this your daughter?" she asked, as she lightly touched Pilar on the cheek.

"Granddaughter," replied Jesus in the Spanish.

"She will be a beautiful woman soon."

"Yes," said Jesus. "Too soon it will come to pass."

The old woman leaned down to Santo and hugged his head to hers and smiled. "You have the eyes of our sky." She stroked his head lovingly and Santo kissed her hand with his tongue as she rubbed his neck and ears. "Well," she finally said, "Thank you for the peppers. I must go home and stuff and cook them now." She got up and started to walk away, and Pilar called out.

"Senora, you forgot your cane." She ran and gave it to the woman, who laughed with surprise.

"So I did, indeed. How did I manage that? Thank you." She tucked the cane under her arm with the bag of peppers and walked away.

Jesus smiled and scratched Santo's head. "Good things never grow old, my friend."

The ride home was a quiet one, as Father Santiago and Jesus said almost nothing. Pilar stood behind the cab of the pickup with the wind in her hair, watching the sun track lower toward the horizon. She wondered what it would be like to be a beautiful woman. Would she feel any differently than she did right now?

Already, the few men who saw her had begun to stare whenever she passed. She didn't understand why. She slid down between the empty baskets and relaxed and tried to turn off the flood of new sensations that had bombarded her senses throughout the day. A hundred images replayed themselves behind her eyes, but the image of the towers of San Antonio de Padua haunted her like some distant memory that would not be dissolved. There was something...a feeling. But she couldn't quite remember what it was. She closed her eyes and fell into sleep.

"It was a good day," Santiago said with satisfaction as he turned on to the road to their village. "How many would you say received Christ's mercy today?"

"I don't know," returned Jesus. Perhaps fifty, it's hard to say. Sometimes I cannot tell."

"Yes, it is still a great mystery to me, too. The more we grow, the less we know, but I felt a lot of love today."

"Do you think...that we should tell Pilar?" asked Jesus.

"She will learn, just as you did learn, in her own time, when her mind is ready. And then she will understand."

"I don't know," opined Jesus. "It was different for me. A man handles loneliness better than a woman."

"But you were never alone, Jesus! None of us are."

"Yes, I was…many times. And if not for Pilar, I would be even more so today. There is a great emptiness in me, and some days it almost consumes me. How can we be doing the work of God, and yet I still feel so very empty at times? Not today, not when I see the faces of those we help, but at other times. Especially when I read the news and I see the world growing crazier everyday. I feel like we should be doing more. I see the murders in the cities and the endless new problems in the world, and I cannot help but think…the devil is winning."

"There is no bad that comes without good," said Santiago.

"Perhaps the greater evils that we see, are preparing us to receive a greater good. Only God knows."

"Yes, that is the problem." Jesus sighed, and they fell back into silence.

In a little while they pulled up next to the old mission in the village, and as he exited, Jesus' truck door squeaked a loud announcement that they were home. It echoed down the quiet street and the heads of several villagers bobbed up and were silhouetted in their dimly lit windows before quickly disappearing again. Jesus walked to the back of the truck cab and looked down at Santo and Pilar, who were both lying undisturbed sleeping.

"Do you think they are dreaming of angels, old friend?"

Santo's tail started thumping the side of the truck wall as soon as Jesus spoke.

"I hope so," returned Santiago. "I will bring you your money tomorrow."

"Put it in the till. We don't need anything now."

"No," scolded Santiago. "You are too generous. You must think of Pilar, and her future schooling. It won't be long before she may need help with that."

"You are right, as always. I keep forgetting how fast the years have passed."

Jesus felt a pit open in his stomach as his mind reeled with concerns. He constantly shoved aside thoughts of the future and how it might unfold. Pilar was his life for so long that the thought of her leaving left a hole too big to imagine. Neither did he want her to stay trapped in the village without exposure to all that the world offered.

She was very bright and read far above her level, and already she was reading science and political journals of her own initiative.

It had been forty-five years since the old sailor had bequeathed Santo to him, and over a dozen since the jihadists had stolen his son and daughter-in-law from him.

"I often find it hard to think about the future," Jesus said absently.

More precise, was that he had a hard time reconciling a disjoint past into a contiguous future. In all the years he had served God he had felt blessed. Even when his wife deserted him because he could not be as carefree a man as what she needed, and left him to raise their only son, he had thanked God for his blessings.

So how was it that his reward was to see that only son blown to bits so senselessly? And how could he ever pass on the responsibility and burden of Santo to his loving granddaughter? Best for her, would be to leave this place forever and find a life of her own and raise a happy family, like the one he had briefly known. He touched her head and whispered her name.

Pilar arose with a smile, and she and Santo jumped from the truck. They bid Santiago goodnight and started up the north road to the cottage, Pilar with her arms wrapped around Jesus' left arm, and Santo walking sleepily beside them.

Santiago watched them walk off up the road, while the Dipper spilled its contents on their heads. "Make thy will known to us, Lord," he prayed quietly. Despite his best counsel to Jesus, and his seeming confidence through the years, he had always been secretly racked with misgivings as to how he had raised Jesus.

The sailor had made him promise never to reveal to the church the existence of Santo, and had told him enough horror stories of his own travails as to make him fearful of breaking that promise to a dying old man. For surely a man of that great age knew far better than a young priest of his limited experience. But through the years, he had begun to see their role as almost a curse.

The healings were erratic, and sometimes no results were obtained. There never seemed any discernible pattern as to who would be helped or by how much. He had to believe it was the will of God that decided, but that didn't make it any easier to watch some children die, while others were miraculously cured. It confounded him and at first tortured his mind, and then, more recently, his soul. How does the mind of man ever understand the will of God? He finally turned and walked slowly into the mission rectory, consoling himself with the memories of those who had been helped.

Chapter 9

Time Shapes Everyone's Life

Pilar made many trips with her grandfather and Father Santiago that summer. Each time they took a different circuitous route, and by the end of the summer she had seen much of the state. Her schooling progressed rapidly and before she knew it, they were at the beginning of another summer, and then another, until after four summers Alita had grown old enough to accompany them.

She had begged so consistently and earnestly, that Santiago and Jesus finally consented to take her, but only because they had purchased a small flatbed trailer so that they could take more produce on each trip, and Alita had promised to help them with the selling. The money was needed, because Pilar had already progressed to the associate level with her schooling, and she was planning to transfer to a university in the fall in Chihuahua.

Jesus had never had so many expenses, nor had there ever been so many things that seemed necessary to buy and own. The outside world had invaded Pueblo del Cielo through a Trojan horse called broadband, and everything had changed overnight. News that often took weeks to filter into the isolated village was now there instantly, twenty-four hours a day. Jesus had felt compelled to purchase the latest technology when it became available to them at an affordable price because he wanted Pilar to have every opportunity, but it was he more than she who spent many hours scanning hundreds of daily news stories across the globe.

The obsession he had once shed of jihadists was again thrust forcefully into his consciousness through a thousand news stories from around the world. Everywhere he looked he saw violence and a growing Muslim menace. He kept reading and studying as if trying to inoculate himself against an emotional response to the terrors he saw daily. But there were many other terrors growing rapidly besides jihadist extremists, and the stories he read of drug cartels and the escalating war between them and the government in the northern border cities made him wonder how men could be so despicable.

The drug lords had taken evil to new depths, committing unspeakable crimes, and acts so vile as to be beyond belief. It made him pray more fervently for guidance, for he felt more impotent than ever in a world that seemed to be growing darker daily. He felt compelled to do more, but could not see the path. He sought his best path in life, one that best suited his individual unique talents, but it seemed obscured by a jungle, with only an occasional clearing for guidance.

Santiago was a pillar of patience, and counseled Jesus always, but Jesus believed him too patient. Show me a patient man and I will show you a man that never gets anywhere, he often thought to himself. Not that Jesus had personal ambitions for himself. He had long since risen above that and was content with his many blessings. He believed that a man so blessed should try to help others. A man so destined as to lose both his son and daughter-in-law to jihadists should try to help cure the diseased minds that commit such acts.

Such was the constant tension that pulled at him, and caused him to oscillate between feelings of contentment and guilt.

For both Jesus and Santiago, their trips were the clear spots in the jungle. No matter how conflicted and confused they felt at other times, they always felt closer to God when they were helping people with Santo. There was no better feeling than to see the sick healed; to see people relieved of their suffering. So they both were more jubilant whenever it was time to market their produce, because it gave them an opportunity to interface with strangers and to use Santo as the gift of grace that he was, to spread the love of the Savior.

Jesus downshifted the truck as they made the final ascent on the north road, and the engine responded smoothly. He looked over at Santiago and smiled.

"It sounds good, no?"

"What?" asked Santiago.

"The rebuilt engine I installed, and the new rear, they sound very good, no?"

Santiago tilted his head and listened, and then nodded approvingly. "Yes, you did a fine job. You are a good mechanic."

Jesus was about to agree but burst into laughter as he saw the contorted face of Alita staring in the right-rear wrap-around window of the Chevy. He motioned, and Santiago turned around and laughed at the face, which by then was pressed up against the glass and smiling.

"It is good that they can both come this time," said Santiago. "Alita will be missing Pilar very much when she leaves for university this fall."

"As will I," sighed Jesus. "I can barely believe that she is already old enough to be leaving. The years have passed too quickly." The pickup truck crested the mountain pass and the morning sunlight broke strong and warm on them through the windshield. Santo began barking with excitement as the truck tilted forward on its descent, and Jesus downshifted, listened, and then nodded with approval to Santiago. "It's good. This will be a good journey."

"Yes," smiled Santiago. "Have you told the girls your surprise yet?"

"No. I thought to wait until after we are done with visiting her school. Otherwise they might be too excited and she would not be able to concentrate."

"You are a wise father."

"I hope so." Jesus thought about the term "father," and how easily it seemed to fit, even though he was after all, her grandfather. A good father, he thought, might have discouraged his son from taking a trip to Spain, and then perhaps his son might be alive today. The pain suddenly came back strong and fast; the emptiness that gnawed at him in times of weakness. If only had he not been so agreeable, but had instead, discouraged that fateful trip.

It was more painful today, with the realization that Pilar would soon be gone too. How would it be in that empty cottage?

How would it be without her laughter and warmth? He pushed it all aside and prayed for strength. He prayed not to hate those who had made such a hole in his life. But today, even with the warmth of the sun and the promise of a fine trip in front of them, his prayers were not answered, and he felt the anger swell up in him. He reached forward and turned on the radio, and the music broke his thoughts.

Pilar stood, and tightened her kerchief against the wind. They were nearing Chihuahua and businesses had started to dot the sides of the road. The highway was the biggest she had ever been on with a grass median strip down the center, and two lanes of traffic on either side. In the median, a line of small trees with whitewashed trunks raced toward them down the center of the roadway. They were neat and trim and could have been in someone's personal garden as easily as on a public highway.

The businesses increased in number, and soon they were driving through a wonder world of development, passing large stores and malls and innumerable small businesses. "How could there be so many businesses in one area?" she thought. "How many people lived here?" She knew that this was a small town compared to elsewhere but it was the biggest town she had yet to experience and she tingled all over with excitement.

Nearing the road to the university, she spotted a tall white spire that was bright white in the sun and she fell awestruck by thoughts of the future. The gleaming spire looked so clean against the bright blue sky that it seemed like an omen to a happy future. She contemplated the geometry of the white obelisk as they drove past it and was surprised to see it change form as her view went from edgewise to diagonal to frontal.

It was in fact a giant keystone over one hundred feet high and surrounded by uniformly spaced blocks. She could not divine its purpose, but it was inspirational and thought provoking, and she felt grateful for the math she had learned over the past few years as it gave her a greater depth of appreciation for its beauty and symmetry. She finally guessed that it was an astronomical clock.

Registration at the university was straightforward and without surprise, and within two hours they were returning along the same road upon which they had previously traveled. Pilar was joyous, and yet the day seemed anticlimactic somehow. She had dreamed of it so many times that the reality did not seem to justify her previous anxiety.

Suddenly, her thoughts shifted, as the truck turned onto a different roadway and headed north. This was not the way home. The road sign said this way went to Ciudad Juarez.

Pilar tapped on the rear window, and looked at Santiago and mouthed the words: "Where are we going?" But Santiago just smiled and nodded his head, acknowledging that he was aware of their route. They were soon north of Chihuahua and crossing many miles of flat roadway past wide fields of brown grass, with mountains all along the distant horizons. She never realized how big Mexico was and the distances made her feel tiny.

In the cab of the truck, Jesus and Santiago were both in deep thought. Santiago broke the silence: "The girls will be very surprised when you tell them where we are going. Are you excited at seeing your sister?"

"I am deeply troubled, my friend. It has been many years since I have seen her and I wonder how she will appear."

"Yes, but love guides the eyes."

"Does it? What will she think when she sees me? I am fifty-six but I barely look forty, and you at sixty-eight, do not look much older. How can I reconcile this? She is sixty now, and she writes that her health is not good. You know what I am thinking."

"Yes. You are wondering if Santo can help her."

"More than that. I am wondering how we will age. The sailor looked old, but he was ancient—and he was still healthy."

"Yes. His teeth were still very good," remarked Santiago. "I wonder how long he might have lived had he chosen."

"And what about those we love? What do we do about this? How do we explain? If they do not receive the gift from Santo, how do we leave them behind and watch them age or grow sickly? This is beyond my ability to reason. And you, Santiago—you have never spoken of loved ones or family. How do you reconcile this?"

Santiago sighed.

"I have no one but you and Pilar, and I maintain distance from the brothers and sisters of our village, simply because it is easier to serve them that way. I too have wondered about the future, and feared that one-day we might have to move away, lest our brethren think something is too strange. I have blocked such thoughts because they confound me, and I have prayed for guidance. I have wondered if we have changed mentally, beyond the obvious changes due to our circumstances.

"My mind feels no more enlightened than it was twenty years ago. Each day brings new questions that I cannot answer, and sometimes I feel an emptiness that tests my faith. Not my faith in God, but my faith in myself. Of course, that is silly, since God helps us all, but even Mother Teresa had very dark times when all she felt was blackness, and she felt weak and alone. But she did not have Santo. It should be easy for us to stay strong, no?" Santiago smiled.

"I have felt great guilt that my wife left me because I could not be the carefree man that she needed. Our many trips together with Santo did not help. God knows, that I have often regretted that I never told her the secret of Santo. There should be no secrets in a marriage. Likewise, had I not later told my son, and then recounted stories about old Sailor; perhaps he would not have gone to Spain.

Perhaps he would be alive today," lamented Jesus.

"Your wife was not a country girl, Jesus. I believe she could have never been happy in our small village. She needed the excitement of the city and that is why she left. Your son's fate was the will of God. You must believe that, since it is true that he oversees all. In the long run, we will all be together. You will see your son and his wife again."

"Yes," Jesus finally said softly. "Of course. It is just hard sometimes."

"So it is...so it is," said Santiago, patting Jesus on the shoulder. "We must trust God."

After a ride of a couple of hours they stopped in a town for gas, and Jesus told the girls his surprise. They were only seventy miles from El Paso and they would be in America in a few hours. Pilar was incredulous.

"America!" She paused in disbelief, thinking. "What about our papers? Can we get in?"

"Yes, yes. I have all that we need," replied Jesus. "Your Aunt Maria is already expecting us. We will sleep there tonight." They sold their remaining vegetables as a lot to a local grocer, and within an hour they were rolling again, this time to a destination of dreams. The landscape flew past them as their truck hurtled along the straight, long, gray strip northward, and Pilar could barely contemplate the veritable moonscape through which they were passing.

Jesus and Santiago on the other hand, talked mainly about the scenery since it was so flat and barren that it made their dry mountain pastures seem almost green. A large, orange fiber optic cable remained uncovered at places, paralleling the roadway, and

Jesus could not help but remark about how the Internet had changed their lives, bringing distant events into their quiet little village everyday.

Now they were following that cable, chasing it to the point of origin of news stories that had both horrified and enlightened him for the past several years. Alita was oblivious to all, as she petted and talked to Santo about where they were going. Santo barely listened, his nose stuck in the wind, he imagined he was running faster than he had ever run before.

The landscape gradually became less desolate and road signs began to dot the highway and far up ahead could be seen buildings, the first signs of civilization in many miles. They stopped at a police checkpoint, and then proceeded onward. Jesus and Santiago became silent after that. Farther on, a giant yellow arch shaped like a rhombus stood atop a hillside by the highway and as they swept passed it Santiago noted that there was a cross beyond it.

They puzzled over what it was, but Pilar recognized a similarity to the white monolith of Chihuahua, and guessed to herself that it was an astronomical clock of some kind. Beyond that, the land changed quickly and soon the highway became divided by trees and populated by bushes and grass, and there was a general greening of the countryside.

Buildings and auto parts yards came quickly upon them and rushed away again behind them. Santo was growing excited and sometimes barked. They passed a freight train that seemed to stretch on forever and Pilar laughed as she remembered how she dreamed of riding a train to the north, all the way to America. Now, she was almost there. It couldn't be a happier day.

The road grew ever wider and with more lanes, and they were

suddenly in a cluttered landscape where strange symbols were spray-painted on walls and numerous signs advertised the small businesses packed along the roadway. Everything seemed busy, and road signs plastered with people's faces and advertising fought for Pilar's attention. The road finally curved to the northwest and Santiago tapped on the rear window and pointed to the right side of the truck, as he slowly mouthed the words: "Rio Grande."

The Rio Grande, thought Pilar. So that was America all along the other side. It did not look impressive from here, no different than Ciudad Juarez, as far as she could see. But her excitement grew nonetheless, and her stomach tickled inside. She felt chilled and goose bumps ran down her arms, and her neck hairs stood on end.

They turned north, to a wide expressway, and were suddenly stuck in a creeping line of cars and trucks waiting to cross the border. They crawled along over the bridge seemingly standing still in time until over their heads was a friendly greeting: "Welcome to the United States" the sign across the highway read. The day couldn't get much better than this, thought Pilar.

In the cab, Jesus and Santiago waved to the girls through the rear window, pointing to the sign overhead, which Pilar had already seen. They laughed and smiled and it was a very good moment that they all could keep in their memory. Jesus was still smiling moments later as he locked eyes with a young man in a truck in the adjacent line of traffic. The young man was lean and dark with a sullen face and empty soulless eyes.

It was a face that looked somehow familiar to Jesus, but he could not place it. The young man stared back at him without smiling. It was an intolerant, menacing face. A narrow, tight little mouth set between clean-shaven, high cheeks whose bones supported deep sunk eyes. They were black shifting voids that darted about too quickly.

"Who is that guy, Santiago?" Jesus tapped Santiago's leg and motioned covertly with his hand towards the adjacent truck. The man looked away quickly and Santiago barely saw his face.

"No one familiar. You think you know him?"

"Probably not, but he reminds me of someone. I'm not sure who," replied Jesus. The cars inched along and Jesus kept turning the face over in his mind, but could not place it. They were finally at the border gates, and Jesus saw a border guard flag the man in the truck off for further inspection, just as they received an all clear from their own inspector. They moved ahead, were inspected, and were soon rolling into El Paso.

Chapter 10

Santo is Shot!!

The grounds of the Chamizal National Monument were packed with throngs of spectators, all wanting to get a glimpse of the fantastically popular Texas governor, Antonio Mendoza, known as "Mendy" to his many fans. His straight-talking, straight-shooting persona had made him wildly popular in Texas and his fame was spreading nationally. Here in the Borderland, he was a hero of immense proportions.

He was hometown El Paso, and the best thing that ever happened for many of his most ardent admirers. Today's event was to celebrate a new collaborative effort between El Paso and Ciudad Juarez increasing guest workers and cross-border cooperation. Mendy had promoted and spearheaded it, and helped back it with state and matching federal funds.

On the parade stands with Mendy were the mayors of El Paso and Juarez, as well as a covey of commercial interests and local politicians. A parade line of baton-wielding drum majorettes was crossing blockaded Paisano Drive, streaming down San Marcial Street toward the park. Hundreds of flag-waving enthusiasts and multiple marching bands accompanied them.

The crowds were unprecedented, and national as well as local news commentators were working the area, capturing the excitement, high hopes, and anticipation. It looked like a presidential event, and the commentators made note of it. Mendy was a phenomenon, an emerging force to be watched and documented.

For good or bad, hysteria feeds on itself, and one could see in the many cheery faces that the enthusiasm of both spectators and participants was soaring. A warm southwest breeze lifted the banners of El Paso, Ciudad Juarez, Texas, Mexico, and the USA, and all waved in joyous harmony in the late afternoon sun.

Jesus snaked the truck and trailer through the clogged side streets as best he could, towards his sister's home in Mission Hills. They heard the drums and music but had no idea what the special occasion was. To them it was just an unexpected hardship.

BAM!

A truck hit into the front left corner of their vehicle, grazed them, and flew across the intersection, smashing into parked cars on the other side.

Several men jumped out of the panel truck and started running around, shouting in an undecipherable language. People started to come towards the accident and one of the men from the wrecked truck pulled out an automatic rifle and sprayed bullets over their heads.

Women were screaming; Santo was barking; Alita was crying. Santiago's door flew open and a man pulled him from the truck and he fell onto the pavement. Jesus tried to open his door, but a gun was thrust in his face.

"STAY!" shouted the gunman. "Don't move!"

Santiago started to get up and his assailant smashed him across the face. He crumpled and fell to one knee, and the man hit him across the head and kicked him, and Santiago rolled to the ground alongside a parked car. The man ran to the trailer and pulled Alita off and she fell on the ground, crying hysterically. Santo growled and jumped at the man as the man grabbed for Pilar.

A blast came from behind Pilar, and Santo yelped and fell to the roadway, his lunge interrupted by a bullet. A fist struck Pilar alongside her head as she was pulled from the trailer, and she was suddenly sitting on the road, half-conscious. She could hear Alita screaming and men hollering but the sounds grew muffled and faint. Her ears rang and she saw white light, like fog all around her.

The men dragged a crate from their crippled vehicle, whose fender had bent into the right wheel well and blown out the tire, making it inoperable. They carried the crate to the trailer and all quickly piled on board. Two of the men dragged their driver who had been knocked out by the collision.

"Leave him!" said the man who had shot Santo and who still held a gun on Jesus. "It was his stupid fault and he's no good to us now."

They dropped the driver obediently in the middle of the intersection and jumped on the trailer. Santiago's assailant slipped into the cab and placed a knife against Jesus' throat, while the man with the gun circled in front of the truck and climbed in beside him.

"Drive!" said the man with gun. "To the airport."

"Which way? I'm not from around here."

"Turn right. I'll guide you."

"And you'd better drive good, Amigo," said the man holding the knife. He pushed it in a little harder against Jesus' throat.

Jesus thought quickly. He saw Santiago starting to stir alongside the truck, and he could see Pilar sitting dazed in the roadway through his side view mirror. Santo was lying motionless in a pool of blood and Alita was wailing pitifully. The driver of the other vehicle was still lying unconscious. The distant sounds of the bands and drums seemed to play in slow motion. He knew what he had to do.

Jesus took off, leaving the others behind in safety, he hoped.

KABOOM! A thunderous explosion shook the ground and a shockwave of compressed air blew passed them. Jesus hit the brakes and everyone was thrust forward.

"What was that?" the man with the knife said, as he pushed himself off the dashboard.

"I don't know," said the gunman. "Go! GO!" he yelled at Jesus, waving his gun. Jesus obeyed and they started again.

Santiago staggered to his feet and looked around. He went to Alita and picked her up and started hugging her, trying to quiet her, and he bent down to Pilar who was silent.

"Pilar...Pilar...are you harmed?"

"No," she said quietly, rubbing a large welt on the side of her head. "I am fine." She took Alita from Santiago, quivering and whimpering, breathing asthmatically. "You are okay. We are all okay."

Alita became quiet. Pilar sat her down and went to Santo. She bent over him calmly and examined his wounds. The bullet had passed clean through his body, a transverse through his left lung. A trickle of blood dripped from his mouth and his breathing was fast and shallow.

"Father, what shall we do?"

Santiago was looking at the intersection at the wrecked car and thinking about Jesus. Blood ran from a cut on top his head. He wiped it from his eyebrow and it smeared across the side of his face. He searched his robe and found a fresh pack of tissues. Then he bent down to Pilar and Santo and wiped some of the blood from the wound. It was starting to coagulate and was only oozing. "We must have faith and trust God."

He instructed Pilar to hold pressure on the wound and she complied.

A small group of people formed in the intersection. Some were examining the truck and others the man in the roadway, while a few more came to Santiago's assistance.

Looking down the hill they saw flames at the park. The music from the bands had been replaced by cries of horror and shock. Distant sirens were echoing from multiple points around the city.

"Jesus, Mary, and Joseph!" one woman whispered as she looked at the mushroom cloud forming over Chamizal Park. "What has happened?"

Chapter 11

The Tragedy at Chamizal Park

The parade stand was a splintered, twisted, mass of wood and material, with bodies strewn everywhere. The entire structure had been up-ended and thrown twenty feet forward and many people were buried in the remains. Patches of dry grass were on fire as well as several cars and media trucks parked behind the original location of the platform.

Mendy's bodyguards helped pull him from under some splintered two-by-fours amidst the unending screaming and chaos that had erupted everywhere. In disbelief he looked around, momentarily unable to get his bearings, and he shook off his guards who were trying to whisk him away.

"Set up a command center across the street at the school. Where are the mayors?"

"I don't know, Sir," answered one guard, who was covered in blood. Are you okay?"

Mendy tore a piece of white cloth from one of the banners and wrapped it around his cut hand. He touched his other hand to his forehead, where a large abrasion was starting to sting in the breeze. "Yeah, I'm fine, how about you?"

"Good to go, Sir. This isn't my blood."

Mendy patted him on the back, and turned to the debris pile, where people were still buried. “Let’s get to work!”

****

Jesus turned the truck as instructed and accelerated slowly.

“Faster!” said the gunman.

“Too fast and we’ll be pulled over.”

“You scared, Amigo?” said the man next to him, as he pressed the knife against Jesus’ ribs. You afraid you going to die?”

“No. Death is certain to us all, only its time is unknown.”

The man pressed the knife a little harder into Jesus’ ribs and smiled. “Maybe you die now, eh?”

“Are you able to drive a clutch?”

“Shut up!” said the gunman, “Both of you.”

Jesus felt the knife penetrate the upper layers of skin and he looked coldly into the eyes of his antagonizer. “If you cut any deeper, you will be driving.”

“Leave him alone! Turn left at the next road.”

Jesus felt the knife move back and his mind cleared.

“What in the name of Allah was that explosion?” said the man with the knife.

“Control your tongue, brother! This may help us yet. Whatever it was, every policeman and emergency crew in the city are on their way there now. We can still make our delivery.”

“Jihadists!” growled Jesus. “I know you now,” he said to the gunman. “I saw you on the International Bridge not long ago.”

“Yes,” said the gunman with pleasure in his eyes. “You stared at me. Why?”

"Because you looked familiar, but I did not place your face until now. I saw you in my village a few days before the explosion. A young woman was killed."

The gunman's face turned solemn. "You are from Pueblo del Cielo?"

"Yes."

"Then that was my sister."

"You are the would-be murderers of children! What is your cargo?"

"Shut up and drive."

"You murder innocents in the name of Allah, but no god would tolerate the murder of children. Yes, I will drive."

Jesus felt the knife return to his ribs. In his mind, an explosion went off, a torrent of thought so fast and clear; memories of his son and daughter-in-law; seeing little Alita lying lifeless and covered by bricks; Santo in a pool of blood. His task became obvious to him. It was no coincidence that these men had crossed his course, or that the driver of their vehicle had been incapacitated so that they would need him. He silently thanked God, and pressed harder on the accelerator.

"Your minds are diseased with false truths."

"Shut up and slow down, you're going too fast."

"I have a beautiful garden, but weeds sometimes choke the plants."

"Shut up you fool. Turn at the next road, we are too far south."

"God gives us freedom of choice, but we must choose wisely." Jesus jerked his elbow back mightily into the neck of the man next to him, crushing his larynx, then reached across like lightning and grabbed hold of the gun while pushing the accelerator to the floor.

He saw the oil tank field ahead of them rapidly approaching. “Death for Christ is freedom!” he shouted as the gun fired repeatedly. “I just rebuilt this engine, she runs very smooth, no?”

The truck and trailer left the road at over one hundred miles per hour and became airborne. The truck smashed through a chain link fence and the trailer flew over the cab passing the truck in midair. It harpooned through the wall of an oil tank, tearing it like paper. Oil gushed everywhere, splashing up around the retaining walls of the field as the truck rolled and slid forward past the tank and finally skidded to a stop in the middle of the tank field. Two of the men on the trailer were squashed and killed instantly, while the third broke his neck upon impact.

Jesus dreamed he was swimming. Pilar and his son waved to him from the shore. He waved back, and swam towards them happily, arm over arm, anxious to be with them again. He awoke scraping along the retaining wall of the oil field, pushed by the flow of oil. Half conscious and dazed, he saw the truck upside down in front of him, gas running to greet oil across dry dirt. He walked like a black ghost towards the truck, still mindless. Inside the truck, a young man lay bleeding. Jesus grabbed him by the collar and pulled him free; then lifted him in a fireman’s carry and walked towards the road.

Along the way he passed the knifeman lying face down in oil, his body twisted unnaturally and missing one arm. He crossed through the torn fencing and kept walking, falling once to his knees, before finally rising again. He gradually felt something dripping on his shoe and looked down to see blood, but he didn’t know if it was his or from the man on his back. He just kept walking, headed for the nearest buildings, a quarter mile away.

The depth of the tragedy at Chamizal National Monument Park was still unfolding. The mayors of El Paso and Ciudad Juarez were both dead, as were numerous other dignitaries, media people, and attendees. The body count was over two hundred and was still climbing. Emergency vehicles completely encircled the park and helicopters crowded the skies as news choppers and Medevacs vied for the same air space. Mendy was outside Bowie High School, which now served as a command center and local triage point. The sun was setting and work crews were rigging emergency lighting for the continuing rescue operations.

"Tell those news choppers to steer clear of this area before they collide with a Medevac," he yelled to a police lieutenant. He was about to turn and enter the school when a bright orange plume soared into the sky from the eastern horizon and caught his eye. It blossomed into a multiple-leafed fiery plant before his eyes. "What the— "

BABOOM!

The sound of the explosion arrived a dozen seconds after the flash, deep and rumbling and accompanied by shaking ground. Everyone hit the deck instinctively, including Mendy.

"We're under attack!" one police officer shouted.

Panicked and crouched emergency workers looked all around, not sure what to do.

"What's happening?" yelled Mendy, as still another explosion rocked them all.

"Oil field fire, Sir," said an officer listening to his radio. "It's over by Chevron Drive...a truck wrecked."

"Jesus!" said Mendy. "What's next?"

KABOOM!

An explosion larger than the first two shook the emergency lights so fiercely that one of the bulbs cracked and burst, setting off another round of screaming and panic.

****

A kind neighbor brought a blanket and Pilar wrapped it around Santo and held him in her lap. He was quiet and didn't move. Santiago watched the new fireballs rising skyward in the east and he touched his crucifix and prayed. Alita was sitting next to Pilar, petting Santo.

"Will he die, Father?" asked Alita.

"I don't know, child."

A squad car pulled up and the officers took statements from all who had witnessed the scene. Then another car came. The officers of the second car roused the driver of the wrecked truck and handcuffed him and took him away. In a short while, the police took Santiago, the children and Santo to the command center for further interrogation and treatment. At the first intersection heading down from the hills, Santiago got a full view of the blazing column of flames and black smoke several miles to the east.

"Officer, what has happened there?" he asked, pointing.

"Truck wrecked into some oil tanks. Another mess."

Santiago's heart sank, but he said nothing. He didn't want to alarm the girls.

They arrived at the command center and it was a war zone. A contingent of Texas National Guard had cordoned off the whole park and there was triple-layered security around the large tent toward which they were led. Media hounds jumped to their feet and ran towards them when they saw them exit the police car, but they were stopped at the first layer of security. Pilar carried Santo in her arms and Alita clung to the blanket trying to help.

Inside the tent, the girls were directed to a quiet corner and they gently placed Santo on the paved parking lot, which was now the floor of the tent. Tables were stacked high with two-way radios, computer servers, laptops, and video monitors. Many of the screens showed aerial views of the park and surrounding area and others showed newscasts from the networks, which were carrying today's news from El Paso worldwide. "*Borderland Under Siege*" read a banner across the bottom of one monitor, and "*El Paso Disaster*" read another.

All anyone knew was that a lot of innocent people had been killed and hurt. No group had yet to claim credit and the forensics evidence was still being collected. The police had brought Santiago and the children to the command center because they thought that the attack at the intersection and the bombing of the parade stand might be related.

After a brief initial interrogation, Santiago was led to the girls in the corner of the tent. A policeman brought them a soda and someone passed a foldout chair to Santiago with a bottle of water and he sat down. A nurse of Mexican descent came and dressed Santiago's wounds while they watched a video clip of El Paso shot from helicopters, interspaced with talking heads trying to decipher the meaning of the day's events thus far.

In a little while, Mendy came over from the far side of the tent. He introduced himself and talked quietly with the girls and Santiago and they told him of their journey and their ordeal. He was very sympathetic as he patted Santo and offered his condolences for their rude reception in America.

The governor's news liaison came over and whispered a few sentences to Mendy and he nodded. He turned around and asked the children: "Would you like to be on TV?" The girls nodded yes and Santiago said no, but the governor overcame his objections, saying it would just be for a few moments, and that this was a human-interest story that captured the senselessness of the violence and how it impacted innocent people.

Suddenly, a bright light clicked on and the governor stood talking with several reporters. He told a heart-rending story of how a group of innocent travelers from deep in the heart of Chihuahua had traveled to El Paso to visit relatives, and how they were attacked by heavily armed men and that one of them was carjacked and their pet dog was shot, and it now hovered near death.

They were here being interviewed to see if what happened to them was related to the tragedy at the park. With that, the governor stepped aside and the cameraman zoomed in on the girls and Santo. Mendy bent down to Pilar who was stroking Santo in her lap. And he gently petted Santo, who tried to lick his hand.

"He's still affectionate," said Mendy compassionately.

"Let him kiss you, Governor!" said a reporter.

The camera came in closer in anticipation of a better shot as the governor bent closer to Santo's head. Suddenly, Santo jumped up and put both paws on the governor, knocking him off balance. He landed in a seated position next to Pilar as Santo wagged his tail and licked him across the forehead.

"Apparently, he is going to recover!" Mendy laughed, trying to push Santo off of him. Santo was suddenly very energetic and he barked and kept licking at the governor who didn't fight Santo off very hard, for he knew it was making great press as several camera flashes went off.

"He's pretty lively for a dog near death," another reporter said as more camera flashes clicked off. Pilar finally pulled Santo toward her.

"Get a couple of shots with the girls, Governor."

Mendy acquiesced and posed for some shots with the dog between him and Pilar, while Santo licked him repeatedly.

"Okay boys, that's enough," Mendy said, and the camera lights clicked off. He stood up laughing, wiping his wet face, and a reporter yelled:

"Hey, look at that! The dog licked the wounds right off your face!"

The camera lights switched back on and the camera man moved back in close on Mendy, who touched his forehead thoughtfully, feeling for the abrasions that he knew should be there, but suddenly weren't.

"I'll be damned," said one reporter. "What'd you do put makeup on for sympathy? What a phony."

In a blur, one of Mendy's bodyguards was on the reporter, and started to eject him from the tent.

"Whoa, whoa...Hold on, Bob. Let him go." Mendy said, still touching his hand to his head. "Anybody got a mirror?"

A female reporter produced a compact and Mendy held the round mirror to his face looking for the deep abrasions that were no longer there.

"What the hell...am I dreaming? What's going on here?"

“I guess the bloody bandage is phony, too,” said the skeptical reporter. “This is pathetic!”

Bob grabbed the reporter by the neck and squeezed hard.

“You don’t know what you’re talking about. I dug the governor out from under that pile of rubble out there myself. He’s lucky to be alive. Show some respect.”

Mendy looked blankly into the camera lights, then looked around the tent at all the faces staring at him for an answer. Then he looked down at his bandaged hand, and rubbed it thoughtfully, and felt no pain. “Well, let’s see just how lucky I am,” he said, and he carefully peeled off the bandages.

He stared down at his open palm, clean and pink, with no sign of a cut or any imperfection whatsoever. Then he held it up to the camera for inspection. A sigh went off from the small group of people in the tent, followed by hushed whispers.

“There were six stitches put in this hand an hour ago.”

Santiago saw the hand being displayed live on one of the monitors across from him. Across the bottom of the screen a banner read: *Live from El Paso*. He sighed, as he realized that the whole world was watching.

The same nurse that had tended Santiago bent down and picked up the discarded bandage from Mendy’s hand and examined it. “It’s a miracle! LOOK!” She held the bandage in front of her for the camera to view and it pulled close on the bandage. On the monitors for the entire world to see were the remains of the stitches that had been in Mendy’s hand, still stuck to the gauze of the dressing. “A miracle,” she whispered.

Pilar looked at Santo who was wagging his tail cheerfully while Alita, oblivious to what was happening, petted him. Pilar carefully removed the cloth bandage that they had fashioned for Santo while waiting for the police to arrive. The cloth peeled away and revealed new flesh where the bullet hole had been. The wound was healed. She pulled Santiago's robe and showed him the healed wound, and the nurse saw them examining Santo.

"The dog is healed, too!" the nurse yelled excitedly. She crossed herself and clasped her folded hands to her face.

"Get the dog! Get the dog!" said the lead reporter. He bent down with his microphone and looked up at the camera as he maneuvered Santo sideways. "As you can see...two round patches of new flesh on either side of the body, on this dog that was supposedly shot and near death less than one hour ago."

"Father, this isn't possible," said Pilar, and the camera panned from her and Santo, to Santiago.

"How do you explain this, Father?" asked the reporter, sticking his microphone in Santiago's face.

"All things are possible with God. Perhaps, in this time of tragedy he sends us a message of hope."

"All right, Gentlemen. We'll have to sort this out later," said Mendy. "We have a lot of work to do here."

"Do you think this is a miracle, Governor?" asked the lead reporter.

"I have to think about other things now."

"But is it a miracle? Is it real?"

Mendy looked at his hand and shook his head, then looked at the reporter and beyond him, into the lens of the camera.

"I have to agree with the father. All things are possible with God. And tonight...we can all use his help."

Mendy turned and walked off.

"There you have it, folks," the reporter said, as he bent down and patted Santo. "A miracle! This is Peter Thomas, live from the scene, of the El Paso tragedy."

The camera lights snapped off, and the reporters were hustled out of the tent by Texas Rangers.

Chapter 12

Mr. Big Takes Notice of Santo

Matt West threw a pillow across the room at his roommate, who was laughing loudly, talking on the telephone.

"Come on, pipe down. I'm listening to this!" he said as he watched the wall screen intently.

"How many times are you going to watch that same clip?"

"This is what I do, Ryan. This is what I am all about. Of course I can't stop watching it. I can't figure it out. It looks like spontaneous regeneration at an impossible rate."

"Don't be naïve, it's a con job, plain and simple," Ryan scoffed.

"It looks real. Look at the progressive still shots that the photographers took. I downloaded them from the net and they are very sharp and clear. It doesn't look like Governor Mendoza was wearing makeup, and they have at least a dozen people who swear that his injuries were real, including the doctors and nurses that attended him."

"Money! They were probably bought and paid for," Ryan said cynically. "How else can you explain it?"

"I can't."

"That says it all. The legendary high-achiever grad student of all time at Hopkins Molecular Biology and Genetics Department can't explain it, so what's that tell you?"

"It's a fake...but how did they do it?"

Ryan laughed, and spoke into the phone. "You tell him, Laurie." He clicked the phone to speaker.

"Shame, shame!" said Laurie's voice from the phone. "You are an atheist!"

"Agnostic!" Matt quickly corrected.

"Atheist!" cried Laurie. "You won't admit what your own eyes tell you is true. I gotta go. Kiss me bye, Sweetie."

Ryan and Matt both kissed the air simultaneously, and the phone clicked off. A second later it rang again. Ryan answered it and tossed it to Matt.

"Are you watching the news?" a voice said in the phone.

"Sure am."

"Come over. I want to see you."

"Be there in an hour," Matt said obediently to the voice.

Matt cut across Hopkins' Homewood campus and through Wyman Park to the Bigelow Building. The doorman recognized him and buzzed him in, and he quickly crossed the lobby to a private elevator. Once there, and after placing his thumb upon a scanner pad, he shot up smoothly in the elevator to his sponsor's office penthouse. This was both the source of money that funded him and a powerful political and economic ally of the university, so he always felt a little nervous when he visited the boss, Philip Bigelow.

Upstairs, another thumb reader passed him through final security and he went in to Bigelow's penthouse. An aide told him that Bigelow (or Big, as Matt often called him) was in the library.

He walked in and found Big sitting in his high-back leather swivel chair, drinking a brandy and watching the wall screen. The same clip that Matt had been watching throughout the day was playing. Big froze the image with his remote.

"What do you think?" said Big.

"It's a great fake. I don't know how they did it."

"Think so?"

"Of course. It has to be."

"Our people say no."

Matt raised his eyebrows. "You're kidding."

"Never." Big clicked the remote and the video started playing again. He freeze-framed it on a close-up of Mendy with Santo and Pilar. "It's almost Spring break and you need to relax. You work too hard." Big tossed a first class airline ticket on the desk in front of Matt. He picked it up and read it and set it back down.

"You don't take any of this seriously?"

"Miracles? We don't know what's behind it all, but something is going on down there. If it's something real that we can figure out and duplicate, it'll be worth billions.

"More snake oil?"

"Look, Matt, I know all of western medicine is crap—anyone with any sense knows that. We treat the symptoms, not the cause. Most of our industry's growth depends on that. We don't want healthy people for Christ's sake. We want sick people who are willing to pay to get healthy."

"Ironic, that you should invoke the name of Christ."

Bigelow turned and looked at Matt with an emotionless stare of contemplation. A small smile finally appeared.

"Funny. I didn't even realize what I'd said. But let's keep the religious aspects out of this, okay? I hired you as a scientist, and that's what I want to explore here...the science. What if we could find something that helps people...actually cures them? Imagine if there is something real going on down there. We could not only help people, we could make billions."

"You already make billions."

Bigelow laughed. "Yeah, but we could do better. Maybe get a lock on something new—something really—"

"Miraculous?"

"I was going to say significant."

"What hope do I have of finding anything out?"

Bigelow clicked the remote again, and then paused the video on a close shot of Pilar. "You're twenty-four years old, good-looking, and unattached. Go have some fun!"

Matt stared at the close up of Pilar, her long shiny black hair gently folded on her shoulders; her big dark eyes and wide full lips set in a strong jaw. It was a face that looked resolute, yet innocent and vulnerable simultaneously. Most of his life was spent studying, with little time for girlfriends, but something about Pilar was mesmerizing. He realized now that she was at least part of the reason he had watched that video clip so many times, and he wondered who she was and what she was like.

"Our guys are collecting all there is to know on the Mexican family and events right now. I'll email you the file as soon as it's ready."

"My budget?"

"Whatever you need."

Matt picked up the ticket and slipped it into his pocket and smiled.

"Thanks, Boss."

"I wish I were twenty-four," Bigelow said softly to himself, as Matt left the room. He took a sip of brandy and clicked the remote, scanning to the point that showed Mendy's dressing, with the six stitches still stuck to the gauze. Then he scanned back to the close up of Mendy's perfect hand. He poured some more brandy and sat back in his chair and slowly swilled it down, while staring at the screen.

"We'll see," he whispered.

Chapter 13

Jesus is Born Again

More chairs and a couch were moved into the command center tent, and FBI agents asked Santiago and the girls many of the same questions that they had already been asked by others previously. Sandwiches were brought in, and an atmosphere of congeniality and cooperation ruled, but it was very difficult to describe and relive the terrible events of the evening. Santiago's voice grew shaky and cracked several times as he retold his version of the day's events.

Jesus was the son he never had, a friend of over forty years. To think that he would never see him again left him incredibly empty. The questioners droned on and on and it was becoming increasingly difficult for him to think. Finally a policeman came in and leaned over to the head FBI investigator and spoke something in his ear. "Okay, bring him on in here," the investigator said in his Texas drawl. The policeman went outside the tent and soon returned with another policeman, leading a handcuffed man in an orange jump suit who was very dark and greasy-looking. "Do you know this man?" he asked Santiago.

Santiago looked up at the man and focused.

"Grandfather!" yelled Pilar in Spanish, as she jumped to her feet and ran to him. She grabbed him with such a hug that he almost lost his balance and the policemen steadied him as Pilar swung from his neck. Jesus' teeth gleamed white in a broad smile made brighter by oil-darkened skin.

"God is great, and Christ is merciful," Santiago whispered with teary eyes.

"Take those cuffs off him, boys. We're punchin' cows riding jackrabbits."

Pilar let go of Jesus and the police removed his handcuffs and Santo jumped up on him. "Santo! You are alive," he said happily as he scratched him behind both ears and then bent and examined his wounds. He had a hard time finding the new flesh, which was mostly hidden by hair. "Good boy," he said rubbing Santo's head between his hands. He hugged the dog and looked up at Santiago. "This day, I am reborn."

The combined police and FBI task force kept them busy another two hours trying to figure out what had happened, but it couldn't be resolved. All agreed that Jesus' heroic action had probably saved hundreds of innocent lives, since the terrorists' cargo was a very powerful bomb that detonated in the oil fires, which were started by the overturned truck.

It seemed a small miracle that Jesus and the gunman had survived, especially since Jesus was unhurt. The conclusion was that his ejection from the cab of the truck as it rolled, had by luck, saved him from injury. The surviving gunman had been taken to a trauma center and was still unconscious and under FBI guard. Finally, they lent Jesus a phone and he called his sister, only to find that she was already outside, blocked from entry by the police security net.

In the inner sanctum of the command center, Mendy and leaders of the emergency response teams were watching the

TV monitors. The situation was going from bad to worse. Although National Guard had cordoned off the park, a massive crowd was growing by the thousands. The border crossings going north into El Paso were jammed for miles with traffic and people who wanted to come to witness the "miracle" that they had seen on television and the Internet.

"More troops are coming, but we have to do something to disperse the crowds. The situation is becoming untenable," said the National Guard commander.

"We have a bigger problem," said a doctor who had just entered. "I believe there are toxic substances in the residue from the bomb, and a lot of emergency personnel are being poisoned."

The room fell silent.

"I've examined at least twenty first-responders who have developed a cough, tightness in the chest, and nausea. Just now, I looked at the governor's personal guards standing outside the door, and they are both feeling sick and feverish. How are you, Sir?" the doctor asked Mendy.

"I was just fine until you started talking."

"We have to immediately declare a biohazard and take appropriate action," concluded the doctor.

"What are we talking about here, Doctor? What kind of biohazard? Is it a virus?" asked Mendy.

"I was at the Senate Office Building in O-four when we had a ricin incident there, and the symptoms here look very similar. If there were ricin in with the vehicle that exploded behind the parade stand, anyone inhaling the dust has already been poisoned. Depending on the amount of exposure and the health of the individual, the symptoms may begin to show anywhere between one and twelve hours or more after inhalation. Death may occur within thirty-six hours."

A uniform sigh went through the room.

"It just gets better and better," said the National Guard commander. "You mean my men have been exposed?"

"Not necessarily. If it is ricin, they aren't in any danger unless they have inhaled its dust or touched or ingested it. The debris field would be tainted, but air filters and HAZMAT suits will solve that. Victims' clothing must all be suspect. I've already ordered field tests for ricin."

"All right, Doctor," said Mendy. "If the tests come back positive, you coordinate with the HAZMAT teams and we'll outfit all guardsmen appropriately. Meanwhile, we take no further chances, until we know what we are dealing with."

"What about the crowds?" said the Guard commander.

"We'll get the police and Rangers to help push the perimeter back to a safe distance until the additional troops get here." Mendy looked at the police chief, who nodded and left the room.

Within a few minutes, the rest of the teams had left the room, and Mendy was left alone with his campaign manager.

"Are you seeing these crowds?" said Graham. This is unbelievable. There's a crowd in Time Square, and cathedrals across the country are being mobbed. It's like the end of the world, with everyone seeking salvation. I don't know how you did it, but this is fantastic. I think I'm looking at the next president of the United States."

"Are you nuts? I didn't do anything. You think I'm part of some hoax? Cracker, look at my hand. You remember that scar I had from where I fell off the ladder while painting last year? Look, it's gone! I don't know what's happening."

Graham shrugged uneasily. "Whatever it is...it's phenomenal—and we can run with it. You are the only one to emerge unscathed from that parade stand today, and that makes you God's chosen candidate. Don't question providence."

Mendy stared at him long and hard and finally nodded.

"Maybe so."

"You know so," Graham said, putting his hand on Mendy's shoulder. "It's your destiny."

Chapter 14

Aunt Maria and a Strange American

Maria did not at first recognize Jesus as her long removed brother due to both the passage of time and his oily appearance, but closer inspection revealed the familiar image of her father that she remembered from when she was a very young girl. Those memories of departed Poppa deepened the sanguine love of a sister to overflowing, and tears rolled down her cheeks.

They kissed and hugged, and Jesus introduced Pilar to the aunt, about whom she had always known, but had never met. The sight of their reunion brought joy to Santiago that was soon extinguished by ambivalent emptiness as he fought the dreaded recall of his own lost family. Alita and Santo nestled in amongst them not wanting to be left out of the happiness.

After brief pleasantries, they walked out past the barricades to where the police had formed a new evacuation zone several blocks west behind the high school. The sight that greeted them was shocking. A sea of people holding thousands of flickering yellow candle bowls had massed along the perimeter of the evacuation zone and along Paisano Drive.

But rather than somber mourners, their faces showed excitement and anticipation. Many held rosaries and were praying.

Media trucks lined one side of Paisano Drive for several blocks, while still more jockeyed for position amongst a caravan that was still arriving. Some news crews were working the perimeter, interviewing candleholders; collecting individual human-interest stories of why they were there. While overhead, a constant procession of Medevacs ferried victims out from the triage center at Bowie High School. Further out in the sky and beyond the evacuation line, news crew choppers flitted to and fro like hungry mosquitoes in search of blood.

They finally arrived at Maria's car. Santo and Alita jumped into the cargo space in the rear and Jesus sat up front with his sister while Santiago sat behind her next to Pilar. Santiago exchanged a quick glance with Pilar as they both ran their hands across the plush upholstery of the large SUV, and made faces of surprise at its luxury.

Maria drove slowly and carefully through the crowded streets that were clogged with both traffic and pedestrians. National Guardsmen were stationed at intersections and many more were assisting the police with crowd control. The traffic thinned as they went further northward and soon there was none. They wound their way through the hills and eventually turned onto a long s-shaped driveway off of Piedmont Drive. It wound up a steep slope and circled back into a flat parking area that gave a wide view to the south, overlooking all of south El Paso and Juarez.

Pilar gave a long sigh. "It's so beautiful." An ocean of yellow light sprinkled with other occasional colors spread out to the horizon. "I have never seen so many lights."

High altitude cirrus clouds reflected back some of the cities' light and revealed a long narrow ribbon of black running from east to southwest and across the border.

"The oil field fires are still burning," said Jesus, pointing to the flames at the source of the black ribbon. They got out of the SUV and stood watching the spectacle far off below them to the southeast. A dome of bright light marked the park area where rescue vehicle lights were flashing and helicopters, otherwise invisible in the darkness, clustered like blinking fireflies. Miles of headlights from lines of cars, all headed towards the light dome, marked the early pilgrimages of tens of thousands of people who had witnessed the "Miracle of El Paso" on TV and across a thousand media outlets.

"You cause excitement when you travel, Brother."

Maria then motioned to Pilar, and they gathered Alita, who was sleeping, and Santo, and went into the house.

"This has been a remarkable day," Jesus said softly. "A day of many miracles. I must confess something to you, my friend he whispered to Santiago. In my darkest hours long ago, when I was wild with torment from thoughts of my lost wife and son, I thought of killing Santo. For if he died, I would be free and my life would be my own, and if he did not, then perhaps I would know once and for all that he was truly the dog of Christ as we believed. Of course, I could not, but when I saw him lying lifeless in the road today and with so much lost blood...now I wonder, will he ever die?"

"Everything dies at its own time. We cannot expect to know or understand God's plans, but he surely has a plan for Santo, and we are part of it. What are years and the passage of time to an eternal being? Time matters to us for we have so little of it, but God can take his time."

Jesus nodded. "That is very true. He took his time with me, of that I am sure. All those years of hollow emptiness fighting hate, feeling impotent and insignificant. Then today, I made up my mind to die to stop the jihadists. I believed it was my final task, to die, that others might live.

"And when I didn't? I saw those dead men around me, the one in the truck who still lived, and without hesitation I pulled him from the wreck. For suddenly, I realized that he could have been my son, he was nearly the same age. He was just a fool who was still a child of God. And as I carried him away," Jesus said, with tears streaking his face, "I felt sorrow, and I wished that I could have saved the other men who died there. I feel sorrow now." He broke down weeping and Santiago put his arm around him and hugged him.

"Christ is merciful," Santiago said through tears. "You are living proof of that. You saved many lives today."

Governor Mendoza listened carefully to all the updates. Their fears had been actualized when the ricin tests came back positive, and consequently, the HAZMAT crews had taken over recovery and clean-up operations. Several hundred cases of suspected ricin poisoning had already been reported and more were showing up all the time. Many, who thought they were safe and had gone home, were now developing chest pains, breathing problems and nausea.

There was not yet proof, but tips received by the FBI seemed to indicate that it was not terrorists but members from a Mexican drug cartel that had organized the attack. The crowd was still growing beyond all manageable size, so Mendy agreed to a curfew and plans were made for a twelve a.m. press interview and announcement to the crowd.

The update meeting over, the team leaders filed out of the inner sanctum, leaving Graham and Mendy alone.

"We couldn't buy this much coverage for ten million," said Graham, looking at some of the monitors.

"I'd gladly opt out of this day," Mendy said, lightly rubbing his temples.

"Just remember, events choose presidents, not elections. We might not have wanted any of this, but it's here, and when you go on the air tonight you won't just be addressing El Paso and Texas, you'll be talking to the world."

"Yeah, and what do I tell them?"

"You tell them the truth, plain and simple," Graham said calmly. "As much as you know. And above all...you look presidential."

The camera crews set up for the news conference along Paisano Drive just outside of the evacuation zone at South Piedras Street. An ocean of people pressed forwards against the barricades as the governor's car pulled up, and yelled as he stepped from the vehicle.

"Mendy! Mendy! Mendy!" the crowd chanted, and they roared with approval as he waved to them. A makeshift podium, packed tight with microphones had been erected on a flatbed trailer and floodlights and a hundred cameras clicked on at his approach. The roar reached a crescendo as Governor Mendoza stepped up to the podium. He shielded his eyes, trying to see past the spotlights, and scanned the enormous mass of people in front of him. The evacuation zone had become like an island surrounded by a mass of humanity, and he was startled to find himself speaking to the biggest crowd he had ever stood before.

Mendy gave a brief appraisal of the current situation and where the investigation stood, announced the curfew, and then fielded a few questions from reporters. He explained that there were many unanswered questions to the events of the day and ended the interview on a positive note, thanking the crowd for their concern and good wishes, and he bid them good night.

"Show us your hand, Governor!" a reporter yelled out, and another seconded. Mendy pressed his spread hand palm-first in the air toward the hungry cameras and the crowd roared approvingly. It soon appeared on the mobile giant screen video displays that had been erected nearby, and when it did, the roar of the crowd increased and they broke back into chants of his name. He climbed down off the trailer, and as the crowd quieted down someone shouted from nearby: "President Mendoza!" and the crowd erupted again in cheers and chants. Mendy stuck his hand in the air and waved as he slid into his vehicle, and it ignited still another outburst.

"Mr. President," said Graham slyly, as Mendy closed the door of the car.

"I can't think about that now," said Mendy, as the car turned around.

"You don't have to," Graham said, patting him on the back, as they zoomed back toward the command center.

****

Pilar stood transfixed with awe as Aunt Maria showed her the private bath of the guest room where she and Alita were to sleep. Never before had she known such luxury. Alita was already tucked into bed and sleeping, so they took Santo to the kitchen to feed him. An amazed Maria watched Santo refuse a ham bone, only to gleefully wolf down a salad with oil dressing and bread.

"This is an unusual diet for a dog," said Maria, as she slid a bowl of water toward him. Santo drank some of the water as Maria stroked his short coarse fur and then turned and thanked her with a series of licks. He smelled the familiar scent of Jesus and knew that the two were family. Her light was similar to Jesus' light, except for a large dark spot near her head. There was something different in the taste of her skin as he licked her. A bitter taste, that told him something was wrong with her.

Jesus and Santiago finally came inside, and Pilar excused herself to shower and retire.

"She is a beautiful girl...very special. You have done a fine job raising her," Maria said quietly to Jesus. "She seems wise beyond her years."

"I have done nothing. She is just rare."

"As is Santo." Maria laughed and hugged Santo and he licked her face, making her laugh even more. "You're a good dog," Maria said, kissing Santo on the head. Her face suddenly went blank and she looked at Santiago. "What happened today, Father? How could this dog have been shot and then healed? Is it true? Yes, I know it is, but how can this be?"

Santiago sighed and slowly shook his head. "God's workings are beyond my explanation. His plans, beyond my understanding. We can only pray and hope for enlightenment. I am still waiting."

"It will come, my friend. Today, I am sure of it. And I am grateful to be here and be able to finally visit with my sister." Jesus helped Maria to her feet and they hugged. "Tomorrow, I will go with you to the doctor, and we shall see what he has to say." He felt Maria quiver and he hugged her tighter and kissed the top of her head. "Have faith, my sister. God is with us."

Maria opened the curtains and bright sunlight streamed in across Pilar and Alita in their beds. “Who wakes up early, God will help,” said Maria. The girls stretched and groaned and Santo raised his head from where he was curled on the floor between the beds. “Join us in the kitchen for breakfast when you have dressed. Your clean clothes are on the dresser.” Maria disappeared down the hallway, humming as she went.

Pilar finished dressing first, brushed out her long hair, and started for the kitchen with Santo at her heels. As she came through the doorway of the kitchen, musical chimes rang out on a diatonic scale.

“Pilar,” said Aunt Maria, while she gingerly folded frying eggs amongst sausages, “Please see who is at the door.”

Pilar obeyed, went to the door, and carefully peeked through the curtains at the sidelights of the door to see who was there. A young, tall man in a light suit jacket with upturned collar stood several steps from the door looking out in the opposite direction, admiring the view.

He wore denim trousers and brown loafers and was rocking up and down on his toes as he looked out across El Paso towards Juarez. Suddenly he spun around and stepped towards the door, and Pilar pulled back behind the solid wood door out of sight. She quickly straightened her clothes, bit her lips and tossed her hair off her shoulders.

The door opened quickly at the first chime and Matt found himself face to face with the beauty he had admired on his wall screen back in Baltimore.

“Oh...Hello...I didn’t know it would be you.” The hair on his neck stood on end and his stomach was suddenly tight and empty.

She had the most amazing eyes that held him in close scrutiny with quiet diffidence. His mind went blank and he couldn't speak as he stared at her hair, face, nose, lips, as fast as he could. He felt like a spider pressed into paralysis by tweezers underneath an examiner's magnifier.

"You speak English?" he finally said.

"Yes." Her voice was indescribably clear and smooth and of such a melodic pitch that it resonated in his ears and seemed to echo. He was impoverished, a pauper with no words.

"Yes?" she said again, this time the tone rising to a question.

"I'm sorry..." Matt fumbled in his jacket pocket for his card and finally found it and handed it to her. "I'm Matthew West from Johns Hopkins University in Baltimore. I saw you on TV."

Pilar watched him with curiosity as he spoke. She instinctively recognized how hard he was trying not to stare at her, without success; the awkward movements; the starch-stiff words. "Yes?" she reiterated.

Matt detected kindness in her tone and gave a sigh of relief. "Anyway...I saw you and your dog..." He pointed to Santo who had come outside and was sniffing around the flowerbed.

"He is my grandfather's dog."

"Your grandfather's dog..." Matt corrected. He stooped to pet Santo and then looked up at Pilar and continued. "My specialization is cellular regeneration, and I hoped I might examine your... grand-father's dog."

"He is just a normal dog as you can see."

"Where was he shot?"

Pilar bent down to show him the scar, searched, and found nothing. "It was here...but it's gone now. You can't see it anymore."

Matt searched the general described area of the wound and found no anomalies. "Has he ever been hurt before?"

"No, he has been healthy all my life."

"You mean all his life?"

"Well, yes." My grandfather had him since I was a small child, since before I can remember."

Matt examined Santo's teeth and gums and eyes. "But you're what...about twenty-two years old?"

"I am nineteen," Pilar returned, with a smile. She liked that he thought she looked older.

"That doesn't seem possible," Matt said as he stood up and looked down into Pilar's eyes.

"I look older than I am."

"No, I mean the dog. His eyes are so clear...and their color..."

"Is almost the same as yours, only lighter blue, like the sky," Pilar said innocently, as she stared up at Matt. He broke her gaze and looked over at Santo, who had crossed the driveway and was doing his morning business on the far side of the garage way in the bushes.

"The lenses of his eyes are so clear," Matt whispered.

"And who is this?" said Aunt Maria from the doorway behind Pilar, where she stood drying her hands in her apron.

Pilar handed Maria Matt's card, and she invited him inside to breakfast. Pilar called Santo, and they all went into the kitchen.

The hand hewn wooden table of the kitchen could comfortably seat ten and seemed overly spacious for the small group that was gathered. Matt sat across from Pilar, who was next to Alita, and Santiago sat one chair up from Matt and directly across from Jesus, while Maria in matriarchal fashion, sat at the head of the table.

Matt's initial awkwardness was soon washed away by the congeniality of his hosts, and before he realized it he had given them a more thorough synopsis of his research and biographical background than anyone except Pilar was interested in knowing. Someone who was just above her age group and who had already experienced all the trials and tribulations at university, and was a highly successful graduate student with very pretty eyes fascinated her. Matt's shyness disappeared completely while talking about his passions. He eventually was emboldened enough to try to ferret out the details of the miracle.

"I saw the time-sequenced photos of Governor Mendoza's forehead injuries and they disappeared in a matter of minutes, is that correct?" he asked Santiago.

"I was not actually watching the governor. We were still very upset from our ordeal with the terrorists."

"But you can verify that Santo had actually been shot?"

"Yes, he was shot," said Santiago. "Of that you can be certain. The bullet passed right through him."

"How can you explain that?"

Santiago smiled. "How can I explain anything?" He slapped his palm down on the table. "This table appears solid, but it is mostly empty space, as is my hand. To me that is a minor miracle. I can tell you what I have been taught, that it is composed of billions of tiny atoms that are themselves constantly whirring in motion, but it seems just as unbelievable as when one talks about galaxies being billions of light years away. Does not that seem miraculous to you, Matthew?"

Matt nodded.

"So on a day filled with horrors, when so many people died,

God performed a miracle that could not be denied, perhaps to give us hope, to let us know that there is more than all we see and feel, just like the atoms in the table, and the invisible galaxies many billions of light years away from us, which we have yet to see. Is that so hard to believe? Because that is how I explain it."

"I understand," Matt said. "Were there any other healings that day, perhaps outside the tent? Or was it only Santo and the governor who were healed?"

Santiago looked across at Jesus and then back to Matt. "I am not sure. You would have to check and see. We left after our interrogation, but it is possible that others may have been healed."

"We have to leave now," said Jesus, as he stood up from the table. "My sister has a doctor's appointment."

Matt stood and began helping to clear the table. "I was thinking that perhaps something in the air was responsible for the rapid cellular regeneration, some previously unknown catalytic reaction between various agents."

Jesus nodded agreement. "That is something I had not considered."

"Yes," added Santiago. "All things must be considered."

"I'm glad you are open-minded," said Matt. "Would it be possible to return later and get a blood sample from Santo?"

"He is just an average dog," said Jesus. "You will find nothing."

"Nevertheless, we should cover all possibilities...don't you agree?"

Jesus smiled at Matt's enthusiasm. "Yes, of course. You are welcome to return at any time."

Matt tried to steal a furtive glance at Pilar, but she was looking at him and smiled and he looked away. "That's excellent…I can't thank you enough."

Jesus patted Matt on the back as the group walked out to the garage way. "No thanks is necessary, Matthew. It is a pleasure to meet such an educated and promising young man," he continued, while secretly watching Pilar, who was studying Matt.

"Thank you, Sir." Matt watched as they loaded Alita and Santo into the back of the SUV. "Goodbye, Pilar," he said quickly, before she could slip into the vehicle.

She turned and looked at him. "Adios," she said softly, with a gentle smile.

Maria started the car, and looked across to Jesus, who in turn looked to Santiago, and they all three smiled. Matt stepped aside as the car backed up and then waved to Alita as it started down the driveway. He slid into his rental car and put the keys into the ignition, but then stopped and got back out. He searched his pockets and pulled out some tissues and walked to the bushes beside the garage way. Then he bent down with the tissues and picked up the droppings that Santo had left there before breakfast.

One hundred feet below him at the end of the serpentine driveway, Maria turned the SUV onto Piedmont Drive and then onto Robinson Ave. He heard a car start up, and a black Denali with tinted windows pulled out from behind the bushes on the far side of Robinson and followed behind Maria at a distance. Matt jumped back in the car, placed the wrapped droppings in the glove compartment, and took off down the driveway. As he turned out of the driveway, a car parked at the corner of the next block turned on to the road behind him and followed.

They drove down out of the hills and Matt followed at a

discrete distance. In heavier traffic, he closed the gap with the shadow vehicle and when Maria turned into the medical center off of Alameda, he saw it turn behind them and follow them into the parking garage. He swung into the entrance circle in front of University and parked by some trees on its far end. Then he dialed Big, who admitted that it might be some of their detectives who were still "following all leads."

Big called his people to verify, and while Matt waited on hold, a car pulled up behind him and parked, and a woman got out of the passenger side and went into University. Big came back on the line and advised Matt that it was his people following Aunt Maria's SUV, and satisfied that there was no need for worry, Matt started back towards his hotel. The car that was parked behind him, waited till he had turned onto Alameda and then trailed behind him unnoticed.

On the way back to the Radisson, Matt's GPS guided him to a UPS Store on Edgemere Boulevard, where he wrapped the napkin containing Santo's droppings in plastic and shipped it overnight. It was fifty bucks to ship a dog turd from El Paso to Baltimore overnight, but Big would pick up the bill, and he wanted the lab to get started on analyzing it immediately.

Chapter 15

A Miracle at University Hospital!

Pilar volunteered to look after Alita and Santo as Jesus and Santiago accompanied Aunt Maria inside the medical center for her doctor's appointment and tests. They split up at the mouth of the parking garage, and Pilar guided Alita and Santo into the shade of some trees in front of the garage, where they could wait comfortably.

Santo tugged at his leash as he tried to explore his new domain while Alita chattered on about all the cars that were passing by, but Pilar barely heard and she took no notice of Santo tugging. She was deep in reverie of the young American who was so different than any boy to whom she had ever spoken. Just thinking about him gave her an exhilaration that was new and exciting and made her long to see him again.

"Excuse me," interrupted a woman from behind Pilar. "I'm Carlota Cabreza." She said the name as if it were supposed to be recognizable, but Pilar turned and just stared at her blankly. "I saw you on TV last night. Is this the dog that was shot?"

"Yes," Pilar answered softly.

"He's so cute," the woman said, as she bent down to pet Santo. "Such beautiful eyes...and he's okay now?"

"Yes."

"My producer drove off and left me. We're here to do a story on some of the poisoning victims that have been admitted at the medical center."

"You are a writer?" asked Pilar.

"No. I co-anchor at KFOX TV-14. You know—I'm See-See." Cabreza smiled and struck a pose, and Pilar smiled softly.

A news van pulled into the entrance loop and stopped and two men got out and started towards them.

"I have a great idea," whispered Cabreza as if the idea were so good that she wanted to keep it a secret. "Why don't you and your dog...what was his name?"

"Santo. But he is my grandfather Jesus' dog."

"Okay, yes. This will be wonderful. You can both help us out with this interview. Would you like to do that? We can take Santo in the hospital with us to visit some of the sick children and make them feel better. Would you like to help us that way?"

"Dogs aren't allowed in the hospital," said Alita from the sideline.

"Oh, they will let Santo in. He is a celebrity now."

"What's a celebrity?" asked Alita.

"Santo is famous, now, and so is Pilar, because they were on international TV yesterday. Everyone will want to see them."

"Really?" asked Alita. "May I help?"

"Definitely," returned Cabreza with a smile.

Cabreza turned and spoke a few sentences to her crew, and they ran to the van and grabbed their gear and the whole group headed for the main entrance.

****

Graham Varner studied the monitors in the command center inner sanctum with voracious zeal while Mendy was busy coordinating with all the emergency response teams in the open tent area. It had been seventeen hours since the parade stand explosion and El Paso was not the same town. Hotels were filled to capacity and people were still pouring into town from all over the world. TV news crews, newspaper reporters, government investigators, and most of all, true believers, had packed the town. The news of the "El Paso Disaster" had been supplanted by news of "The El Paso Miracle," and Christians from all over the world were irresistibly compelled to pilgrimage to the site of the most widely viewed miracle in history.

Mendy came through the doorway and collapsed into a leather recliner that had been brought in overnight. "I can't think anymore. I need food."

Graham pointed to the table without taking his eyes off the monitors. "Boneless chicken with Spanish sauce in the big bag, fresh from the L and J."

"I'm actually craving some salad."

"The other bag," Graham said, with his eyes still on the monitors. "Look at these crowds. It must be two hundred thousand people out there. Don't they have jobs?"

"Maybe not," said Mendy, finally looking at the screens.

"Look at that," said Graham, pointing to one screen where a man was holding up a sign that read: Pray for Mendy, God's chosen candidate. Another was holding an effigy of a hand on a stick with blood running from a cut across its palm. A sign below the hand read: Christ heals!

"Is that supposed to be you or Jesus?"

"I don't know."

The screen suddenly blinked to a banner that read: "*KFOX Breaking News*" and soon after, a close up of Carlota Cabreza appeared. "This is Carlota Cabreza and we are live at University Medical Center here in El Paso where poisoning victims from yesterday's disaster at Chamizal National Park are still streaming in." The camera pulled back to show a busy emergency room, and then panned right, on Pilar. "With me here today is Pilar Munoz and her miracle dog, Santo, who was shot yesterday by terrorists and then was mysteriously healed in front of a world-wide television audience." Carlota pointed the microphone at Pilar and continued—

****

Maria's palms were damp with perspiration as she sat with Jesus and Santiago, waiting for the doctor to come back with her X-rays. The door of the office swung open and the doctor walked into the room, but did not make eye contact with anyone. He slipped two X-rays onto his wall viewer and started talking with his back towards the seated trio. "I'm sorry for the delay but I wanted to be sure, and that's why we took that second set of prints."

He turned around and looked Maria in the eyes before speaking further.

"Frankly, I just don't understand it."

He switched on the viewer and pointed to the two prints that he had just placed there. "The first print is the one taken on your last visit here, which clearly shows the tumor on your left lung, which the biopsy found to be malignant. The second print shows your lungs today."

He took the first print down and clipped another one in its place.

"This is the second print that we took today, and as you can plainly see, both prints show no sign whatsoever of a tumor. I want to wait to get your blood work back, but as far as I can see, the tumor is inexplicably gone, and you have had a spontaneous remission."

Maria squeezed Jesus' hand tightly and began to cry. He smiled and thanked the doctor and the doctor cautioned that they still needed to see the blood tests to be sure. Then they left, with Jesus steadying Maria as they walked slowly down the hall.

Santiago suddenly froze in front of the nurses station and pointed to a TV that was playing there. A woman had a microphone in front of Pilar and was speaking to her.

****

Matt walked into his hotel room and tossed his carryout bag on the table. He put some ice in a glass and poured some aloe water across it, then grabbed a sandwich from the bag, plopped in a chair, and switched on the TV using the remote. He flipped through a few channels and suddenly; there was Pilar, big as life on the TV.

Her eyes looked right out at him as the camera closed in and her face filled the screen. His stomach turned hollow and he mindlessly took a bite from the sandwich trying to fill the void. She was talking, but he didn't hear the words. He fumbled for the mute button and finally switched on the audio.

"He is not truly my dog, he belongs to my grandfather. But he was shot trying to protect me from the men who attacked us." The camera pulled back to show Santo sitting next to Pilar, then zoomed in on Santo, whose eyes luminesced in the bright camera light.

"How do you explain what happened yesterday?" said Carlota as the camera pulled back.

"I can't," Pilar said thoughtfully.

"Do you think it was a miracle?"

"My friend, Father Santiago, says miracles teach us to rise above visible things, to help us understand that there is more than all this, and to know that God exists. So much evil happened there yesterday...maybe God just wanted to do something to give us all hope. For me, it was a miracle."

Pilar reached down and scratched Santo's head. "I am happy Santo is alive, and his cure gave me great hope."

The camera went to Carlota and she continued the newscast with doctor interviews about the arriving poison victims. Matt rewound the clip to the close-up of Pilar and freeze-framed it. He got up from his chair and walked close to the screen and studied her face in detail. What made her face seem so special to him? He couldn't pinpoint it, but something just reached into him and grabbed hold of his insides and twisted when he looked at her.

It had him now, tight in its grasp, and the scientist in him wanted to analyze and understand it. You like chocolate cake because it's sweet and high in fat content that appeals to the taste buds, but that's a learned response that becomes Pavlovian. He knew nothing about this girl except what he saw, which was irresistible, but he couldn't figure out why. All he knew was what he felt.

****

Mendy muted the monitor showing Carlota's interview.

"That means we could be looking at a lot more fatalities. You know what I'm thinking, Cracker? I'm thinking it could have been a lot worse. What if it were a dirty bomb that spread nuclear radiation across the city? Who is responsible, and what was the final target of those terrorists that were killed at the oil tank field? Were the two acts related?"

"That's not what I get paid for, and I don't have a clue," returned Graham. "My job is to get you elected, and as terrible as all this stuff may be, I still have to do my job. We have a press conference in a little while. The speechwriter is finishing up something that will blend just the right amount of sympathy and eloquence with executive command. We have to make you look like you're on top of this."

"I **am** on top of it!"

"I know that, but we have to communicate that fact."

Mendy paused, rubbing his palm in thought. One of the networks was showing copies of his medical records that proved he had received stitches in his hand.

"Where did they get that from?"

"We released it to them. We had to counter any claims of possible falsehood."

"Of course," Mendy scoffed.

"What's wrong?"

"Nothing. It's just that sometimes I wish things could be a little more honest."

"We're honest!"

"Yeah, but we're guarded. We're always so confound guarded. I would just like to get up there and speak from my heart for a change you know? Something amazing happened here yesterday… something that I'd like to talk about and try to explain."

"Oh, Brother. You do have a death wish! We'll let others do the explaining. You just need to get out there and look presidential." Graham laughed. "Let's talk about it. Sure! A rainbow appears over our heads with a pot of gold at the end, and you want to talk about it? Just thank God for putting it there!"

Mendy took a long look at Graham.

"Yeah. Thank God," he finally whispered.

"Right," Graham said, as he turned away. "Just don't talk about it."

****

Pilar faded into the background as Carlota continued her interviews with doctors of the emergency room who were describing the symptoms of the poison victims from yesterday's event at Chamizal. Santo always seemed to gravitate towards children and he led the way towards some young people who were waiting for care by emergency room staff. A young boy and his older sister were seated together with their mother, who was visibly distressed by her children's symptoms. They both had a bluish tinge and were suffering labored breathing.

The mother saw Pilar and Santo and jumped to her feet. "You are the girl from Chamizal Park...I saw you on TV...Bless my children, please!"

The little boy smiled as Santo nudged his arm with a wet nose and laughed as Santo licked him. His sister, reached over and began petting Santo, too, and they forgot their fears as they petted the dog that they knew from the television.

Pilar and the children's mother both smiled at the instantaneous change in the children's dispositions and the mother put her arm around Pilar and hugged her. "Thank you," she said.

Pilar hugged her back and whispered: "Don't worry."

"It's the miracle dog," said an old Mexican woman who was seated in a nearby chair. Several hushed comments of recognition rolled across the room and more children and their parents came forward to pet and touch Santo. The tension evaporated as quiet chatter filled the room amid laughter from children.

Pilar took Alita by the hand as more people surrounded them so they wouldn't be separated, while Alita, completely unafraid of the strange environment began telling total strangers of how much Santo liked to chase the stick. The emergency room was getting crowded as more patients with breathing problems were arriving and visitors from other floors who had seen the recent TV interview had become curiosity seekers and were jockeying to get a view of the miracle dog. Pilar slowly worked her way toward the entrance as many outstretched arms vied to touch Santo. She was almost to the door when a woman screamed.

"A miracle! It's another miracle. My cut arm has been healed!"

"It is a miracle," said a man next to her. "I brought her here, and her arm as bleeding, cut by an accident with a box knife. Look!" he said, holding the woman's arm up for all to see.

"I saw it, too!" said a woman next to them. "It just healed right before our eyes."

Sighs went through the room, and then some people who didn't get to touch Santo started to push towards him.

"Let me touch the dog," cried one man. "I can't breathe.

Please!" People stepped aside to let him pass and he bent down and began petting Santo. "Help me, merciful God, my family needs me to put bread on the table. Forgive me for my sins."

"He is just a plain dog," said Pilar softly. "But I will pray with you."

A bright light flashed on and a couple of startled women screamed. It was the camera lights from the film crew with Carlota. They had finished their interior shoot and stumbled on this fresh opportunity to feed. They kept taping as Pilar huddled with the man and said the Lord's Prayer. Several other people joined in. When they were done, Pilar bid the man goodbye and wished him God's blessing. He thanked her profusely and melted back into the crowd, consoled but not cured.

Santiago intercepted them at the door and shepherded them toward the parking garage. Aunt Maria and Jesus were already parked in the entrance circle and waved them over. They climbed into the SUV and it took off towards home along Alameda.

"This does us no service," warned Santiago. "Such fanfare could make our lives impossible. Jesus, you tell her," he said, pointing to Pilar. "Tell her of the dangers."

"What dangers?" asked Pilar.

"Notoriety," answered Jesus. "Notoriety in a media-obsessed world."

"And worse. Remember the sailor's words, Jesus, and all the troubles that befell him in Spain. The same dangers exist today."

"Yes. I remember. But certainly it is God's plan that these things have happened, for how else can we explain the events of the last two days? We have sought no notoriety and yet we find it thrust upon us."

"Nevertheless, I must recommend that we seek anonymity, and that we return to Pueblo del Cielo as soon as possible. The shrimp that falls asleep is swept away by the current."

"As you wish, my friend," said Jesus. "I accept your counsel."

Pilar felt her heart sink. Despite the terror of the last twenty hours she was enjoying the excitement of being in a major city and meeting so many people. Returning to the village suddenly seemed like a prison sentence and confinement. Thoughts of Matt filled her head as the car chased its shadow into the hills.

Chapter 16

The Chosen One Speaks

The crowd gave a tumultuous roar and chanted his name as Mendy stepped up onto the trailer. He waved, and they roared even louder and waved their banners. Mendy ran through the written itinerary, detailing all that had been done, what was still being done, and the research to date about who had set the bomb at the parade stand. He thanked the crowd for their good wishes and was about to leave the podium when a reporter yelled out: "What about the miracle?" The crowd picked up on it and several more people hollered requests for him to address the spontaneous healings. He paused and reflected and finally waved down their shouts, waiting until they had all become quiet.

"I was told not to speak about that, because it's an uncomfortable subject in our modern world. Miracles are something that we all pray for, but few of us ever see...at least not up close...not to the point that it distorts our sense of reality and makes us afraid. Because we are often smug, and we like to think...that we know all there is to know about the world. Many of us say we believe in God, or a higher power...but we never expect to see indisputable proof of such power. Such things just don't happen in today's world."

He paused and surveyed the crowd and there was silence.

"Then what are we praying for?"

The crowd roared its approval and he waited for it to die down. "Yesterday...a lot of innocent people lost their lives. Still more may die. I..."

Mendy's voice quivered as he fought back his emotions.

"I...was the sole survivor from the parade stand. You could call that a miracle, or maybe it was just luck. But later that day, I saw, and you all saw on television, a dog that was shot by a bullet suddenly heal...and my own wounds on my forehead and my hand suddenly melt away."

He held up his hand to the crowd for their inspection and they roared again.

"My campaign manager advised me not to speak about this. But there is an old saying: Who is silent consents. That could be rephrased to say: Who is silent denies.

"I do not deny the existence of God...and I will not be silent! I believe we saw a miracle yesterday, and I will not deny it.

"Thank you, and may God bless you all."

Mendy held his hand high and pointed to the scar-free palm for everyone to inspect, and the cameras zoomed in on it. The crowd's roar was deafening and they waved their signs and banners frantically as he left the podium with a final salute.

Graham Varner stood with the governor's press secretary and speechwriter in the command center and silently watched the performance on the video monitors.

"Well, I guess he must have found a new speechwriter," said the press secretary.

"Shut-up, Dildo," replied Jerry. "Let's see how you word that in your press release tomorrow."

Graham stood silent, still studying the many screens. Honest, refreshing, the Texas straight shooter; were all terms that network reporters were using to describe Mendy's speech. The crowd was exuberant and showed no signs of diminishing as they continued to cheer and wave their signs.

In a short while, Mendy came through the door of the tent and locked eyes with Graham.

"Well, you really did it, didn't you?" said Graham.

Mendy just stared at him, and the air grew tense.

"I mean you did it! Holy shit!" Graham shouted, laughing. "Just look at that crowd! They ate it up. Next time...how about giving me some advance notice, so I don't leave my lunch on the floor."

Mendy sighed. "I just had to say something."

"Well you said a mouthful. The liberal left is going to be screaming about this for weeks. Let'em scream. Just look at that crowd!"

A "News Alert" banner flashed across one of the monitors and Mendy hushed Graham to silence as he saw a video clip of Pilar next to Santo, praying with patients at University Medical Center. Carlota Cabreza appeared on the screen: "And now we are getting reports of spontaneous healings at this center, where many poison victims from yesterday's disaster have come for treatment."

"Turn that off, Jerry," whispered Graham.

"Leave it. I want to hear," said Mendy. He watched, entranced, as Graham flashed an unseen look of grimace to Jerry and the press secretary, Kenneth Shroud.

****

The phone rang, and Matt jumped for it reflexively.

"I'm watching the latest news from El Paso," said Big's voice in the phone. Matt clicked it to speaker and sat the phone down on the table. "New healings have occurred."

"So they say, but I'm still skeptical. It's probably just people seeking attention."

"We've got a narrow window on this. Have you made any progress?"

"I sent a stool sample from the dog to the lab, and I am supposed to meet up with the girl later this afternoon. I need to talk them into letting me take a blood sample."

"Okay. I've got our people working on getting a sample of the governor's blood."

"You can do that?"

"Of course. I didn't grow this company from pushing vitamin pills to making four billion-a-year without making connections."

Matt made a face.

"And don't be making faces at me, Matt"

Matt looked around the room.

"I wasn't."

Big laughed. "Okay. Our people are checking the latest claims as we speak. I'm counting on you for the rest."

"Right."

"Have fun," Big said, and the phone went silent.

Matt picked it up and slid it into its holder and onto his belt, then looked warily around the room. It had to be a lucky guess, Big couldn't be watching him, he thought.

****

Maria packed a few things in a bag and gave the maid her instructions as to what should be done during her absence. Jesus bid her hurry, since they didn't want to drive in the desert after dark. She soon finished, gathered up some necessary papers and collected a bag of sandwiches and snacks from the maid and they quickly said their farewells.

A car pulled up across the garage way as they exited the house. Pilar's heart raced when she saw Matt get out of the car and walk towards them. He smiled and waved and they all greeted him.

"I saw you on TV today," Matt said to Pilar.

"Yes." Pilar smiled and stopped to speak with him as the others walked on towards the car.

"Goodbye, Matt!" Alita said as she waved.

"Where are you all going?"

"Aunt Maria is taking us back home."

A lump formed in Matt's throat and his mouth turned dry. When he tried to speak again, his voice cracked.

"You're leaving?"

"Yes," Pilar said sadly. "Our plans changed. We are going now, back to Pueblo del Cielo."

"I was hoping..."

"Pilar!" Jesus called. "We must hurry."

"Sorry," Pilar said, as she turned and walked towards the car. Matt walked along with her.

"What about the tests? I brought my sample kit to get—"

"There's no time now," said Jesus. "We need to cross the desert before dark."

"It'll only take a minute."

"Sorry, my boy, but we must make haste." Matt's shoulders

drooped.

"Come and visit us in our village. We will be happy to have you as our guest."

"Adios," Pilar whispered as she slid into the car and closed the door, disappearing behind darkened glass.

Matt knocked on the window, and it rolled down.

"When? When can I come and see you?" he asked Pilar through the open window.

"Come anytime," Jesus said before she could answer. "You are always welcome."

The car backed up and Matt walked along with it, his eyes locked with Pilar's. Then it rolled forward slowly down the driveway leaving him standing alone, looking after it. Suddenly, Pilar's head popped out of the window and she smiled and waved.

"Until later!" she said as the car drove off.

"Later!" Matt returned, his face lighting up with hope. He waved, and watched the car disappear around the bend. He stood frozen a few moments looking south towards Juarez, but seeing only Pilar's smiling face, echoing in his memory.

Chapter 17

The Revolution Begins

It began in Juarez the next day; the beginning of what some would later call la Nueva Revolucion Christiana, or the New Christian Revolution. Others called it the New Christian Renaissance. Either way, the English acronym remained the same, and NCR can be traced to Mexican Chamizal Park just a few days before Cinco de Mayo. People began to spontaneously appear in large numbers, as if they were a mirror image of what was happening on the other side of the river in El Paso.

Promoters sensed an opportunity, and secured permission to set up a stage, amplifiers, and video screens. They brought in bands that they wanted to promote, and played popular music, interspaced with periodic clips of the miracles in El Paso.

The crowds grew. Juarez, long oppressed by both gangs and government, wanted nothing more than the promise of freedom, to live free from fear. Speakers representing various citizen interest groups set up their own podiums around the park and began making speeches and handing out literature. Speeches commemorating the fallen mayor, and about the chaos in the streets, as well as economic conditions and the future were all put forth.

Thousands of travelers who had intended to visit the site of the miracles in El Paso, but who were deterred by the massive backup at the border, pulled out of line and parked and walked across to the park to see what was happening. Vendors took fast advantage of a lucrative new venue and hundreds of street marketers selling food and drinks and collectibles gravitated to the park and all along the clogged highways.

Students from the university made a giant paper-mache sculpture of Santo and carried it through the park, finally parking it on the stage next to the live performing bands. Later, a sculpture of Jesus Christ with outstretched hands was placed behind the sculpture of Santo. It looked like Christ was presenting Santo to the world.

At mid-day, Father Luis, a Juarez priest, performed mass on the stage, while the bands rested. Afterwards, his sermon echoed through the park over the loudspeaker system. He was in his fifties, a strong speaker, and the events of the day had inspired him.

"My friends, many of us can remember a time, not so long ago, when our city was safe enough to sleep on the streets when it was too hot indoors. We would linger outside, and enjoy the cool of the evening with no fear. But now, too many of us hurry home after dark and lock ourselves behind closed doors. Why?

"I am not supposed to speak of these things, I know, but seeing all your smiling, happy faces here today, reminds me of how vibrant our city used to be.

"Nobody loves a miracle more than a Mexican, and God knows, a miracle is what our city needs right now."

BANG! BANG-BANG!

Hysterical screams and shouts filled the air, as the crowd nearest the gunshots simultaneously dropped towards the ground. About one hundred feet out from the stage a small circle formed around a man lying on the ground and many women were crying.

"They have murdered Father Alfredo!" someone shouted.

Father Luis jumped from the stage and ran to where the fallen man was lying. He reached down and pulled his mentor, and friend of more than twenty years toward him, but he was already gone. "Why? Why an eighty-four-year-old priest?" he asked.

"It was a cartel member," a man standing next to him said. The man bent down and spoke softly to Luis: "Father Alfredo took the wrong person's confession, I think."

Luis nodded silently, and then performed the last rites over his fallen friend. That was how far Juarez had fallen; that a priest need concern himself whose confession he received, lest it contain facts that a rival gang member might fear. He finished his administration, and asked for help from the crowd, and they carried Father Alfredo's body to the stage, where they laid it next to the sculptures of Santo and Christ. Luis covered his friend's face with his jacket and stood looking down at him. After a while, he walked back to the microphone and stared out across the audience. Many women and men were crying. Some knew Father Alfredo, while others, were just in shock.

"Brothers and sisters!" His voice echoed mightily through the park. "We gathered here today to celebrate the promise and love of God. Let us still do that!

"Yesterday, we lost our mayor, and today I have lost my friend...but from this day forward, forevermore, let us stand united for good, and be undiminished in our faith.

"For you cannot create evil without creating a corresponding good, and good will always destroy evil.

"God is on our side, and he will show us the way!"

Shouts erupted from the field and spread towards the stage. "They got him! They got him! They caught the assassin!"

Four men carrying another pushed their way forward and dropped their load like unwanted baggage in front of the stage.

"That's him," said one man proudly. "He shot Father Alfredo."

Luis jumped from the stage and briefly examined the man on the ground and then stood up. "This man is dead."

"Well, they hit him a few times. Maybe too much."

"Maybe not enough," said another man. "I still want to hit him."

"I say we kill them all!" a man hollered from the crowd. "There are thousands of us, they can't stop us. Kill them all!"

The crowd shouted its approval.

"Kill them in the name of God!" one woman shouted. They deserve to die! They murdered my daughter."

Father Luis jumped back up on the stage and spoke into the microphone. "Wait...Wait! Hear me, please. That is not the way. But you are right! They cannot stop us all. We must stand together in righteousness and demand an end to such lawlessness. In our numbers we have strength, and in our hearts we have light, not darkness, but light. He turned to the sculptures and looked down at his friend lying next to them.

"God has united us with courage. Now we can make our own miracle for Juarez by standing strong together and demanding what is right!

"Let none of us ever forget our brother, Alfredo."

The crowd roared and took up the chant. "Alfredo! Alfredo! Alfredo!"

On the south side of the park a group of about two thousand

men had splintered off from the rest and a few leaders were stirring them to action. They knew which cartel the gang member was from and they had had enough. They knew where his safe house was and how many men were there. They guessed how many guns. They didn't care. All they saw was red. Fear and common sense had left them, over-powered by righteous indignation. The mob grew as it traveled, and by the time they had reached the safe house, they were over three thousand strong.

They stormed the safe house, destroying everything. Flying glass injured some, as rocks and bricks shattered all the windows. A few more were shot in the hail of gunfire that erupted when they stormed in, but none of the righteous died, and they wore their wounds like badges of courage.

The occupants of the safe house were beaten into unconsciousness. A few died on the spot. They were all dragged from the building, dead or alive, and hauled away by cars that arrived to assist. Then they drove them south of the city and dumped them in the desert, warning them not to return to Juarez.

The news spread of what was happening and more men of conscience joined the vigilantes. A nearby police station was known to have active gang members, and it was demolished, and the crooked police were never seen again. Probably, they were killed, but no one knew. It went on like that for hours, and the frenzy fed on itself growing larger and more unstoppable.

People who had suffered injustices and cowered helplessly for years were suddenly empowered and could command the mob with information on any that had harmed them. A name, a location, and implied membership in any gang were enough to be sentenced summarily. The vigilante justice delivered was not always accurate, but it was swift. Word spread, and still more people spilled into the streets.

Thousands went to Chamizal Park, while thousands more joined with vigilante mobs throughout the city. Juarez was becoming ungovernable and the people were the ultimate authority. Their numbers were too great to control, their rage too sanguinary to pacify. The Juarez crusade was unstoppable.

At first, these events were unknown at the park, and the crowd continued to grow gradually as before. Father Alfredo's body was taken away and Luis accompanied him. The bands returned from their lunch break and music filled the park again. To those still arriving, who had not yet heard the news of the riots, it was just a pleasant day in the sun, and a nice family outing.

Chapter 18

The Purification of Juarez

Matt stared hypnotically at the second hand of his alarm clock as it noisily jerked out the seconds. He was getting old. It seemed like just a short time ago that age twenty seemed old to him, and now here he was twenty-four chasing thirty. Pilar was nineteen and just beginning university, he thought. What could they possibly talk about? If he were to follow her to Mexico, it had to be about career and work.

The stool sample from Santo had showed nothing dramatic thus far. There were no parasites and the bacterial flora seemed okay. No traces of any unknown substances. It was just a healthy turd. If there were anything going on that was detectable, it would take a blood sample to find it. He had to go to Mexico.

Matt had already stopped by the car rental place and purchased Mexican liability insurance. Big had forewarned him that they operated under the Napoleonic code in Mexico, and that you were guilty until proven innocent. Even a simple fender bender could be considered a criminal offense, so he wasn't taking any chances. He had his passport, had picked up a tourist card at the airport, and had printed out the necessary maps from the hotel's computer. He stuffed the ticking alarm clock in his travel bag and headed out the door.

Travel anywhere near Chamizal Park was impossible due to the crowds, so he headed southeast to another border crossing. In a couple of hours he was deep in the state of Chihuahua headed south across the flatlands. The highway ran out in front of him to the mountains on the distant horizon, while dust devils chased the electric towers parallel to his course, and nothing reminded him of home. He wondered if there weren't gradients between people propelling them together, which sometimes changed, and then pushed them apart.

****

Mendy listened attentively as the team captains brought him up to date. It was suspected that a Juarez cartel had blown the parade stand to kill the mayor of Juarez, although none had claimed credit to date. The oil tank field explosion was unrelated, and the surviving terrorist had named the armory at Fort Bliss as their final target. Their goal was to strike deep in the heart of one of the largest military bases in the country and spread as much havoc and destruction as possible to demoralize the populace.

This was not yet proven, and was only the confession of the survivor. Finally, the medical situation was appraised and it was expected that more fatalities would occur within twenty-four hours from ricin inhalation. Among those not faring well were Mendy's bodyguards who had dug him out from the debris of the parade stand. Mendy dismissed the teams except for a few Texas Rangers.

"Look," Mendy said softly when they were alone. "Our two guys in the hospital are not looking good right now. I don't pretend to understand any of this, but every person who that Mexican girl and her dog visited with at the medical center yesterday has either stabilized or has achieved a remission of symptoms to the ricin poisoning. I want you to get that girl and the dog and take them to see Billy-Bob and Joseph right now."

"I don't think that would be wise," injected Graham. "It could be used against us in the campaign."

"Damn the campaign. Get her in to see them secretly if you have to, but get her! Maybe it will help them."

"Yes, Sir," the ranking trooper said, and they departed.

Mendy looked at the bank of news monitors, which were starting to flash stories of the riots in Juarez. An aerial view from a news helicopter showed the massive crowds on both sides of the river in the Chamizal areas.

"What do you make of all this, Cracker?"

"I don't know, but I do know this...it can make us, or destroy us."

"That's all it means to you?"

"That's what you're paying me for."

Mendy studied the screens thoughtfully for a few seconds more, then turned back to Graham.

"I can't help but think that there's more than that; that this is a pivotal moment in history."

"It is, and we need to be on the winning side, because the winners write history, not the losers. So let's be careful."

Mendy looked at Graham carefully and felt empty. Cracker just didn't get it. The world still looked the same to him as it had two days ago, but Mendy's universe had changed irrevocably and they were now on different planes.

"Okay," Mendy finally answered. "Let's wrap it up here and get back to Austin before someone burns the mansion down."

"Now you're talking!" Graham patted Mendy on the back and walked out of the tent, leaving Mendy studying the monitors.

Pilar and the family had arrived home late the previous night, so Alita slept with them at the cottage rather than waking her family. They awoke the next day to the smell of sausages and eggs, and discovered Aunt Maria had prepared them a hearty breakfast.

She was a good cook and happy to have family to care for again. Maria had been lonely since her husband had passed, but had not realized how much so until the girls and Jesus had arrived at her home. Suddenly, she felt young and reinvigorated, and glad to be alive. She hustled the girls to the table and happily filled their plates with food.

Pilar finished eating and went out to the front porch. Santiago and Jesus were already there, sipping coffee sweetened with brown sugar and cinnamon. They had been up all night talking. Pilar bid them good morning and floated past into the garden where she walked slowly along the perimeter staring out across the fields to the village below.

"She has suddenly blossomed," whispered Santiago to Jesus.

"Yes, the trip has changed her greatly. Her childhood is over and adult thoughts fill her mind. I saw it when she met that boy. That is probably what she thinks of now. I am sorry for her that we had to return so quickly."

"God's will be done, my friend," returned Santiago. "I confess I am glad he protected us all from harm. I thought we had lost you."

"Perhaps you did in a way, for I am not the man I was, and I am very glad and content to be back in our peaceful village. Should I never leave again, I would be happy. I am finally free." Jesus nodded towards Pilar who was still looking towards the village. "I wonder what she is thinking."

Pilar saw a small dust trail coming up the road from the village. She watched it mindlessly as she filled her lungs with the clean mountain air faintly scented with early blooming sage. It was good to be home after all, and memories of the crazed events of the last days were fading.

She wondered about the American boy she had met; where he was, and what he was doing. She remembered his eyes, and how excited he became when he talked about his work. And she remembered how she felt while she talked with him, like something missing had been found, and she smiled.

The approaching dust trail grew closer and revealed the silhouette of a woman walking, and soon she recognized it as Isabel, Alita's great grandmother. She kept a brisk pace that denied her years and she was soon at the cottage.

Isabel opened the gate and went straight to Jesus and Santiago on the porch, not seeing Pilar in the garden.

"Thank heaven you are back. How could you get into so much trouble selling vegetables?"

Santo jumped up from beside Jesus and went to Isabel, wagging his tail. She bent down and patted his head.

"What about Santo? You said no one should know—"

Jesus quickly raised his finger to his lips, and pointed to the garden where Pilar was looking towards the village, and Isabel stopped talking.

"It is over now, and we are all safe," said Jesus.

"Over? Have you not seen the news? Ciudad Juarez is in a state of revolution…there are riots and murders in the streets, all because of Santo!"

Jesus and Santiago both sprang from their chairs.

"What craziness are you talking?" said Jesus.

They went into the house, and Jesus logged on to his computer and searched the news, while Santiago introduced Isabel to Maria. Pilar turned and followed them into the house, having heard every word that was spoken in the still mountain air.

Jesus clicked on a link labeled: *Crisis in Juarez*. Images filled the monitor screen of gangs of people running wildly through the streets, attacking suspected cartel members. Gang members' cars were fire bombed, safe houses burned to the ground, gang members murdered and mutilated, some strung up by ropes and tortured.

Then the clip shifted to Juarez's Chamizal Park, a reverse schizoid shift towards sanity, where throngs of people were celebrating, singing and dancing to music. The camera zoomed in close on a group of people who were parading a large sculpture of a dog through the park on their shoulders. The shot pulled tighter and Alita spouted excitedly: "It's Santo!"

Santiago let out a sigh. "It does look like him."

The announcer explained how the random murder of a priest had cascaded into chaos throughout the city. Dozens of people had already been killed, hundreds injured, and there was no relief in sight. Jesus listened to several more news clips before finally turning off the computer. He turned and looked at Santiago.

"It appears we escaped notoriety none too soon."

Santo suddenly started barking, and Jesus went to the front

porch to investigate, with Santiago close on his heels. Santo was barking into space towards the north mountain crest, but nothing was there.

"This is very unusual behavior," Jesus said warily.

"I have a bad feeling," whispered Santiago.

Suddenly, the quiet pasture exploded with sound.

Thup-thup-thup...the pulses came at them Doppler-shifted as a helicopter roared past the crest of the mountain. It soared over their heads and circled, revealing a large, gold five-pointed star on its fuselage with "State of Texas" arced around the star in gold letters. They all ran out the front gate and watched as the helicopter completed its circle and then landed in the field in front of them.

A man in a white cowboy hat and ranchero boots jumped from the helicopter and ran towards them with his head ducked and his hand holding his hat steady against the prop wash. The entire family stood transfixed with surprise at the sight. He ran up to Jesus and greeted him with a big smile and an outstretched hand as the blades of the helicopter rapidly slowed.

"Howdy," the man said, and smiled again. Jesus noticed a gold star on the man's shirt. "I'm Sheriff Elrod of the Texas Rangers. It was a little hard finding you. Your village isn't on any of our maps. Mighty purty country up here."

He shook Jesus' hand while he was talking.

"Governor Mendoza sent me to ask you a favor. Two of our men are in a very bad way from inhaling poison the other day, and seein' as all the folks that your little gal there and the dog visited at the medical center got cured, the governor would sure appreciate it if they could come back and see our two men, in the off chance that it might help them."

Santiago wagged his head no to Jesus, but Pilar stepped forward before he could answer.

"We will be happy to go."

"I don't think that would be wise, Pilar," Jesus added. "There are things to consider. We do not want publicity."

"Well that ain't no problem, Sir, because the governor wants to do this on the QT. In other words, ain't nobody needs to know about it."

Jesus looked to Santiago who was still shaking his head no.

"Grandfather, we cannot refuse. I want to help."

Jesus looked at the ranger.

"We'll have her back in just a few hours, Sir."

"Very well, but I will accompany her."

"May I come, too?" asked Alita.

"No problem," said the ranger. "We got plenty of room."

Pilar ran to the house and fetched Santo's leash and then they all boarded the helicopter. The blades swished ever faster and louder through the air and they were soon airborne and sailing high above the pasture. A crowd from the village was running up the road towards the cottage, and Alita waved and hollered greetings as they flew over them in a great arc.

Many waved and shouted back, but only their mouths could be seen moving and they couldn't be heard above the noise of the helicopter. Their faces showed mutual excitement of the great event, for never before had a flying machine of any kind been to Pueblo del Cielo.

They passed back over the cottage, and Santiago, Aunt Maria, and Isabel were waving. They shrank quickly as the helicopter climbed towards the mountaintop. In another minute they had cleared the mountain and were traveling north towards El Paso.

The mountain ranges flowed beneath them like waves in an ocean and as far as the eye could see in every direction was Mexico. Jesus hugged Pilar and Alita, expressing the shared joy and exhilaration that all three were feeling at their first aerial adventure, while Santo stretched against his collar, sticking his nose into the rush of wind from the door vent.

The time passed quickly, and after a while Sheriff Elrod pointed to the horizon in front of them.

"Look at that mess."

Columns of smoke stood like trees in a forest, rising hundreds of feet into the air before bending and meeting with the trails from other columns.

"What is it?" asked Jesus.

"That's Juarez."

They watched in silence as the helicopter went straight towards the trunks of the aerial forest, finally weaving in amongst them on its path to El Paso. The sky above them darkened as they moved beneath the smoke ceiling of the forest, which trailed off into the distance towards the east. Below, fires were burning everywhere, mostly unattended, and crowds were in the streets.

"It's purification," Elrod said to no one in particular. "You have to burn the diseased parts to save the rest."

Chapter 19

The World Comes to Pueblo del Cielo

Rocks popped from beneath Matt's tires as he crested the final peak on the road into Pueblo del Cielo. Wide open pastures spread out below him and far off to the right along the lower roadway he saw a familiar vehicle parked by a fenced cottage on the dusty road into town. When he reached the cottage, he pulled off the road into a patch of blue wildflowers and gave a light toot of the horn as he exited the vehicle. By the time he got to the gate, Santiago and Aunt Maria were on the porch, and they waved with surprise when they saw him.

Santiago explained that he had just missed Pilar and Jesus, and that they would be back in a few hours. Matt asked if there was a local Internet connection that he could use, and when he found out there was, he used the opportunity to email Big, and update him. Then Santiago took him on a tour of the village and its main street. Santiago explained the history of the village and how it had shrunk in recent years due to droughts, and the fact that younger people had moved away to find more opportunities in the cities.

Begun as a spur in the El Camino Real, it had existed for several hundred years, and was never abandoned by a small core populace, some, who could trace their roots to Spain. The settlement had become isolated in the indigenous peoples' uprising of the late sixteen hundreds, but being self-sustaining and with natural water sources in those early days, the settlers had remained unmolested by warring factions and the trail was forgotten by many. That culture of independence and isolation still existed in the surviving locals and most were not very anxious to participate in the modern world. They eked out a living as their parents and grandparents had done, seldom venturing to the larger towns.

Matt and Santiago walked towards the mission, having already seen the small town.

"So you see," said Santiago, "until recently, isolation was a tradition here. All that started to change about twenty years ago, as several shopkeepers opened stores, and began to pull in customers from farms further away, and then the Internet changed us again, bombarding us with continual news of the outside world. The droughts reversed the trend of growth for now. I wonder, what is your real interest here? Is it Pilar?"

"Pilar?" Matt felt his stomach squirm. "She seems like a very nice girl."

"She is," returned Santiago. "Probably very different from any you know."

"Yes." Matt stopped walking and cast a long glance up the north road towards the cottage. "But my visit here is strictly business. I came to study Santo."

"And what could you possibly hope to find?"

"Maybe the cause of the spontaneous tissue regeneration. Maybe some answers."

"Answers?" asked Santiago. "Yes, that is what people always want answers."

"That's what science is all about."

"I suppose." Santiago put his hand on Matt's shoulder. "But every why begets another why, and then another. Is that how you plan to spend your life, chasing answers?"

"That's the plan."

"It sounds lonely."

"Are your parents alive, Father?"

Santiago grew rigid. "What?"

"I only ask because one never knows what it is like to lose a parent, until it happens. I lost my father as a child. Now, my mother grows old. I will tell you something crazy, Father. My dream is to find a cure for death, perhaps even before my grandmother dies of old age. I don't think we have to die. Our cells can be immortal, but they age and die. Cancer cells are an example of cells that don't age and continually reproduce. If they can do it, then so can other cells. I think that people could live to be thousands of years old. I think that what we saw with Santo, and how his bullet wound healed, was an example of spontaneous rapid cellular regeneration that might offer a clue to my quest."

"I see. And you feel the answer is something biological within the dog, and nothing more?"

"Of course."

Santiago's face turned solemn. "If that were true, you could find it with your modern equipment at the university?"

"I think so. Something must be different about Santo. Perhaps he is a genetic mutation. Perhaps his body's cells were forced into some altered state by the trauma. Vigorous examination should reveal how he is different."

"Interesting." Santiago reflected carefully. "So then it is your belief that Noah and others in the bible, might have indeed lived to have been over six hundred years old?"

"It could be possible."

"God would not be a factor?"

"Not directly," Matt said softly. "Not in the strictest sense of the word. I believe that physical laws control the physical universe, and require no interaction from God."

"But do you believe in God?"

"I guess that would depend upon your definition of God," answered Matt. "I am still not certain of how I would define God."

"I will pray for your enlightenment, and perhaps you will pray for mine." Santiago patted Matt on the shoulder, and they started the climb back up the north road to the cottage.

****

The helicopter passed from under the smoke canopy and broke into bright sunlight as it crossed the border. In minutes it landed at University Medical Center's helipad and the passengers disembarked. The group was discreetly led past the nurses station in intensive care, and Sheriff Elrod guided them into a room that held one of the two stricken sheriffs. He was still able to talk, but his color was very poor, and his breathing was labored. He recognized Pilar and Jesus from the command center and asked how their dog was, not seeing Santo standing by the bed.

Jesus cradled Santo and picked him up for Sheriff Billy-Bob Allen to see, and the man managed enough strength to raise his hand and pet Santo as Jesus held him close to the bed. He smiled weakly as Santo licked his hand, and it was obvious that the man was a dog lover, as his composure changed and he immediately became more relaxed. After a few moments, Jesus put Santo down, and the sheriff thanked them for coming and slipped into sleep. The visiting group followed Jesus' lead and bowed their heads in prayer for Sheriff Bob, before moving on to the next room.

The sheriff in the next room was far worse, unconscious, and with an ugly purple hue. His wife was stationed at the bedside holding his hand. She immediately recognized Santo and stood up from the bed, wiping tear streaks from her face.

"The miracle dog," she said in a quivering voice. "Can you help us?"

"He is just a plain—" Pilar started to speak, but was stopped by Jesus.

Jesus smiled warmly at the woman and grasped her hand.

"Only God controls all, but we can pray." Jesus led them in a prayer and then bent down and picked up Santo and carried him to the bedside. He bid Pilar to assist him and asked that she take the hand of the man in bed and to pet Santo on the head with the man's hand.

"Why?" she whispered to Jesus.

"Just do it," he said quietly.

Pilar obeyed, and Santo turned and sniffed at the man's hand, and began licking it at the web of the thumb and forefinger. Then, as instructed by Jesus, she turned the man's hand palm upwards and Santo also licked the man's palm.

Jesus finally put Santo down and then quietly beseeched mercy for the sheriff and his family. He turned to leave and the sheriff's wife stopped them.

"Thank you so much for coming, thank you...muchas gracias,"

she said though tears.

"Trust God," said Jesus, "no matter what outcome." The woman nodded, greatly relieved, and went back to her husband's bedside. The group left the same way they had arrived, and they were soon back in the helicopter headed home.

Pilar was silent, contemplating the events at the hospital. She wondered why Jesus had made sure that Santo should come into direct physical contact with the patients, and whether he believed that Santo had some specific connection to the spontaneous healings, as Matt had suggested. But surely he could not believe that, for Santo was just a dog, she thought.

Below them, the streets of El Paso were crowded with Cinco de Mayo festival attendees. They soared higher over the border and the throngs of people at Chamizal looked like many thousands of swarming ants. Pilar felt a rush of fear and excitement. The world was turned on its head and her life of a few short days ago was like a faded dream, erased by an ambivalent reality of occurring impossibilities.

****

Governor Mendoza walked through the double doors of the mansion command center with Graham Varner close on his heels. Already seated and waiting, were the Texas Attorney General, the Lieutenant Governor, the acting Mayor of El Paso, the head of the Texas Army National Guard, and the Director of Texas Homeland Security. Live video links with the Whitehouse, DHS Headquarters, and El Paso, were being displayed on the control consoles. Also on display were local news feeds from El Paso providing live pictures of the on-going invasion.

General Beaumont was arguing with an ICE manager as Mendy entered.

"This is a dream come true for you guys, isn't it!" railed the general. "Thousands of new Democratic voters pouring into the state."

Mendy cut short the general's tirade. "General...how are things up in Amarillo?"

"We're Texas strong and ready, Sir."

"Good. Bring me up to date."

"We've reinforced the previously established perimeter around Chamizal Park and the monument, and the lines that were protecting the quarantine and clean-up areas from domestic intrusion are now the first line of defense against the foreign invasion."

Mendy watched the command console screens as the general spoke. Thousands of Mexicans had already crossed the border and were spilling through cut fences and across the border highway into Chamizal Park. One news feed zoomed in for a close-up and showed a group of people carrying something up over the north wall of the river. The camera pulled tighter to reveal a large paper mache sculpture of a dog. Others cheered the group as they carried the dog along Cesar E. Chavez Highway and into Chamizal Park.

"This isn't an invasion, General," Mendy said as he pointed to the screen. "That's Santo, the dog of Jesus Munoz."

"The miracle dog?"

"Yes," returned Mendy, shaking his head. He clicked the volume up on another screen that had a close-up of Carlota Cabreza. She was describing a new miracle healing of two Texas Rangers that had occurred at University Medical Center a short time ago. "Is that

Bob and John? They're okay?"

"Yes, Sir," said a Ranger in the group.

"How'd See-See find out so soon?"

"One of the trauma nurses is her cousin."

Mendy shook his head and laughed. "She has a big family."

"We have more munitions coming from Fort Bliss," said General Beaumont.

"Munitions? As I said, General, this isn't an invasion. There will be no shooting."

"They've breeched our border, Sir. It's invasion."

"Incursion will be the watchword, Gentlemen. This is a case of overzealous religious fervor, not one of international intrigue. We will not be shooting our neighbors. I've already spoken to the Mexican President and we have agreed to create a temporary international zone that includes both the Mexican and Texan Chamizal areas. We are erecting a barrier wall and fence around both parks and monuments until this event stabilizes."

"This may be a false flag operation," said the head of Texas Homeland Security.

Mendy pointed to the video screens, which showed the Cinco de Mayo revelers triumphantly placing the statue of Santo in the park. "I am still very concerned about terrorist activity, due to the plan that was foiled this week. There may be other cell members acting locally, or they may use these festivities as a cloak to conduct operations elsewhere. But these people at Chamizal are no threat to our security. Are we all on the same page?"

Mendy looked around the room, making eye contact with each person there, and all were in agreement. The President came into view on the White House link, and Mendy took his position in front of the camera. The President asked what he needed and Mendy responded politely that the situation was under control.

The President acknowledged, bid all a farewell, and was gone as quickly as he had appeared. Mendy, then called the hospital, while all were still there, and spoke directly with his personal guard, Bob, and sent Bob all their best wishes. His voice quavered slightly, as he expressed how happy he was about Bob's recovery. Then he made his exit, with Graham still following closely.

****

The helicopter crested the mountaintop and Pueblo del Cielo appeared far below, bathed gold in the evening sun and looking like a tranquil paradise. Jesus, Alita, and Pilar squeezed towards the window as they passed over the cottage, still excited by the aerial view of their home and village. In short order they were on the ground. The pilot leaned back to Sheriff Elrod and said something, and Elrod smiled and shook his head in acknowledgement. Then he turned to the others as they waited for the blades to slow.

"Folks, the pilot just gave me the word that our guys are going to be alright. I don't pretend to understand any of this, but I sure want to thank you all for helping us out. Those two men both have families that are going to be mighty happy. Thank you all again," he said as he slid open the door of the helicopter. He smiled warmly and shook their hands.

"Vaya con dios."

"Thank you," said Jesus. "It was our great pleasure. Thank you for the ride," Jesus said, as he waved his arm across the sky.

"Goodbye," said Pilar and Alita simultaneously.

The blades sped up and the group stepped away from the helicopter and all waved to Elrod as the craft lifted from the ground.

"Adios!" Elrod shouted from the still open door. He continued to smile and wave as the craft shrank upwards into the blue sky, finally turning to the north and disappearing over the mountaintop.

Pilar turned round towards the cottage and saw three figures standing at the front gate; Santiago, Aunt Maria, and a third person. Her heart jumped when she recognized the third figure as Matt.

They made their greetings and went into the cottage. Pilar and Matt were conspicuously quiet in one another's eyes, each trying to act nonchalant towards the other. Despite his best effort, Matt could not keep his eyes off of Pilar, and she caught him staring at her several times. Her hair was so straight and thick and shiny, he wondered how it would feel to run his fingers through its length. He imagined gently lifting the swirl that gracefully curled over her shoulder, and exposing the nape of her neck. Suddenly he locked eyes with Pilar, and realized that she had been watching him steal a long glance. His face started to burn red, but she smiled a saintly smile that instantly freed him of any guilt, and he smiled back before looking away.

Pilar was already used to having men stare at her, although this time she liked the attention. Matt was not just intelligent and interesting and handsome, he was an American, and that fascinated her. What could she learn from this older man whose blue eyes studied her so carefully? She imagined what it would be like to be alone with him and have long casual conversations. She pictured walking the mountain trails together, whilst he entertained her with tales of his homeland so far to the north.

Jesus turned on the television as Aunt Pilar began taking out food for the returned travelers. The TV screen was immediately filled with video clips of Cinco de Mayo revelers, first in Juarez, and then at Chamizal in El Paso.

"Look at this, Santiago!" Jesus watched in disbelief as he saw a close-up of the sculpture of Santo. "It's a very good likeness."

Alita squealed with delight, but Santiago watched solemnly. His face drooped as pictures of rioters in the streets of Juarez appeared. More videos of Monterrey showed open revolt against gangsters, and thousands beat gang members to death with sticks, chains, and tire irons; anything that they could use as a weapon. Some of the army had joined forces with the vigilantes, and were assisting the cleansing of lawless mobsters and malefactors.

"God forgive us," Santiago said quietly.

"To the contrary, my friend," returned Jesus. "God leads us now, I am convinced of it."

A video clip of Carlota Cabreza standing in front of the University Medical Center appeared. She was speaking English with Spanish subtitles, and she described the miraculous healings of two Texas Rangers earlier that day.

"Is that where you were?" Matt asked Pilar.

Pilar nodded yes to Matt from across the room.

"Yes," replied Jesus, without looking away from the screen.

"Interesting," Matt said with curiosity, as the screen changed to a new shot. The announcer was speaking Spanish and the shot was a house with a rose-covered trellis at the front gate of its yard.

Someone knocked at the front door, and Aunt Maria wiped her hands on her apron and walked to the door and opened it.

A mutual sigh went through the room as Aunt Maria suddenly appeared on the TV screen in her apron. "*En Vivo de Pueblo del*

Cielo" (Live from Town of the Sky), scrolled in bright yellow letters at the bottom of the screen and everyone looked towards the living room door where Aunt Maria stood transfixed, staring into the lens of a TV camera with a microphone thrust in her face by one of the news crew.

Jesus looked over to Santiago, who looked pale and ill.

"Now we have troubles," murmured Santiago. "They have found us."

Jesus said nothing and got up and went to the door to talk with the reporters.

Matt exited through the kitchen door and used the opportunity to call Big and apprise him of the latest developments. He watched through the glass panes of the back door as Jesus let the news crew into the living room and they took photos and video of the trio; Pilar, Santo, and Jesus. Pilar reached out and pulled Alita into frame and hugged her, and Alita beamed with delight. Santiago watched from the sidelines with a concerned look of disapproval. He remembered more clearly than Jesus, he thought, the warnings of old Sailor, and why he had fled Spain. "Shun notoriety!" the sailor had warned. "Lead a long life of anonymity." The words still echoed in his memory.

Matt turned away from the door and walked into the garden along a neatly tended row of vegetables and small trees, while Big talked dollars and cents, and the importance of securing an agreement with Jesus concerning Santo. He sat down on a wooden bench in an alcove in the shade, and took a deep breath of the clean mountain air. Then he mindlessly snapped a leaf off the tree under which he was sitting and chewed it. A mild taste of cinnamon surprised his senses. Big finished talking and signed off, and Matt leaned back against the tree and relaxed.

An unknown bird twittered above, and the ageless beauty of his surroundings suddenly struck him. He looked out across waving acres of blue wild flowers to the village below and recalled some of the stories that Santiago had told him earlier in the day. What was it like for Pilar to grow up here? No wonder she seemed so unworldly and pure.

The news crew had packed up and was leaving, and Matt noted "XEJ-TV" on the van as it spit dust and passed him, headed down the road to the village. They were probably going to interview some of the locals to personalize the story. The bobbing helical antenna element of the satellite dish atop the van seemed anachronistic and unholy, and he dreaded what he knew was to come. Civilization and modernity were about to unweave a timeless tapestry of simplicity and beauty, and it seemed a sin.

"That's my favorite spot," Pilar said from behind him.

Matt turned and smiled and watched her float gracefully past him, before she turned round and smiled. Her face radiated something that he found hard to label; a dichotomy of innocence and intellect that was devoid of carnality.

"I can see why," he said.

"I used to come here and sit, and look off toward the west across the canyon, and imagine what it was like in China and beyond. I traveled there in my mind many times, so I never really had any wanderlust, not like Alita. She always has dreamed of going to faraway places and visiting great sights and cities. But I've already been there in my mind. Traveling is a fool's paradise, or so it's been said. Do you believe that?"

"I'm not sure. What do you mean?"

Pilar smiled and slid onto the bench beside him. She was glad that he didn't blurt out a simple answer and gave her a chance to explain.

"Well..." she began slowly and slid just a little bit closer, like she was about to tell a secret. "I think it means that some people travel, thinking that seeing things like the pyramids or Eiffel Tower is going to make them better, but when they get there, they are still themselves, and then they just feel empty and cheated. They diminish themselves by trying to steal greatness from others. But who built the pyramids or the Eiffel Tower? They were just slaves or common workers who probably never traveled anywhere, and yet they built great things that people have admired for centuries. What if they would have spent their lives traveling to see great sights? There wouldn't be a Great Pyramid of Giza or an Eiffel Tower."

Matt smiled and nodded, slowly bobbing his head in agreement.

"A valid point," he said slowly, as if pondering her profundity. He watched the way her face moved and how her eyes always seemed to drift skyward to some teleprompter in the clouds.

"I have a theory," Pilar continued, "that one doesn't need to travel. If one achieves greatness, then the entire world will come. Pueblo del Cielo is a great place, I think. So many generations of people have struggled here and survived on their own, with no help from any of the outside world. Maybe someday the whole world will circle our little village, and all the people of the globe will travel here to see what made the people so strong and pure that they did not need the rest of the world.

"My grandfather and Santiago are both great men. Grandfather knows almost everything that is happening in the world. He studies the news day and night and has read many books. And Santiago is very intellectual and thoughtful and has studied much philosophy and all the religions of the world. I have listened to them chatting in the garden many times, without their knowledge, and they made my mind explode with thoughts about creation and the universe and God. They are thrilling to listen to.

"What do you think?" Pilar asked softly. Her eyes were wide and her smile angelic.

"About what?"

"My theory. What do you think about it?"

A loud thupping sound filled the air and grew rapidly louder as a helicopter crested the mountain ridge just north of the cottage. As it circled overhead "Fox News" sprang into view along the fuselage. Another helicopter appeared and turned the air to warring pulses that drifted in and out of synchronization. They both landed in front of the cottage, sending oscillating blue waves through the field of blue wildflowers. From the village, the earlier news crew returned, and several new vehicles followed them up the road. People from the village came on foot behind them, and more vehicles crested the ridge on the north road.

"I think you might be right," Matt finally answered.

The following week was a trip into ever-increasing insanity. Pilar's fanciful theory turned out to be prophetic, as news agencies from around the globe picked up the stories that had been running about "miracle cures" in Texas. The leaked news of Santo being flown by helicopter from Mexico back to El Paso, and of the miraculous cures of the Texas Rangers lit the imaginations of millions and caught fire worldwide. Reporters from China and Japan, to Australia, India, Italy, France, and Russia, all vied for personal interviews with Jesus, Santo, and Pilar. Reporters grasping for enhancements to their stories made comparisons to the Holy Trinity and alternately labeled Santo as Miracle Dog, Holy Dog, or Jesus Dog.

One effect of the non-stop news was that it acted as a catalyst to the civil unrest that had begun in Juarez and was quickly sweeping the country. Mexico was non-stop world news, and a nation tired of corruption rose to cleanse itself, bathed by holy events that brought the focus of the world to a small town high in the mountains of its central interior.

The reporters were only the first wave, and behind them came thousands of religious pilgrims, curiosity-seekers, the afflicted seeking cures, and entrepreneurs. The world had come to Pueblo del Cielo, accompanied by a growing hysteria that made normal life there impossible. The lack of infrastructure and limited road access compounded the problems of the besieged town, and long-time residents, used to isolation, immediately rebelled against the onslaught.

In an emergency conference at the mission, it was decided that the only way to defuse the situation was to remove the cause of the problems; Santo had to go.

Matt disclosed to Jesus that his employer had made a very attractive offer, a cash advance of two hundred and fifty thousand U.S. dollars for the privilege of studying Santo at their lab in Baltimore. It was to be a joint research effort with Johns Hopkins supplying expertise and facilities as needed. The term would be six months, and Bigelow Pharmaceuticals would take care of everything, including visas, transportation, housing, and getting Pilar admitted to school.

Jesus and Santiago conferred with Pilar, and the decision was made. For the good of the village and to restore some sense of sanity in everyone's lives, they would relocate to an undisclosed location. It would be like a vacation of sorts, and a chance to learn and experience new things.

The field in front of the cottage had become a heliport, and police had arrived to hold the crowds at bay. Reporters were worse than the religious pilgrims and cure-seekers, as they pushed their way through the throngs, carrying boom-mikes and cameras. Pilar had seen such craziness on television at Hollywood awards, but she never expected to see such sights outside her home.

It wasn't all bad. Santiago suddenly had a flock of thousands, and he conducted outdoor masses twice daily. The coffers of the mission were over-flowing with more money than anyone could have ever hoped or prayed for, and the local merchants who were able to get supplies through, sold out their wares in a few hours each day. The bakery grew to occupy two previously vacant buildings and added more ovens and a new eatery. And Hector's part-time machinery repair shop, became a full-time operation with two new employees.

To Pilar, the frenzy, the wild-eyed hysteria of the people, was frightening. She appeared with Jesus twice daily at the conclusion of mass and greeted long lines of people who had come to see Santo. Villagers acted as temporary security guards to protect against the over-zealous and the occasional mental case. One man had pulled a knife while petting Santo and tried to stab him, demanding that God show his power. After that incident, a stage was constructed for the services, and people had to file past the guards and be searched before being allowed to climb the stairs to the stage to pet Santo.

Most did so with divine reverence as if they were receiving a holy sacrament. But the hopeful faces of the sick, most of whom saw no immediate amelioration of their symptoms, were hard to bear for Pilar, and she prayed for all who came, and for strength and guidance for herself.

Despite the change for the better of the local merchants' finances, most villagers were relieved when they learned that a helicopter commissioned by Bigelow had surreptitiously carried Santo and his family away in the night. There was some anger in the crowds, especially those who were still arriving from many miles away, when they found that they would not get to see the miracle dog.

However, despite his absence, people still continued to come and visit, and in short order, a statue of Santo was commissioned, donated by an anonymous benefactor, and it was erected in the field just north of the mission. A large canopy was raised over the stage where mass was held, and as time passed, although the numbers were greatly diminished, there was still a continuous flow of people, and the financial fate of Pueblo del Cielo was permanently improved.

Chapter 20

The Vatican Takes Notice

Mendy finished shaving and dragged his fingers across his face searching for vagrant whiskers. He stared at the face in the mirror and it stared back at him. It looked foreign and strange, as if it weren't really his. "What are you looking at?" he asked to no reply.

A large thunderclap exploded overhead and Mendy flinched. The sounds of screaming echoed emptily in his memory and he saw the faces of some of the people with whom he had shook hands at the parade stand in El Paso. He gave one last glance to the stranger in his mirror, and walked into the adjacent bedroom, where his wife was brushing her hair. He watched her silently, the way she gave a twist to the brush at the end of each stroke, and remembered the young beauty he had married over twenty years ago. Claire saw him watching and turned around and smiled warmly.

"I remember you watching me like that, twenty years ago."

"Yes," Mendy said softly.

"But not lately."

"Because you have a stupid husband." He smiled and studied her face, and the young innocent girl was still there, still beautiful, and warm and kind, devoid of any pretense.

"Are you okay?" Claire said, and stopped brushing her hair.

"Yes." He crossed the room and bent down and kissed her forehead. "I was just thinking that it would be nice to go to church together this Sunday. Maybe Saint Mary's. I haven't been for quite a while."

"I know," she said with a sweetness that scolded. "You sure you're okay?"

"Better than okay." He touched his hand to her cheek and looked deep into her eyes with warmth that she hadn't seen in a long time. "I was just thinking how lucky I am to have you."

Claire's eyes filled as she smiled, and she quickly grabbed a tissue and dabbed them dry.

"Get out of here, you charmer," she said with a smile.

Mendy hugged her and rubbed her on the back and went out to his study. Graham was already there, waiting for him.

The media control console was turned on and Graham was monitoring six stations simultaneously, constantly flipping through channels to view campaign results and developing issues. Mendy watched silently, momentarily mesmerized by the man and his method.

Graham was good at what he did, not just because he was a news junkie, but also because he had an innate ability to connect the dots of seemingly disparate events and project future possibilities. Beyond that, he was a brilliant broker of human emotion, knowing what buttons to push and when. He knew what would sell, and more importantly, he knew how to sell it.

Carlota Cabreza appeared on one of the screens, and the camera panned past her to a shot of a makeshift shrine to Santo. Grown up around his sculpture were many candles, bouquets, and remembrances that had been carried to Chamizal Park by enraptured believers. Some had erected crosses on either side of the sculpture, and it was surrounded with thousands of flowers and gifts left to commemorate those who had died there.

Many offerings were designed to specifically honor miracles now associated with Santo. The crowds had not diminished and were constantly replenished by those returning with fresh flowers and new offerings.

"What is she saying?" Mendy asked. Graham flinched, snapped his head around to Mendy, and then looked back at the screens for an instant, before clicking the remote he held in his hand.

"The overall tone here has changed." Cabreza's voiceover narrated a series of scenes, beginning with crying mourners of days past.

"It has gone from initial shock, horror, and despair..."

The scene changed to a live shot of people queuing past the shrine, placing flowers and mementos, many wearing smiles on their faces.

"To one of reverence and hope for the future, perhaps buoyed by recent positive events in Juarez and elsewhere."

A montage of scenes from Juarez, showing vigilantes escorting bound cartel members through the streets and delivering them to police and army troops, was followed by similar scenes from other cities including Monterey, Los Angeles, Detroit, and Miami.

"Now this phenomenon, this inspired spirit of individual activism associated with Santo, seems to be growing, and has spread across the country. But it's also more than that. Many have called the unexplained healings after the disaster here miracles, and the dog, Santo, owned by a poor Mexican farmer named Jesus Munoz, has alternately been labeled the Miracle Dog, Jesus Dog, and the Dog of

Jesus. A new Christian fervor has gripped America and Mexico, and many are calling it...a revolution."

The camera went to Cabreza, live at Chamizal, with the sculpture of Santo flanked by crosses in the background.

"And it all started here...in El Paso."

Cabreza signed off, and the screen went to national news, and Graham clicked the mute.

"Maybe we should fly over there tomorrow. You could hold a news conference and update, right at the monument. Especially now, with the tie-in to national events, it could work very well."

"Claire and I are going to mass tomorrow at Saint Mary's."

"Even better," said Graham. "We can tape you and Claire walking to mass in the morning, and then do El Paso at the monument in the afternoon. It shows you working seven-days-a-week, but still taking time to worship."

"For god sakes, Cracker, don't you ever turn it off?"

"No! And neither should you. We don't have that luxury, not if we want to win, not if we really want to lead this country to a better place. Don't demonize what I do. Do you want to win?"

Mendy looked at him blank-faced.

"Do you want to win? It's an easy question, one whose answer should have popped out of your mouth immediately. If you don't have the guts for it, just say so, and I will understand. No sane man should want to be president of the United States…unless he thinks he can bring something to the table that the others can't...unless he thinks that he is the best thing for the country. I'm here because I think you do bring something better to the table. I think you are what this country needs and that you will work tirelessly to push us all forward to a better future. Am I wrong?"

"I hope not."

Graham laughed and threw his arm around Mendy and hugged him. "I'm not wrong, and you know why I know I'm not wrong? Because you are the only living survivor of that parade stand… because some force beyond my understanding not only chose to save you, but also to heal you....on national television."

Cracker paused and looked Mendy in the eye.

"Most of all, because you're my friend, and you're the best man I know. I think you're better than you know yourself, and I know that if you win, you will never let this country down. You'll take command, just like you did at the parade grounds when you were bloodied and shaken, and you will give it your all. That is why I feel no shame or shyness about pushing you at every possible opportunity. If not you...who? Who would you choose?"

Mendy stared long and hard at Graham. He rubbed his thumb back and forth across the palm of its opposing hand, thinking.

Finally he smiled.

"You're right, Cracker. There is no one else, and it's only eight years, and after that I'm free. Let's do it!"

"Now you're talking. I'll get things lined up for tomorrow."

Graham whipped out his phone and turned away as he switched back into campaign mode, leaving Mendy to study the display screens. A banner along the bottom of one of the screens read: *Where is Santo?*

****

Pilar stared through the oval window into blank whiteness and an uncertain future. Her life had changed so dramatically in the past several months that it was hard to grasp reality. She glanced across the glass tabletop to where Jesus sat reading the Wall Street Journal and he seemed to sense her stare and looked up at her and smiled.

"There is much information in this newspaper. I wish my English were better. So many things are happening in the world right now."

Pilar smiled as Jesus turned back to the newspaper and she studied him as if seeing him for the first time; this man whom she had always known only as Grandfather, but who had raised her as a loving father and had recently ballooned in front of her, into a hero who had saved many lives. People are often so much more than we know, she thought.

She turned her attention to Matt, who was sitting across the aisle in an opposing adjacent seat, examining Santo's teeth with curiosity.

Santo saw her looking at him and took it as an invitation to escape, so he bounded across the aisle to Pilar and jumped into her welcoming arms. She hugged him and kissed him on top his head and then scratched him gently behind both ears the way he loved it so much, and he leaned in towards her as she spoke soothing nothings to him while she looked out at breaking holes in the diffuse whiteness beyond the window.

The white disintegrated into passing powder puffs and then disappeared entirely as the Gulfstream dropped beneath the cloud ceiling, revealing a wrinkled, rolling emerald blanket of mountainous hills. Pilar sighed, and Jesus looked up from his paper and followed her lead when he saw the scene below them.

"Never, have I seen so much green," Pilar said.

"That's West Virginia," said Matt, pointing to a flight monitor.

"We'll be crossing into Maryland shortly."

"And is Maryland so beautiful?" asked Pilar.

"Some of it is."

The sun suddenly streamed in through the window and bathed Pilar's face with radiance and Matt found it impossible to break his stare. She smiled serenely, unfazed by his careful inspection, as his eyes traced the details of her beauty into his memory.

Her penetrating eyes that seemed to change from black to blue, depending upon how the light hit them; the lean, athletic quality of her skin, stretched so tight across her face and cheekbones that she might have been a long-distance runner; the perfect pearl-white teeth that would make her the instant love of any dentist, set behind full luscious lips that never needed lipstick to enhance them. She exuded the clean, guileless beauty of a desert flower, untainted and undiminished by anything near it.

Pilar turned back to the window and Matt continued to stare in abandon.

Within the hour, they had landed and disembarked at BWI, and they were then whisked north to Baltimore by a company limo.

The building manager met them at the entrance court of the Bigelow Building in Wyman Park, where he directed a quick and successful battle for the luggage between Jesus and Pilar versus several building staff members. They were then guided through a plush lobby to the elevators, one of which took them up seven floors to a spacious four-bedroom apartment provided for them by Bigelow Pharmaceuticals. The staff triumphantly deposited their newest tenants' luggage and left unceremoniously, while the building manager conducted a tour of the apartment and its many amenities. Jesus and Pilar watched and listened in silent awe of the luxury.

Upon completion of the tour, they were scheduled an hour respite, whereafter they were extended an undeniable invitation to lunch with their benefactor, Philip Bigelow, at his penthouse above them. With that, the building manager left, and Matt also excused himself, promising to return within an hour to escort them to lunch.

The door closed behind Matt, and the apartment went silent. Pilar and Jesus momentarily stared blank-faced at one another before bursting out in laughter.

"Bienvenidos a los Estados Unidos," Jesus said, laughing.

"Welcome to the United States," Pilar repeated in English.

Jesus went into the kitchen, removed a glass from a cabinet, and placed it under a dispenser on the door of the refrigerator. Ice clinked noisily into it. Then he moved it to the next dispenser and it filled with water. He smiled and took a big sip from the glass. "This I like...but not the taste."

He wrinkled his nose, and poured the water down the sink.

Pilar laughed, then searched and found a bowl, and filled it with water for Santo, who was hurriedly nosing his way through the apartment. There were many new smells that he needed to explore; aromatic pine base moldings that mixed with the scent of fresh latex paint, a new carpet smell, and a smell in one bathroom that reminded him of a field of sage that he had recently played in with Pilar. He smelled people, too, but no one that he knew.

Pilar and Jesus chose their respective bedrooms, she, the one with a southerly view of the downtown skyline of Baltimore, and he, one with an easterly view looking down across Hopkins' Homewood Campus and the clock tower. They were both in the middle of unpacking, when the sound of horns playing El Harabe Tapatio (the Mexican Hat Dance) filled the apartment.

Pilar ran from her room, and found Jesus searching in puzzled bewilderment throughout the living room while Santo barked loudly in the background. Suddenly the music stopped playing. Pilar looked at Jesus and he shrugged.

"I don't see any radio or audio unit."

They both turned to go back to their unpacking, when the music started again.

"It seems to be coming from speakers in the ceiling," said Pilar, as Santo ran barking through the living room. It stopped a second time and they both paused before finally returning to their rooms.

Suddenly, there was a loud knock at the door, and Santo ran toward it, barking. Pilar opened the door to Matt, whose face quickly lit with a smile.

"I like your door chime," he said, while pointing to the push-button switch on the doorframe. "Nice touch."

Pilar looked at the illuminated button and nodded, not really understanding the inference.

They went inside and collected Jesus and Santo, and then Matt escorted them down the hall and into the private elevator that went upstairs to Philip Bigelow's penthouse. Once in the elevator, Matt tried to make small talk with Pilar and her grandfather, hoping it would hide the awkwardness he felt in Pilar's presence. She was younger than he, but his newfound emotions made him feel out of control and sheepish.

She wasn't dazzled by his knowledge or accomplishments and she seemed to be toying with him at times, as she swung between warmth and aloofness. Jesus watched Matt with sympathetic amusement, recalling his own early days of courtship with Pilar's grandmother. A smile crept across his face as Matt struggled to look at ease and calm while talking, but his sweating palms that he innocently wiped dry on his pants legs telegraphed his nervousness to Jesus.

It had been a long while since Jesus had remembered those days of youth and their exquisite tortures, back in the days when just one look from the object of his affection could torment or enrapture. He looked briefly at Pilar, who in complete innocence was a master of feminine wile. Matt had catalyzed her transformation into womanhood, and every motion she made while in his presence seemed new to Jesus. His little nieta had emerged as a butterfly. Finally, he rescued Matt from his torment.

"What is this Mr. Bigelow like, Matthew?"

"It's hard to say, I don't quite have him figured. Sometimes I feel like he's my friend and mentor, and other times it's like I don't know him at all. He lives alone. I've never seen him with a woman, but I don't think he prefers men. He has a lot of books, and he reads a lot. He likes history and zoology. I know that, because he always quotes guys like Marcus Aurelius and Confucius, and he likes to compare human endeavor to the actions of primates and other animals, and insects, too. He seems to know a lot about everything, but he never lauds it over my head. Most of the time, I think I like him."

"When do you not like him?"

Matt laughed. "When he's dismissive. I don't think he means to be, but sometimes he can be abrasive and short. Maybe that's what being a billionaire does to you, I don't know. He's the only billionaire I know."

The elevator doors slid open and they stepped out into the penthouse atrium. Sunlight shafted down from its crystal dome through waving leaves of planted trees and danced brightly on a polished white marble floor. A softly scented breeze carried the gurgling sounds of a terraced waterfall from on the far side of the atrium, whose opposing glass curtain walls gave east and west exposures that assured perfect views of the sunrise and sunset.

Jesus looked through the eastern curtain wall, down at the clock tower, and then scanned outward across Hopkins campus. Then he walked towards the waterfall and stared at the western horizon and distant hills.

"One man owns this entire building?"

"Yes," answered Matt. "This and a lot more."

"Impressive." Jesus nodded.

Pilar was struggling to keep Santo from drinking from the waterfall and seemed oblivious.

"Mr. Bigelow is expecting you," a voice said from the far side of the atrium.

They turned to see the tall, well-tailored figure of the building manager standing at the entrance to the penthouse. He conducted them to the library study, where several other guests were waiting and introduced them. Among them were Joseph Tydings, from the law firm of Tydings and Turner, Bigelow's legal counsel, and Ian Worth, of Bigelow Pharmaceuticals. As soon as the introductions were completed, and as if on cue, Bigelow descended the spiral staircase from the observatory above the library and greeted everyone.

"A sincere welcome my friends," Bigelow said with warmth as he shook hands with Jesus and Pilar. He bent down and patted Santo on the head, and then scratched him lightly behind one ear as he examined him with curiosity. "So this is the fellow who has caused such a stir. He looks very plain, doesn't he? Except for those blue eyes."

"He is just a plain and simple dog," Pilar said sincerely.

"Is he?" Bigelow searched Pilar's face and then glanced to Jesus. "The world doesn't think so. Have you seen the latest headlines?"

Bigelow rose and walked to a table where he pressed a button and a large wall screen switched on. A news clip from China was playing that showed thousands of people protesting in the People's Square in Shanghai. A close-up showed people carrying a statue of a dog, while a speaker talked to the crowd through a bullhorn.

"That's a pretty good likeness of Santo."

Jesus sighed.

"It's on all the news channels. Over a thousand people have been killed in riots throughout South America, and the vigilante justice groups that started in Juarez have spread throughout Mexico. South Korea, Japan...even Thailand is experiencing massive rallies, as are many cities here in our country. We seem to be standing at a cusp in history, my friends, and Santo has become a global phenomenon."

"If we are, it is God's will," said Jesus.

"Isn't everything?" Bigelow replied, with a warm smile. "Come, let us eat," he said, as he guided the group into the dining room.

****

At the Vatican, inside the papal private library several men watched the news detailing world events. The smallest of the group, dressed in a white cassock asked the man next to him:

“What is the latest from the Americas?”

“The turmoil is still spreading, Your Holiness.”

“What have our people turned up on this dog?”

“The dog and its owner have disappeared, possibly gone into hiding. We are searching for them, even now.”

“They must be found as quickly as possible and protected. You understand the dangcrs that thcy facc?”

“Yes, Holy Father. We have our best people on it.”

The Pope looked back to the wall screen where a massive Chinese throng was pictured, praying in the People’s Square.

“Could it be, that after all these years...we find that the legend of Saint James was truth?”

Chapter 21

Pilar's First Kiss

Santiago swept the never-ending dust from the sidewalk between the mission and his garden. The sidewalk was in shade from the grape arbor that covered it, but still he perspired from the rigor of his movements. Sweeping was a tonic that helped him clear his thoughts, which these days were too many, and often conflicting.

"Good day, Father," came a voice from the fence. "You have a very orderly garden."

Santiago looked up from his sweeping to see a man and a woman at the fence; the man, dressed all in white and wearing a white Panama hat; and the woman, dressed inappropriately in black, which was foolish in the mid-day sun. They seemed like a matched pair of salt-and-pepper shakers. "The garden is not what it used to be. There is not much time to keep up with it lately."

"May we enter?" said the man, as they walked through the gate.

"Of course, come right in," Santiago replied, directing them towards a shaded table in the yard. "How may I help you?"

"We traveled very far to see Santo," the man said.

"I see. I am very sorry, my friend, but the crowds became so large that the townspeople grew weary, and Santo has been taken away for a while."

“We had hoped to see the dog perform a miracle.”

Santiago smiled glumly.

“Only Christ performs miracles.”

The man looked at the woman and they both smiled.

Maria emerged from the rectory behind them carrying a pitcher of water with sliced lemons in it and a glass. She slid it onto the table, wiped her hands on her apron, and walked away.

The man looked at the water, and Santiago invited him to drink. A lemon slice splashed into the glass as Santiago filled it for him, and the ejected water wet the table. The man lifted the glass and took a long drink and set the glass back down upon the table.

“You have never asked for anything for yourself, Santiago.”

“Do I know you?”

The woman started down the sidewalk to the gate.

“Enjoy your sweeping,” the man said as he followed the woman down the walk. He turned round at the gate and stopped. “Look to Juarez.”

“What?” asked Santiago.

“There, you will find your son.”

The man smiled and turned, exited the gate, and walked out of sight around the front of the mission.

“Wait!”

Santiago leapt from his chair and ran fast through the open gate before it could close, but when he rounded the front of the mission, the man and woman were no where to be seen. He stood stunned for several seconds as he searched Main Street for a glimpse of them, but they were not there. Finally, he turned and walked back into the rectory yard. He felt dizzy and sat back down at the table, trying to think.

"Maria!"

Maria quickly appeared.

"Did you recognize those people?"

"What people?"

"The man and woman that were with me here."

"I saw no one," Maria replied. "Are you going to drink your water?"

Santiago looked down at the table and saw the full pitcher. The glass was empty and dry, as was the tabletop.

"Yes," he said. "In a moment."

Maria went back into the house.

Santiago stared at the water pitcher for several seconds before pouring a glass. He watched a lemon wedge splash into the glass, just as before. He took a slow drink of water and then wiped tears from his eyes. A gust of wind threw dust back onto the clean sidewalk and blew cool across his perspiring brow.

"My son," he whispered to the wind.

****

The chopper flew a half-doughnut path high above the crowd, which looked like so many ants below in the new International Zone. It was unrecognizable compared to a few months previous, and a double line of ten-foot high concrete barrier walls now separated the high school and surrounding neighborhood from the former park, with military patrols on constant vigil, patrolling the space between the walls.

Paisano Drive had been transformed into a new marketplace lined with street vendors hawking their wares to a never-ending stream of pilgrims, and the makeshift shrine housing an effigy of Santo had been enlarged to include the names of those killed in the El Paso tragedy, which was now old news to the world at large. The site of the tragedy and Santo had become irrevocably linked through what were now viewed as connected miracles, and the International Zone was a political bullhorn pointed at the administrative powers in both Mexico and the United States.

They spiraled lower, and Mendy's stomach muscles felt like a stretched rubber band as he looked down on a new stage that had been built. He suddenly felt cold, and shivered invisibly from a surge of adrenalin.

"Maybe this wasn't such a great idea," he said quietly to Graham. "I didn't realize I would feel..."

"Remember what we talked about. Events are beyond us. All that matters is what we make of them."

Mendy nodded. He took a deep breath and sank his fingernails into the sides of his knees, squeezing as tightly as he could to stop the adrenaline shakes.

People were packed tightly up against the stage barriers, enrapt listeners of Father Luis, who had become a premiere character in the Mexican vigilante justice movement. Ironically, his was a message of peace, but also one of personal responsibility, commitment, and a call to action.

"Love one another! These were the words of our savior," Luis said to the crowd, as he paced the front of the stage like a lion. He glared down into the crowd, meeting many eyes as he spoke. "Turn the other cheek. And yet, innocent men, women, and children still were murdered in our streets.

"We came to doubt, some of us, if God were really watching.

And so, he sent us signs of his love through numerous miracle healings. He chose an unknown man from a small mountain town to save possibly thousands of lives through an act of individual heroism, and then he miraculously cured Santo, the dog of that man, Jesus Munoz, of Pueblo del Cielo.

"My friends, his message could not be more clear. From tragedy comes grace...if we choose to make it so. But it takes individual action...it takes courage and determination...and faith! Across Mexico, and now spreading across the world, we are seeing individuals taking action, standing up for Christ!"

Suddenly, a line of Texas Rangers ringed the front of the stage, complementing the guards that were already stationed there. Additional camera crews pushed through the crowd to join their comrades on an elevated platform in front of the stage that looked like an island floating on a sea of people. A man came out on the stage and spoke a few quiet words to Father Luis, who nodded his head and returned to the microphone.

"My friends," he said, first in Spanish and then in English. "Governor Antonio Mendoza is here, and he would like to say a few words." Father Luis extended his arm to the north side of the stage, and Mendy walked out to a roar of approval.

Mendy raised his hand in a broad wave and the roar grew thunderous.

"Thank you. Thank you, friends and amigos," he said, as a thousand camera flashes winked through the crowd like diamond snowflakes.

"It is fitting and proper that we meet in this liminal zone, a space that between our two nations, was so long disputed, and which has now been hallowed by slaughtered innocents of both our countries. Across Mexico...and America...and the entire world...a united voice is growing, that demands to be heard. It is the voice of millions of individuals who recognize that the love of God and good is stronger than any group, sect, or government.

"God made each of us in his own image, and we are therefore each of us, valuable beyond calculation.

"I come here today not as a candidate for president...but as an individual...to make a statement."

A cracked cloud moved in front of the sun and a beam of light shined silent gold upon the stage.

"There are no Chinese!"

He paused, and let the crowd hunger for a few long seconds.

"There are no Mexicans...no Arabs...no Americans. There are only individuals...all created in the image of God. And as such, the most precious resource that we share...is each other.

"Many do not yet understand. They believe that whatever banner they wave...or whatever goal they crave...justifies their trespasses against others. Such were the beliefs of those who murdered many of our friends on this very spot. Yet out of such darkness came light...out of our grief came hope...and a new resolution to do right.

"My statement as an individual is this. I believe that we are at an inflection point, and that each of us through his or her personal choices can tip the world toward light or dark. I resolve and promise in this hallowed place...to all who can hear my voice...to devote the rest of my life to helping others without fail. So help me, God.

"Furthermore...as a candidate...if I am elected...I will use the full power of the presidency to make life, liberty, and the pursuit of happiness the realized goal of not just every American, but every individual on the planet. I will also devote every possible effort, both diplomatic and legal, to insure that the Mexican people are helped in cleansing their nation of crime and corruption.

"Finally...I want to say...that I believe we will win, because America has always been a nation under God, and Mexicans share our love of God and country. Whatever it takes, we can do it together. Thank you, and God bless you all."

In Austin, in the governor's mansion command center, several staff members earnestly watched the network coverage of Mendy's short speech.

"I must say, Jerry," said Kenneth Shroud, "that was a stellar speech you penned. I think you've just given our governor a very good chance of being elected president...of Mexico!"

"Shut-up, nitwit! The only two words of that speech that I wrote were thank you. If I thought—"

Jerry Blackwood's cell phone sounded, as did Kenneth Shroud's and they simultaneously looked at them to see a text message from Graham Varner:

"*Start working damage control!*"

Jerry looked up from his phone. "I guess that means get busy writing a speech that explains why the previous one didn't get read."

"Just be glad you're not me," moaned Shroud. "The secular crowd is going to beat me with a stick. This will be tough to spin."

****

The luncheon was over and Philip Bigelow directed his guests into the activity room, where they could relax and occupy themselves with any of the many toys he had collected. Meanwhile, he and Jesus and his lawyer retired to the library office to take care of some necessary paperwork. Jesus skimmed the contract that spelled out his responsibilities as far as providing free access to Santo for testing over a six-month period. There was an option to renew the agreement for up to a year, for an additional sum. Also specified, was that Bigelow Pharmaceuticals would pay for all their expenses, lodging, and Pilar's university tuition.

Jesus picked up the pen and signed without hesitation. This solved all of their short-term problems and seemed without pitfalls. Having done so, Bigelow picked up a check and handed it to Jesus with a warm smile, and they shook hands. The red stamped numbers and written amount jumped into focus against the green background of the check as Jesus stared down at it: *Two hundred and fifty thousand dollars and zero cents*.

"That's a good deal of money," said Joe Tydings.

"I could start my own country," replied Jesus, as he stared at the check. "But you know, I have never really cared about money, except for Pilar's sake. I was always happy in our village, and I never wanted. Still, some of this money can be used to buy more books for the school, and it is security for Pilar and her future."

"What about you?" asked Bigelow. "What do you want?"

Jesus paused in thought, remembering for a brief instant his son and daughter-in-law. Then his face lightened and he smiled.

"Nothing, for myself, I have all that I need."

Tydings looked uncomfortable, excused himself, and left.

"Lawyers are always busy," said Bigelow. "They never seem to have what they need, and they are as wary as insurance salesmen.

Come along, and I'll show you what makes me thoughtful."

They went up the spiral staircase to the observatory, and from there, up another stairway to a rooftop deck above the building. The air gusted warmly past them, lifting the hair on both their heads so it danced in the wind. Bigelow spread his arms and spun round, pointing out the three hundred and sixty degree panorama of Baltimore that was spread below them.

"Up here, I have seen many perfect sunrises and sunsets. I have watched the sun and moon track across the sky in succession, and always, I am struck with the wonder of life, and how short a time we have upon this earth." He looked at Jesus and smiled. "Why do you suppose that God made life so short?"

"It seems long for those that suffer."

"Yes," replied Bigelow. "I hope we can change some of that."

He extended his hand to Jesus, and they shook hands in agreement to that common cause. Then they sat in the shade of an ornamental awning on chaise lounges and swapped stories, as men of older age are often prone to do. Bigelow explained how he had built his company, and Jesus regaled him with tales of some of the miracle healings that he had beheld throughout his life. As the hours passed, they came to realize that in their own way, they had each been serving the same purpose in life, the amelioration of mankind.

Downstairs in the activity room, Matt had introduced Pilar to the game of pool. They played for a couple of hours before tiring, and then Matt asked Pilar if she wanted to accompany him to visit "someone special."

She agreed, and in a short while they were driving north of the city along Dulaney Valley Road. Pilar was struck by the fertile, rolling green countryside; the lovely trees; and the manifold quantity of large, well-maintained homes with plush green lawns along the way. Santo imagined that he was running very fast as he held his head out the window and felt the rush of air in his nostrils.

They turned into the grounds of Stella Mariss, a Catholic managed-care facility, and Pilar felt suddenly at home when they exited the car and she saw the outstretched arms of the Holy Mother greeting them at the edge of the parking lot. Santo sat in front of the statue and waved his raised paws in the air, causing Matt to look at Pilar and question.

"What is he doing?"

"Grandfather said that is how he got his name. He loves the saints," said Pilar laughing. "I don't know why he does it."

Matt watched Santo for several seconds and shook his head in wonder. "Wait here for a minute and I'll be right back," he said, and he disappeared into the building.

Pilar stretched the dog leash enough to sit on a bench in the shade, and watched Santo paw the air for a few more moments, before he gave up and came and sat next to her.

"Why do you do that?" she said, as she scratched him behind both ears.

It was warm and humid, and Santo's tongue dripped a small puddle on the pavement. In a few minutes Matt reappeared pushing a wheel chair.

In the chair was an old woman with neatly combed white hair and pale sky blue eyes. She was alert and her eyes locked on Pilar and Santo immediately and she smiled.

"Pilar, this is my grandmother, Violet May West."

The woman stuck out a shriveled, bony hand that was attached to a bony arm with sagging skin. The bags beneath her watery blue eyes looked as heavy as suitcases and they seemed to be pulling her eyelids wider open.

"Pilar. That's a lovely name. You look Spanish."

"I am Spanish, from Mexico."

"What a nice dog you have," said Violet, as she patted Santo. He smelled and licked her hand and she laughed. "He's very friendly. Dogs are much nicer than people, don't you think?"

"Yes."

Violet went on to talk about people, and how she used to pick blackberries at the edge of Baltimore City on the hills where Hopkins Bayview Hospitals presently stood. She told of how when she was small, they were so poor that she used an ear of corn to make a doll with golden hair. It was stream of consciousness memories that flowed out of her like an on-turned water faucet. Finally, an attendant appeared, and advised Matt that it was time for Violet to go to lunch.

"Goodbye, it was nice meeting you," said Pilar.

Violet smiled and said goodbye, and looked up to Matt.

"Who are you?"

"It's me, Matthew."

"Are you my brother?"

"No, Grandma. I'm your grandson."

"I used to have long, beautiful hair."

"Yes," Matt said. "I've seen pictures."

"And who are you?"

"I'm your grandson, Matthew."

"Goodbye," Violet said, as the attendant wheeled her off to lunch. Matt turned around to Pilar, who had tears streaking down her cheeks.

"I'm so sorry."

"It's okay," Matt said, as he handed her a tissue to dry her tears. "I don't mind that she forgets who I am. But it's sad, you know, the way she remembers past events so vividly sometimes, and then can't even remember her own name."

"She's very sweet."

"Yes. That's part of why I wanted you to meet her. My research may one day help restore people like her to their former selves. I sometimes dream of how wonderful it would be, to be able to give families that gift."

Pilar reached out and touched Matt's cheek.

"You are a good man."

Matt was mute, overcome by a surge of irresistible attraction to Pilar. She smiled and took her hand away, and his face felt like it was on fire. His lips were pins and needles and he felt light-headed. He finally reached down and took her hand and they walked beneath the trees around the grounds of the facility saying little, but feeling very much.

When they got back to the car, Pilar slid in to the front seat and pulled Santo in with her, so that he sat next to the window, leaving no excuse for her to not sit close up against Matt. They followed a circuitous route around Loch Raven back towards the beltway.

Matt was unusually quiet, thinking about the consequences of an involvement with Pilar. He was on the verge of the biggest research project of his life and he wanted to compartmentalize his feelings for her, put them in a box and save them for later, when it might be more appropriate and timely. She leaned in against him and lightly combed her fingers through the hair on his neck.

"You need a haircut," she said softly.

He felt like he was going to explode and turned into a parking area that looked west across the reservoir. The late afternoon sun sparkled off a million small ripples that blew across the water, and a scent of pine filled the car through the open windows. They sat there without speaking for a long minute, while Pilar continued to softly scratch the hair on his neck.

"Santo loves it when I do this," Pilar said innocently.

"It's beautiful here," Matt said, trying desperately not to look at Pilar, while also trying to fight the goose bumps running everywhere across his body. This wasn't going to happen, he said to himself. It was a gigantic mistake, especially at this juncture. He turned to tell her firmly to her face.

"Pilar..."

Her eyes looked up at him and shined so innocently, reflecting the light from the water, and before he knew what happened he had pulled her toward him and his lips were pressed against hers. They were soft and full and firm, and an image of her formed behind his closed eyelids of the time when she had said goodbye to him from the family car as it drove from Aunt Maria's driveway. "Adios," she had said. But now she was here in his arms, and her body pushed back against his as he slid his arms more tightly around her, and their nervous systems intertwined in rapture. She gradually went limp in his arms and he pulled back to look at her.

"I can feel your heart beating," she whispered breathlessly.

"So can I," Matt said, as he gulped a deep breath.

Pilar placed her hand on his chest and her eyes widened.

"It feels like it's going to jump right out of your chest."

Matt smiled, embarrassed at his uncontrolled passion.

"It's getting late...your grandfather will worry."

He turned and started the car and they started back towards the city. Pilar nestled in against him and squeezed his right biceps gently with both hands.

"Thank you," she said with a shy smile. "That was my first real kiss."

The confession took Matt by surprise until he thought on it. Despite her serene demeanor and apparent maturity, she had lived in a very small town in the mountains with a conservative older man and a priest for adult supervision. It made him feel like he had taken unfair advantage of innocence. It also made him realize that he was transporting a very special individual, someone pure in an impure world. Beyond her beauty, maybe it was that purity that made her seem so serene.

Maybe that is what he had sensed from the first that was so special about her. He sneaked a glance down at her, as she watched the passing reservoir through the trees, and he felt warmth that he couldn't pinpoint.

Suddenly, a wet tongue lapped the side of his face and he yelled a complaint at Santo, who had reached over Pilar and was licking him. She pushed Santo back to his window seat and she and Matt both laughed tears. Santo studied the aura of colors that enveloped Matt and Pilar and watched curiously as it danced between them. He jumped back across Pilar and tried to wriggle in between her and Matt, and they both laughed and hugged him as Matt carefully kept one eye on the road.

They arrived back at the Wyman Park condo before sunset and Matt parked in the entrance circle. He jumped from the car and ran and opened the passenger's door for Pilar, who thanked him graciously. Then they walked slowly to the front door, where they bid one another farewell until the next day.

Pilar stood on her toes and gave Matt a quick peck on the cheek, hugged him a final goodnight, and then walked backwards through the spinning door into the building. Matt watched her through the glass curtain wall until she caught the elevator, waved, and then finally turned away. He dream-walked back to the car, seeing nothing but her face and smile as he remembered kissing her.

Pilar stood quietly in the elevator for several seconds before she realized that she had forgotten to press the floor number. She reached forward, pressed her floor, and leaned back against the wall with a sigh. Santo jumped up and she reflexively scratched his neck, while mentally counting the number of hours until she and Matt would meet again.

****

Jesus searched the news clips while he waited for Pilar to return from her afternoon outing with Matt. His rebirth had taken away his anger, but not his need to know, and more, his need to understand. His was a compulsion to make sense of the world in spite of the many years of tutelage by Santiago, which dictated that it was not possible. This he still could not accept, even though each day the world seemed to make less sense to him. Now, more than ever, the puzzle pieces of the big picture seemed to cry out for him to assemble them, despite their incongruous form.

The vigilantes of Mexico, the riots in American cities, the rise of the Chinese Christians, all swirled outward from a series of miracles in which he had been a participant, so surely, he should be able to fathom an intent from these things, if there were one. Was it not some of these very events that had pushed him to the United States? He looked down at a dime that lay on his desktop. "E Pluribus Unum" it read on its back, "out of many, one." He turned the dime over, and as if in answer to an unspoken query, he read aloud: "In God we trust. "

Jesus turned back to the monitor and clicked on more headline news stories. The US news was filled with rants about Texas Governor Mendoza and how his most recent public statements proved that he was mentally ill, probably suffering from post-traumatic stress disorder from the El Paso tragedy.

It was, according to most of the reports, an embarrassment to the Republican Party to allow him to continue in office, and he should be asked to bow out of the presidential campaign entirely. The same news stories from Juarez were completely opposite. In those stories he was championed as a man of vision and honesty. In particular, one news interview with a Father Luis was very impressive. The father was very convincing, very sincere in his evaluation of Governor Mendoza, and he painted a noble picture of a man that he believed, was touched by God.

Jesus liked this version of reality much better, partly because it seemed to make more sense to him, and also because there was something about the priest's voice and gesticulations that made him trust his analysis.

Just then, his cell phone rang, and Jesus picked it up to hear the welcome voice of Santiago, who was calling just to make sure that they had arrived safely and were situated. He explained that they were fine and gave Santiago an encapsulated version of the day's events, including the award of the check. In closing, he mentioned the news stories that he had seen and in particular, the video clip of

Father Luis of Juarez. He advised Santiago to check it out for himself, since he found the clip very moving. Pilar returned, and after getting her to parrot a fond hello to Santiago, he said goodbye.

Santiago sat quietly thinking after he signed off with Jesus. This was only the second time in over forty-six years that he and Jesus had been apart, and he was still filled with many doubts about the wisdom in their decision to submit Santo to tests in the USA. He and Jesus had agreed that nothing would be told of the true origination of Santo, just as Sailor had counseled. Nevertheless, the very pressures that had forced them to vacate the village could follow them if word leaked out of where they were. He crossed himself and asked a blessing for them, and then switched on his media center. A quick search brought up news clips of the speech of Father Luis.

Santiago's face floated ghostlike in the evening twilight of the rectory media room, flickering reflected colors from the video display screen that mesmerized him as he sat frozen in front of it. He watched the speech repeatedly as the last of the day drained from the room, then switched it off, and sat in darkness contemplating. He wondered if atonement for certain sins was possible, or if even a lifetime of penance was only a prelude to final dispensation.

In the darkness Santiago saw her face, unchanged by the decades in his memory; the tan skin stretched tight against high cheekbones, and her beautiful almond-shaped eyes that looked up at him at an angle, one eye half-eclipsed by the curved meeting point of the rim of her eye socket and the bridge of her nose; those eyes that hypnotized with feline wild beauty, irresistible and magnetic.

The Asian influence of twenty thousand years previous was still there, from the time before her people crossed the land bridge that would later become the Bering Sea. Her full and pouting lips displayed a perfect cupid's bow, which when stretched to a smile showed brilliantly white teeth of perfect size and proportion. How he had loved her, or more accurately, how he had longed for her, until she finally conquered him completely and they both indulged their passion, which led to such penurious results.

She was only fourteen, a Yaqui, but was a full-grown woman, and he was an ancient seventeen years old at the time. In fear of her violent father, he had cowered and run away, and when he regained his courage and returned, he found that they had sent her away to live with family elsewhere, as was often done in such cases. A story was fabricated to explain her fatherless son.

Disgraced, Santiago left his home state of Sonora, and traveled aimlessly for several years, before finding a path with Christ that led him to Pueblo del Cielo and the burden that the old sailor would place upon him. In a way, Jesus was the son that he would never get to know and love, and that part was not a burden, but a blessing, despite the many challenges that they faced through the years.

"Aurora," he said softly, speaking her name for the first time in many years. Tears wet his cheeks in the darkness.

"Forgive me."

Chapter 22

The Spear of Christ is Found

The next morning found Matt prowling the lobby of Pilar's condo as he waited for her, Jesus, and Santo to emerge from the elevator. He had called and told them he was in the lobby and ready to take them for a tour of his lab. Ambivalent feelings about Pilar were pushing him to the point of distraction, and his prowling was symptomatic of the displacement activities of wild beasts.

The elevator doors slid open, and he immediately saw Pilar's smiling face, with her eyes locked on him. His eyes darted to Jesus and he greeted him warmly, almost ignoring Pilar. But his demeanor was tense, and Jesus immediately discerned the abnormally cool lack of focus on his granddaughter, and he smiled inside, knowing what was going on. Matt spouted superfluous conversation and pleasantries as he led them all to his car. Pilar enjoyed seeing Matt acting out of character, knowing full well that it was because of her, for she had seen the passion in his eyes as soon as the elevator doors had opened. She said nothing and listened to him drone on, wearing a tight little smile on her face. At the lab, Matt was back in character, surrounded by the objects of his other passion. He took them through the incubation room and explained about immortal cells versus senescent cells, and some of the things that they were studying, and he showed them the microscopy lab and the high-magnification images that were possible. Pilar was enchanted by all the technology and completely impressed at how knowledgeable Matt was. Jesus looked for signs of anything that might be dangerous to Santo.

They finally stopped in an examination room, where Matt began the process of a cursory examination of Santo and entering his pertinent data into the computer system. He entered Santo into the system as Sam Bowser, and asked Jesus: "How old is Santo?"

"That is what you will tell us, no?" Jesus laughed. "At least I should hope you could tell with all this fancy equipment."

Matt laughed good-naturedly. "I don't even need any equipment to tell that." He patted the examination table and called Santo, and the dog jumped up onto the padded table and sat happily down, wagging his tail. Matt opened Santo's mouth and examined his teeth and tongue. "Has he been eating mints?"

"Not today, but he does eat wild mint plants at home. He eats no meat at all," said Pilar.

"Really?" said Matt, still looking into Santo's mouth. "That seems a bit unusual." Matt turned to Pilar and Jesus, and smiled. "Your dog is between one and two years old," he said confidently.

Jesus choked a laugh, and Pilar looked disappointed.

"No, Matthew," she said with sad surprise. "He's at least nineteen, I told you before. I've had him all of my life, and he was my father's dog before I had him."

She turned to Jesus. "How old is he, Grandfather?"

"That's impossible!" Matt interjected. "His teeth are bright white, and there is no tarter at all. They are smooth and without barbs or sharp points, but they are still not worn. Therefore he must be about two years old. I'll stand by that."

"Then you would be wrong," said Jesus softly. He is older than you think."

"How old do you say he is?" Matt replied.

Jesus smiled.

"How old? Let's just say that Pilar's father played with him all his life. He died when he was only twenty-two."

"I'm sorry," said Matt as he studied Jesus' somber face. "Sorry for your loss of a son at such an early age. But that would make Santo well over thirty years old or older, and that's just not possible. That would put him older than Bluey, the oldest dog ever, and he was only twenty-nine."

"I only tell you what I know to be true," said Jesus.

"Of course," said Matt. "I only meant that it goes against everything I know to be true, so it is difficult to accept as fact. I'm sorry for being a skeptic."

"I understand completely, and if Santo were not thought to be special, we would not be here." Jesus smiled. "Perhaps we will all learn, no? After you have completed your testing."

"Yes," agreed Matt. "That's why we're here."

Pilar stepped in between Matt and Santo and began scratching Santo behind his left ear. Matt felt his stomach muscles involuntarily stiffen as she brushed up against him, and his face flushed.

"He is just a plain dog, but his heart is very big. Can your tests prove that?" Pilar asked, as she locked eyes with Matt.

"Yes...they can." He laughed nervously, jerked his eyes from hers, and reached over and patted Santo. Pilar moved her hip slightly toward him and he could feel the heat of her body through her dress. He stepped away from her, carefully lifted Santo off the table and gently set him down. "We can take an MRI, a magnetic resonance image, of him that will show everything. Come-on."

Matt led them out of the examination room and they took the elevator to a lower level. They went into a large room, where several people were attending a dog that seemed to be anesthetized. There were tubes going into the dog's mouth and he was lying on a movable table that went into a giant, doughnut-shape. Matt explained that they were just about to create an MRI image of the dog, and he explained briefly how the machine used magnetism and pulses of radio energy to take pictures of internal organs with more detail than any X-ray. This system was also safer than an X-ray because the frequencies of the energy were much lower than X-rays, so there was no tissue damage from radiation.

The ready command was given and the machine was switched on.

Santo yelped, shot upwards off the floor into the air, and let out a howl of pain before falling back down in convulsions.

Pilar screamed: "Santo!" and bent down to tend him, as did Jesus.

"Turn it off!" Matt shouted as the technicians at the machine turned around in surprise. "Shut it down! Now!"

The scan was halted and Matt bent down with Pilar and Jesus to the quivering body of Santo. Matt scooped him up and took him out into the hallway, where he placed him on a mobile transport table, and then quickly rolled him to the elevator, with Pilar and Jesus attending.

They took him upstairs to the veterinary center and two doctors began to examine him immediately. Suddenly, Santo's breathing calmed and he became perfectly still.

"Santo?" Pilar said softly, while stroking his head.

The dog's eyes popped open and he tried to get up, but he yelped in pain, and lay back down.

"Has he ever had seizures before?" asked Matt.

"Never," Jesus said solemnly.

Santo tried to stand again, but again yelped and lay down.

"Something's wrong...he's in pain." Tears streaked Pilar's face. "What has happened to him?"

"I don't know. Let's get a quick X-ray of him, he might have cracked a rib during his muscular spasm when he hit the floor."

"I think not," Jesus said sternly. "No X-ray."

"It won't hurt him. It's perfectly safe, only a millisecond exposure with minimal radiation."

"Like the MRI was safe?"

"We don't know that it was the MRI?"

"You saw him. The convulsions stopped as soon as they switched the machine off. Maybe Santo's body can't take these tests," said Jesus.

Matt looked into Jesus' eyes. "Maybe. But right now he is in pain, and there has never been any person or animal that I know of, who has ever been hurt by a low-level X-ray photograph. He might have hurt himself internally, and if so, we need to treat him."

"No. We will wait, and see if he improves."

"And if he doesn't? What if a rib has punctured his lung? He could be bleeding internally."

Jesus scoffed. "Are you kidding me? This dog was shot through by a bullet and healed. If God did that, then why would he not heal him again now?"

Matt searched the floor for an answer but found none.

"We will wait." Jesus reiterated.

"Okay, he's your dog." Matt wrapped a blood pressure cuff around Santo's forearm and hooked up a Doppler pad to his paw. After a few moments he frowned. "I don't like his blood pressure. It's too low, his breathing is fast and shallow, and his pulse is racing, too. We don't want him going into shock."

"We will wait," Jesus said calmly.

They took Santo down to Matt's floor and Matt made some tea as they waited. During tea, Matt talked with Jesus and Pilar about the events that occurred on the day that Santo was shot. After about an hour, it was apparent that Santo was not getting better and his breathing had become more irregular. Matt took his blood pressure again. Santo's blood pressure was lower and his heartbeat higher.

"He's getting worse," said Matt. "Let me take one X-ray."

"No, we must have faith."

"Well if you have faith, don't you also have faith that God will protect Santo from any effects of a single X-ray? Maybe he wants Santo to get an X-ray, how do you know?"

"Grandfather, I think Matt is right. He is getting worse."

Jesus' face suddenly lightened, and he stood up from his chair. "Perhaps you are right, Matthew. Let us take him for an X-ray. It was, after all, God's will that we come here. We will leave it to him one more time. A simple X-ray may be what is called for."

A short time later, they were in the X-ray examination room where two doctors and Matt explained the results of Santo's photos. The X-ray was illuminated up on a view screen and the problem was clearly visible.

"You see here..." said the first doctor, "this pointed object near the heart is actually scraping on the lung, and may even be touching a nerve. It's probably quite painful."

"It's dangerously close to the heart, too," added the second doctor."

"It seems to be metal due to the strength of the image. Notice how opaque it is compared to the ribs," said Matt. "It's shaped like part of an eccentric, pointed ellipse. Almost like—"

"A broken spear tip," interrupted Jesus.

"I was going to say an arrow head, but you're right. It's too big to be an arrowhead, and not as sharply pointed. It does look almost like the shape of an old-time spear."

"Like a Roman spear tip, " Jesus whispered.

"Yes, that's a pretty good description. The thing is, that it needs to come out of there, before it does any more damage."

Jesus turned abruptly, and walked quickly out into the hallway, and Pilar and Matt followed after him. He turned his face to the wall as he wiped away tears.

All these years, and still I doubted, he thought. He crossed himself and whispered softly: "Thank you, Lord, for revealing yourself completely."

Pilar put her arms around him and hugged him.

"Grandfather, don't cry."

"Santo will be alright," Matt said sympathetically. "It's a simple micro-surgery operation that we can perform immediately."

Jesus dried his eyes and hugged Pilar. "I am not crying. I could not be happier." He looked over to Matt and smiled. "You have just proven that the story of an old sailor who gave Santo to me, is true. He was my friend, and he was a very great and wise man. I know that now."

"What was the story?" asked Matt.

Jesus pried Pilar's arms from around him and reached for his phone.

"I must call Santiago," he said, and he walked to the seclusion of the far end of the hallway.

Pilar watched Jesus with concern.

"I never see him cry...not in all my life."

"Don't worry, Santo will be alright."

"I wonder," said Pilar, as she continued to stare down the hallway. Matt slipped his arm around her shoulder and hugged her, but she didn't seem to notice. She was deep in thought.

Matt dropped his arm, excused himself, and went back into the examination room to confer with the doctors. Pilar sat down on a bench next to the door and waited, all the time watching her grandfather.

In a little while Jesus returned. As Pilar stood up he gave her a hug and kissed her on the forehead. They went into the examination room and Matt and the doctors explained the plan they had to remove the object from inside Santo. Jesus agreed, but with the stipulation that he observe the entire operation, and that he would be given the object immediately upon its removal from Santo. With everyone in agreement, Santo was prepped for surgery, and within the hour the operation was underway.

Jesus watched with scientific curiosity as the Microsystem with robotic assist was swung overtop a sleeping Santo on the operating table. A large video display showed the small incision and the insertion of the endoscopic tools. The operating doctor gave a detailed description of what he was doing as the operation progressed, but Jesus could not discern the various body parts that were named as he went deeper into the thoracic cavity. Except for the nearby lung, everything seemed to be red tissues and blood, and he prayed that this was the right course of action.

"Got it!" the doctor finally exclaimed, as the robotic forceps grabbed hold of the object. With some difficulty he maneuvered the object backwards towards the opening, and finally retrieved it. "That's strange," he said, as he wiped the incision clean. He swung the Microsystem aside and pulled a boom microscope over the incision and switched on its camera feed.

"Look at that." He glanced up from the binocular eyepiece and pointed to the display screen. "It looks like—"

He quickly turned back to the eyepiece, adjusted the magnification, and wiped the incision clean again. "It's closing!"

On the video viewer at a magnification of twenty-five times, the incision filled the screen like a gaping bloody zipper that seemed to be closing at both ends simultaneously. The doctor wiped the incision clean again, and the incision showed visibly smaller than moments before, and the bleeding had slowed.

"So it's true!" Matt said, grabbing Jesus by the arm. "Rapid tissue regeneration. It's just like in El Paso!"

"God Almighty!" gasped the doctor.

"Exactly," Jesus said softly.

The three of them watched in awe as the incision shrank before their eyes. It closed by itself as new cells sprang into existence along the open walls of the cut.

"This is beyond belief," the doctor panted, as he took off his glasses, wiped them and his forehead, and put them back on. "It's like...witnessing a miracle."

Jesus smiled. "Does it make you uncomfortable?"

Matt became so exuberant that he jumped up and down and

pulled on Jesus' arm. "This is fantastic! It's more than anything I ever imagined. Do you know what this means?

"We have a living example to study, a real live miracle dog, just like the newspapers named him! This is big, really big. Which reminds me..." Matt took out his phone and speed-dialed Philip Bigelow to give him the news.

Jesus reached over to the tool table and picked up the object that had been removed from Santo. The doctor pulled out several wipes and they cleaned it off.

"That's interesting," said the doctor, "it seems to have an unusual coating, almost like glass. "What is it?"

"It is the last testament of a very old injury," replied Jesus, as he wrapped the object in a clean wipe and placed it in his pocket.

Suddenly Santo stirred on the operating table. His eyes opened into slits and his body began to squirm beneath the restraints.

"I can't believe he is already coming out of it," said the doctor as he turned to Santo and tried to calm him.

One of the restraints slipped and Santo pulled his head out from under it, and quickly wormed out from under the last remaining belt. He sat up and his eyes opened fully and he licked the doctor, who was still trying to hold him down.

"He's very strong said the doctor," as he tried to hold Santo still.

Jesus reached over to Santo and gave him a hug and patted him on the head. "He's okay. Not to worry."

The doctor let go, and in shocked disbelief examined the incision. "It's completely closed! I can't believe it."

Matt hung up from Bigelow and joined the doctor, inspecting the shaved area of the previous incision.

"Except for the pink color of the newer cells there isn't even a scar. Remarkable."

Matt's phone rang and he answered it. "Okay. Okay. Will-do," he said before hanging up.

"Big wants me to pull all the video of the operation and the healing, and hand-carry it over to him now."

The doctor complied and handed Matt the file. Then Matt went to the computer and erased the backup files.

"This is all covered in the non-disclosure papers you signed, Doctor. No one else is to know about this. Do you understand?" Matt said sternly.

"Who would believe me? I don't believe it myself."

"For the record, I need you to answer in the affirmative that you understand."

"Yes," the doctor replied.

"This never happened. The dog was never here, and there was no operation."

"But the log—"

"The log will show that you spent the afternoon in the pathology lab with Doctor Greene."

The doctor nodded understanding. "Yes."

Matt carefully lifted Santo from the table and set him down, and Jesus reattached his collar and leash. Then he turned back to the doctor.

"Thank you, Doctor," Matt said. "You did a great job."

He shook hands with the doctor, and patted him on the back.

"I'll finish up in here."

The doctor turned to Jesus, who also shook his hand and thanked him graciously. He bent down and patted Santo goodbye, and then he left, looking like a man who had forgotten where he parked his car.

Matt turned back to the table and wiped it down with alcohol pads. He collected all the spent gauze pads, emptied the trashcan, and sealed the trash bag containing the spent gauzes. Then they went out into the hallway, where Pilar was waiting for them on a bench, busily reviewing class schedules for the current semester. Matt momentarily excused himself, walked across the hall to a storeroom, and returned. He locked the operating room and slapped a big yellow and red biohazard sticker on the door that read: "*Do not enter*." Then he turned to Pilar and Jesus, who were both petting Santo and examining his almost invisible scar.

"Okay, folks," Matt said with a smile. "Let's go home."

Pilar gathered up her things and they started down the hallway. Jesus put his arm around Matt and patted him on the shoulder.

"That was quite a day, Matthew," he said with a smile.

Matt took a deep breath and exhaled.

"Yeah...day-one of Project Santo."

Chapter 23

The Research on Santo Begins

Philip Bigelow watched the video screen in stunned silence as Matt played the recording made two hours previously in the operating room showing the rapid healing of Santo's incision.

"Play it again," he said, as he poured a decanter of brandy. He swirled the brandy around in the glass and sniffed its bouquet while he watched the recording repeat, occasionally taking small sips.

"What do you think?" he finally said to Matt. He refilled the decanter as he waited for Matt's answer. His hands were shaking.

"Well, there's no more doubt as to authenticity."

Bigelow laughed, downed the brandy in the decanter, and then poured another.

"As for the mechanisms, and the why and how of it, I've got a million questions. Jesus claims the dog is over thirty years old. I scoffed when he told me, especially since he seemed cryptic about it when I tried to nail him down, but after seeing this, I don't know what to believe."

"I want you on this, Matt, fulltime. Forget everything else. You'll head the team, and I'll put any and all resources at your disposal."

"But my doctorate—"

Bigelow laughed, and slapped Matt on the back.

"Are you kidding? You'll not only get your doctorate, you'll probably get the goddamned Nobel out of this. Not that it means anything anymore.

"Did you sweep the room?"

"I got all the big stuff," Matt said. "I sealed it and scheduled a complete sanitization immediately, just as you asked."

"Good. I've put the building into complete lock-down and all elevator keycards have been rescinded for the pathology lab and the third floor. No one, except you and your team will have access. Starting tomorrow, I've also commissioned a security team to escort Jesus to and from the lab, and round-the-clock security for his quarters. Furthermore, there is to be no storage of any data on hard drives. Everything will be locked up daily. Internet connections will be strictly limited and monitored, and none will be tied to any computers that host data. All gene sequencing will be done in-house, and again, under top security measures.

"By the way...tomorrow, I want Santo to be moved to the lab. I'm not taking any chance on even one strand of DNA getting out of here."

"Did you ask Jesus about that? He may not want Santo to be housed at the lab."

"It's in the contract that he signed."

"Does he know that?"

"It doesn't matter. He signed it and deposited the check. That ratified the contract."

Matt's stomach squirmed. "If he didn't know—"

"Make it happen, Matt. We can't take any chances now."

"Okay. I'd better get going, I have a lot to do."

Matt turned and started for the door, and Bigelow called after him. "This is everything we dreamed of, Matt."

"And more," Matt said softly, as he turned and faced Big. "Much more."

Bigelow looked thoughtful for a moment. Then he smiled, toasted Matt, and downed the last of the brandy in his decanter. Matt saluted a goodnight, turned, and went through the door into the hallway.

Bigelow stood silent for a few moments, thinking. Suddenly, he noticed a man much older than himself staring at him from the mirror on the far side of the room. The man looked worn and empty. He turned back to the video screen and replayed the recording and wondered: Could absolution vanquish emptiness?

****

The door snapped locked behind Matt and echoed off the marble tiles of the hallway into final stillness. He walked in front of the elevator and its door slid open and waited for him to make up his mind about getting in. He finally stepped inside and the closing door sealed him in with his thoughts.

Big knew that Matt would never be able to resist the offer to go to El Paso to check on an event that appeared to be the nexus of all his research. But he also was cunning enough to recognize that Pilar was key to getting Jesus to agree to any research on Santo.

Matt pressed the down button and his heart sank with the elevator cab. He was a Judas goat. If not for him, Jesus would not be here.

The cab stopped. Matt exited, and walked to the first apartment and pressed the doorbell. The muffled barking of a dog could be heard amidst the tune of the Mexican Hat Dance. No one answered, so he knocked on the door.

The door finally opened, and Jesus looked at Matt with a curious expression.

“That’s very interesting,” said Jesus. “The last time you were here, the same music preceded your arrival. It seems to be coming from the ceiling.”

Matt smiled and pressed the doorbell and the chime sounded again and Santo barked.

“Very interesting...clever,” said Jesus as he examined the push-button switch on the doorframe.

“You can program it to play whatever you like. Big must have chosen that selection.”

“I like it. I like him…he is a good man.”

“You think so?”

“I do. I think we two are much alike.”

“I doubt that,” Matt said sarcastically.

Jesus raised one eyebrow. “Come-in, Matthew, I was just watching the news.”

Jesus extended his arm and guided Matt into the living room where a large wall screen was playing the evening news, and they sat down on the couch.

“Pilar is in the shower.”

Matt answered, “Oh,” indifferently, as he tried to shake that image from his head.

“Look at this,” Jesus said, pointing to the wall screen. “That is a statue of Santo in Tiananmen Square in Beijing! Can you believe it? The people are demanding more freedom of religion. Look at that crowd. They say it is over two hundred thousand people!”

Jesus bent down and patted Santo on his head.

"He has no idea how famous he is. And in my country, there is even more change. The people have taken control of the corrupt power structures that have failed us for years. There is great hope for the future. Around the globe—"

"I have to tell you something."

Matt rubbed his hand across the evening stubble of his beard as he searched for the right words, but finally, just spit them out.

"Bigelow says that we need to move Santo to the lab."

"Yes?" responded Jesus.

"We can't take a chance on anyone getting any of his DNA. It would ruin the exclusivity of our testing."

"Yes, this is understandable."

"I'm sorry, I feel like a Judas."

"Judas Iscariot? The one who betrayed our Savior?"

Matt looked down at the floor.

"Do you know, Matthew, that there is one school of thought, that claims that Judas did not betray Christ, and that his actions were done in obedience to instructions given to him by the Lord. He actually helped Christ to fulfill his mission."

"Really?"

"But don't be so silly, as to cast yourself in that role anyway. It was specified in the contract I signed that Bigelow Pharmaceutical could enact any means necessary to ensure their rights of exclusive examination of Santo."

"You knew that?"

"Of course. I would not sign something I did not read. But if you read the contract, you will see that I have the right to be present at all times and at all phases of the examination, to protect and watch over Santo. So I will be moving my residence to the lab with him."

A door opened, and Matt turned to the sound.

Pilar was silhouetted in the doorway against the light from inside her bathroom. Her hair was wrapped in a towel and she was wearing a white terrycloth bathrobe pulled tight at the waist, which revealed her hourglass figure.

"Buenas noches. I heard voices."

Steam from the hot shower wrapped her like an angel floating in a cloud and Matt's face started to burn.

"I will be out as soon as I dress."

She clutched her robe closed at the neck and rhythmically swayed the few steps to her bedroom. Matt dragged his eyes off her hips just in time to watch her calves disappear through the doorway.

"I must ask you a favor, Matthew," Jesus said. "Pilar will be here all alone while I am staying with Santo, and I ask you to watch over her while I am gone."

Matt's mouth was dry cotton and he felt light-headed.

"She will be lonely, so I hope that you can take some time from your schedule to entertain her."

"I don't think...I'm going to be so busy that—"

"Please, do me this favor."

Matt shook his head and laughed. "Isn't that like giving the fox the keys to the hen house?"

Jesus looked puzzled.

"You know what I mean," Matt said awkwardly. "Your granddaughter is a very beautiful girl."

"Do you like Pilar?"

Matt's face flushed. "Yes...of course. Very much."

"Then why do you belittle her and yourself with such a statement? Do you think she has no will? Have you none? Do you liken yourself to an animal that I should not trust?"

"No. No, it was just an American saying. I was only kidding. I didn't mean anything like that."

Jesus burst out laughing, and placed his hand on Matt's shoulder.

"I got you! I was only joking, Matthew."

Matt exhaled a sigh of relief and collapsed into a seated position on the couch. "You did get me." But Matt wondered if the joke were not some sly, manipulative trick, since it placed him in a compulsory position of conscience that would constantly weigh on every interaction he had with Pilar.

Jesus sat down next to him and smiled warmly, and Matt wondered what he was actually thinking. This man who superficially seemed so plain and simple, might not be simple at all.

"Look at that!" Jesus said, pointing to the wall screen. A news clip was playing that showed an enormous crowd in Seoul marching with crosses and carrying a statue of a dog. One demonstrator held a sign that read: God is man's best friend.

"Santo is everywhere," mused Jesus.

"It's mass hysteria. What do they hope to accomplish?"

"Hysteria? Perhaps for some it is that, a sympathetic response to the stimulus of the crowd. But I think there is more to it. When I see the positive changes happening everywhere around the globe, and in particular in my country, I see it more as an outpouring of love for God and all that is good."

"Maybe," said Matt. "But mobs seldom achieve any logical agenda that betters mankind."

“Perhaps society needs a mob to cleanse itself. Perhaps it takes the threat of the mob, to finally force change. I wish you could hear the words of a man called Father Luis—”

The bedroom door opened, and Pilar walked through it into the living room. She wore a simple, flowered cotton dress that fit her to perfection. Her hair was still a little damp and she was lightly brushing out the tangles as she slowly glided across the distance to the couch and blithely took a standing position next to Matt.

“What’s that statue?” she said carelessly.

“I believe that is supposed to be Santo,” replied Jesus.

“It looks like a sick llama.”

“It’s the Doggy Lama,” Matt said laughing.

Pilar hit him playfully on the arm with the hairbrush, and he looked up at her and their eyes locked. She smiled narrowly and her white teeth reflected light from a lamp in the ceiling that made them sparkle. She lightly touched the tip of the brush against his arm and slightly puckered her lips before wetting them with her tongue.

Matt’s mouth went dry. His heart raced and he looked away.

Jesus studied their interaction with curious amusement, amazed at how fast his innocent granddaughter had acquired womanly wile. He excused himself to take Santo for an evening walk, so the two young people could have some time to themselves.

The door closed and Pilar sat down on the couch next to Matt.

“What were you two talking about?”

“World events.”

Pilar leaned a little closer and a soft fragrance titillated Matt.

“You smell good.”

She smiled, and with confident familiarity placed the palm of her hand lightly against his chest. His heart was thumping.

"You have a healthy heart, Matthew."

"I hope so."

****

Jesus crossed the park with Santo and followed a brick-lined sidewalk to some stairs that led to the upper quad on the Hopkins Homewood campus. The clock in the tower of Gilman Hall read eight o'clock and it had taken ten minutes to get here from the condo. He thought to linger longer for Matt and Pilar's sake, but not too long. "Young people," he said to Santo as he bent down to pet him. "They need their time."

A man in a black suit and hat approached along the walkway.

He removed his hat and said hello, and Jesus noticed the white of a clerical collar.

"It's a very pleasant evening," the man said.

"Yes."

"I am Father Gianfranco Saldana," the priest said, handing his card to Jesus.

Jesus read it and looked impressed.

"You are from Rome?"

The man stooped and patted Santo, studied him with some curiosity, and then stood up.

"God bless and protect you, Jesus," the priest said in Spanish.

Jesus started, and looked quickly around.

"How do you know my name?"

"There is concern for your welfare. I have been sent here to offer you an invitation of asylum at the Vatican."

"Asylum? From what?"

"From those who may wish to harm you and Santo."

"How did you find us?"

"The helicopter pilot told me the private plane that you boarded, and I checked the flight schedule. Then I made a few inquiries when I got to BWI. Many people are helpful to a priest."

Jesus nodded.

Santo pulled at the leash and the three of them walked slowly along the walkway back towards the condo.

"I followed you through the park. That was imprudent. Even here, you are in danger."

"Why should I be in danger?"

"There is often danger in truth. Santo has upset the status quo, and many people have noticed. Governments have become unstable...great fortunes have been reversed. Do you think that such events will go unchallenged?"

"But these things are not because of Santo, but because of God. Surely, you must understand that."

"I am not anyone who matters. But this dog has become a symbol, and the Holy Father does not wish to see any harm come to him or your family."

"His Holiness, the Pope, knows of Santo?"

"Who else would have sent me?"

Jesus froze. "Do you have any other identification?"

The priest pulled out his passport and wallet, and Jesus examined them carefully.

"Very well," Jesus said, as they began walking again. "You have succeeded in making me worried. I thought we were safe here. We have commitments."

They walked back across the park to the condo, and Father

Saldano saw Jesus to the door.

"Don't forget," he said, "if you change your mind, the church will still welcome you. Just call me."

A black Mercedes pulled up to the curb. Father Saldana shook hands with Jesus, said goodbye, and stepped into the waiting car. Jesus started into the turnstile of the revolving door, and the tinted window of the Mercedes rolled down.

"Vaya con dios," Father Saldana shouted with a wave, and the car sped off.

Jesus walked slowly through the lobby, heavy with thought. The old sailor had been right all along. Sailor had fled Spain for the anonymity that the New World offered, but where could anyone flee in the computer age that would be safe? How would life be now, having to always look over his shoulder, no matter where they went? But the offer of sanctuary by the church was no more than a prison sentence in itself, and he would never inflict that on his granddaughter. For now, he was committed to this current course of action, but his mind began turning over many possible scenarios that might afford a decent life for Pilar, after their current commitments were fulfilled. Such thoughts filled his mind as he rode the elevator up to his floor.

Jesus placed his keycard into the apartment door and a green LED blinked on. The door bolt clicked open as he turned the handle and slowly opened the door. Inside, two heads visible above the back of the living room couch quickly moved apart as he opened the door. He smiled and removed Santo from his leash, and Santo raced into the living room and jumped up onto the couch with Matt and Pilar.

Jesus dallied in the kitchen for a few moments before finally going in to talk with Matt and Pilar. When he related the details of his meeting with Father Saldana, Matt's face turned pale.

"Are you sure of his identity?"

"Yes," Jesus calmly replied. "I checked his passport and papers."

"I've got to go tell Big." Matt excused himself, and rushed upstairs to Bigelow's penthouse where he retold the details of the story.

Bigelow's response was instantaneous, and he called his security firm to immediately implement a high security lock-down of the condo building, as well as ordering bodyguards for both Jesus and Pilar. From this point on, they would never be able to go anywhere without guards.

Bigelow suggested that Matt take up temporary residence in the guest quarters of the penthouse. It was closer to the lab than Matt's apartment and would make it easier for them to interface each day as the tests progressed. It would also save having to detail any security to Matt's apartment quarters.

"You think I am under any threat?" Matt asked.

"I think we'd be foolish to not suspect that anyone connected with this project might be viewed as a potential pry bar to gain an advantage, or to extort some gain. It was shortsighted of me to not have taken these precautions earlier on. Maybe I delayed, because deep down I didn't think things would go this way. Deep down, I think I thought it was all a hoax."

"That priest won't leak anything...so I guess...as long as nobody knows that Santo is here...we are safe." Matt said it slowly, with growing apprehension, like a man on thin ice who hears cracking. He looked to Bigelow, hoping for some reassurance.

"This thing has grown beyond any predictable proportions, and the hysteria has become autogenous. It just keeps growing, even in the absence of Santo. I've paid our press people to plant some news stories saying that Santo has been sighted at various places around Texas. No specifics, but enough to keep the speculation in that area."

Matt nodded agreement and turned to leave.

"Hold-up, Matt."

Big turned to his desk, reached into one of the drawers, and handed a keycard to Matt. "This is to the guest quarters. Stay here tonight."

"You serious?"

"There's no sense kidding ourselves, we are all now prisoners of this project. Tomorrow, I will have my driver and a man help you move whatever things you need over here."

Matt shrugged. "That's fine with me. There are too many distractions at my apartment." He smiled, said goodnight, and left.

Reflected floor lights and the orange glow of a rising moon dimly lit the penthouse atrium. Matt paused at the waterfall and contemplated the scene, so tranquil and serene, as compared to the rapidly unfolding, riotous events of the world. He wondered how many people would die in the few minutes that he stood there watching the ascending moon, how many more would be born during that same time.

Maybe life and death were like two states of a vaporous liquid in a container, changing from liquid to gas and back again. But Buddhist notions of reincarnation held no sway with him. Dead was just dead, like his father, and there was no coming back. But did it have to be that way? Maybe there existed a path to biological immortality.

He finally turned from his thoughts, looked down at the suite number on the keycard, PG1, and followed the nearby hallway to his temporary new abode.

Matt opened the door and slid the keycard into its home berth on the wall, and the pre-programmed lighting schedule switched on the interior lights of the guest suite. LED spots lit several pieces of Native American art and some scenes of the Desert Southwest that adorned the walls. The electric curtains slid slowly open around their curved path to reveal a breath-taking panoramic view of Wyman Park, Johns Hopkins Homewood Campus and Baltimore beyond it, from northeast to southwest. Proximity detectors switched on lamps as he crossed the living room, revealing in full detail, a western motif with rough-hewn wooden beams and a sand-colored stucco ceiling above a wood planked floor that was dotted with hand-woven rugs holding couches embroidered with arrowheads.

Through the curved window wall, he gazed down on the tiny people far below, scurrying to and fro along the cross walks of Keyser Quad. His undergraduate years seemed but a dim memory now, having to kowtow to the whims of professors and their schedules. They were all somewhere beneath him with the other tiny people. He'd left them years behind. If they only knew of the Santo project, they would sell their wives and mothers to stand where he was, at the precipice of a new frontier of knowledge, and the possible dawning of a new age for humanity.

Matt flipped out his phone and called his roommate Ryan, to let him know that he wouldn't make it home for pizza as scheduled. He advised Ryan of the new temporary boarding arrangements, and that he would be removing some of his things the next day. He didn't want Ryan to think that they had been burgled. Ryan advised him that his grandmother had called, and Matt figured that the message had just been garbled, since his grandmother had never called before, and in her condition, she never would call. It was probably just the front office, and he would call them the next day during business hours. He hung up, and then scavenged the kitchen and pantry, finally finding a jackpot of frozen pizza in the fridge.

He took his microwave pizza and a glass of ginger ale back to the window wall and sat down in a chair facing east. The moon had climbed several more diameters above the horizon and shed its orange skin. He wondered how many lives had begun and ended in that time.

Matt slid lower in the chair and tried to relax; tried to freeze the moon in its rise in his mind. It was funny, he thought, how things like the moon seemed to move so slowly; how time always seemed like there was so very much of it, when in fact a man's life was painfully short after all. For what was the interval of a human life, any life, no matter how extended compared to geological time? Life was like some grand joke, lasting just long enough for a man to appreciate its intricacies, only to have it snatched away.

He thought of Pilar somewhere on a floor below him, and he refused to allow himself to envision her old like his grandmother, even though that time would inevitably arrive. It needn't ever happen, he thought, if the biological clock could be switched off, if cells could keep reproducing forever.

Chapter 24

A Meteor Message from God?

Santiago stopped the truck at the customs checkpoint just south of Juarez. NCR vigilantes had taken control and all identities were being checked, but as a priest, he was treated with great respect. The commander at the checkpoint gave him directions to vigilante headquarters, and two men were assigned to go with him as security. It was still unsafe at some flash points around the city, as the combined citizen forces were cleaning out the last vestiges of corruption.

At a mass grave near the checkpoint, they passed several trucks bringing more bodies to be deposited at the gravesite. Several doctors and a priest were checking the bodies for signs of life as they were pulled from the trucks. Other men searched the bodies for any identification. This was the final dispensation that had come to the malefactors of Juarez.

Santiago felt sick to his stomach, but it was too late to turn back. In a short while, they pulled up in front of headquarters and his security guards accompanied him inside. He asked to speak with Father Luis, which would normally be impossible without an appointment, but as a fellow member of the church, and having traveled so far, they were happy to pass him through to the front of the line. He sat in the hall on a long wooden bench with about ten others, who were on one of six benches in the hallway, and many more people were standing in line, waiting for their opportunity. In about ten minutes, a man leaned out of the office and motioned for Santiago to come inside.

Santiago walked through the door of the office and immediately locked eyes with Father Luis, who studied him with curiosity from behind his desk. Both men paused, as each took the measure of the other. Luis was rather muscular but lean, and his frame was about the same size as Santiago's. He had piercing dark eyes that scanned Santiago quickly and made up their mind that he was no threat.

"How may I help you, Father?"

Santiago held his breath, like a man plunged in water over his head. He smiled, as he focused his thoughts. "Actually," he finally said, "I need nothing at all, and this may seem strange, but I saw you on the television speaking, and you looked so very familiar to me, that I thought I might know your family from a very long time ago. Curiosity got the best of me, and I came to ask."

"Ask away," said Father Luis with a laugh.

"What is your actual name?"

"I am Luis Banderas Maldonado, formerly of Sonora."

Santiago's face paled. "Aaah," he whispered. "Then it was only my imagination, and I am sorry to have bothered you."

"It's nothing," Luis said, staring intensely.

"I will leave you to your work."

Santiago turned to the door.

"One moment, please."

Father Luis stepped out from around the desk and placed his hand on Santiago's shoulder. He pointed with his arm to an adjoining office. "I was about to have lunch, please join me."

The two men walked through the door and Father Luis closed and locked the door, before turning back to Santiago.

"I know who you are," Luis said quietly.

Santiago stood transfixed.

"You do?"

"Yes. I knew there was something very familiar about your face, but I did not place it at first."

Father Luis opened a closet and removed a bag lunch. He took out two sandwiches and placed them on either side of a small table that sat beside the room's only window. It overlooked a courtyard where enemies of the revolution were being held and questioned before transport from the city. He poured two glasses of water from a covered glass pitcher, and removed a bottle of Hermosillo wine from a small refrigerator and poured two small glasses. Then he took two pears from the refrigerator and placed them next to the sandwiches. He gestured for Santiago to be seated, and they both sat down.

Santiago began: "I was not sure...I did not know if I should say."

"You were wise to say nothing. It would have caused a great commotion, I am sure."

Santiago looked puzzled. "How?"

"For you, the companion of Jesus Munoz and his dog Santo, to be here, would undoubtedly cause a great stir. I am glad that no one recognized you. In fact, when we are through, I will ask that you wear your hat and leave by the rear door, just to avoid that situation."

"Of course," said Santiago. "No problem."

"Now tell me, please, what is your mission here?"

Santiago sighed. "It was as I said, merely curiosity. I thought you might be the son of an old friend, but I was mistaken."

"I see...an old friend. What was it that made you reach that conclusion?"

Santiago smiled as he studied Father Luis.

"It was your eyes, and your smile, and certain mannerisms that seemed very familiar to me. Just a very strong feeling that I knew your family from those similarities."

"What was your friend's name?

"It doesn't matter. I am getting old, and when one gets old, they sometimes prefer the past to the present. The past is like a comfortable old friend, whereas the present lacks warmth. And the future...is a stranger, who perhaps brings bad news."

"We are about the same age," laughed Father Luis. "Don't paint us gray yet!"

"I am old enough to be your father," said Santiago. "I do not look my age."

"Really?" Father Luis looked at Santiago carefully, as if seeing him anew.

They chatted over their sandwiches and wine, primarily about current events. Father Luis asked the location of Santo, and Santiago explained that he had temporarily been taken to a safe, undisclosed location, due to the hysteria that had overrun his home village. Santo would probably return when things calmed down, if they ever calmed down. Their personalities resonated, although Santiago was much more conservative, having lived an agrarian lifestyle in his isolated mountain village for so many years. They finally made a parting toast to God and Mexico, and Father Luis made a firm promise to come and visit Santiago in Pueblo del Cielo, the home of Santo, as soon as events allowed it.

That evening, Santiago was driving southward toward home, breathing deeply the clean desert air, and feeling completely happy in the desolation that always took him closer to God. Everything in life is a miracle, he thought, and for the first time in nearly fifty years, his heart felt whole.

In a spiritual and mental epiphany, Santiago suddenly saw vividly the unity of all things. Through all the years during which he thought he had been denied a son, he realized that God had granted him stewardship of a different son in Jesus Munoz, whom he now knew and loved even more than his own biological son. And yet God, in his infinite mercy, had finally allowed him to meet his lost son, and to learn that he had become a great man and a leader, who was now directing the conscience of Mexico.

The hairs on his neck stood on end as he finally fully realized that all the past forty years were spent as more than just a penance, but also as God's plan that had built a matrix of events to support the work of his son, Luis. For if not for Santo and all the events surrounding him, there would be no leader of a vigilante movement cleansing Mexico. Tears of joy filled his eyes as his humility before God was complete.

"Thank you, Father," Santiago said to the star-filled Chihuahuan Desert sky. "You have given me more than any man needs." And just then, a shooting star trailed green copper flame across the sky in recognition. "Thank you," he whispered.

****

"Make a wish," Claire said softly to Mendy as they watched a meteor streak across the southern sky beyond Tenth Street.

"I've got all I need," Mendy whispered, as he slipped his arms around her from behind. They continued to watch the sky through the mansion house window.

"Then I'll wish for you."

"Don't be greedy, let it pass to someone else."

"Too late. I already wished."

Mendy pulled her closer and kissed her softly on the neck.

"It will get tougher the next two months," he said. "They will hit us with everything they've got, and fabricate what they don't have. Are you sure you're up to it?"

Claire squirmed in his arms and turned and faced him, and smiled.

"It's not about us any longer. I know that now. That makes it easy." She kissed him lightly on the lips and rested her head against his chest. "Once one removes oneself from the equation there is no fear or anxiety."

"That's right," Mendy said, while stroking Claire's hair. "I'm glad you understand. It's only about what's best for the people. For a little while, we give up our right to be human, in an effort to make a better world."

****

Zhang Zhuang looked out his jail cell window through swollen, bruised eyelids just as a fireball streaked pale green across the morning sky of Guangdong. In the street below, villagers were mulling about, trying to decide what to do next. Roadblocks had been constructed on the main roads and there was a temporary standoff between villagers who claimed their rights of land ownership and those in authority who were trying to steal their farmland for financial gain. Zhuang had stood strong and was the most vocal, defending the rights of individuals to follow their chosen destiny, farming land that had been in their families for many generations.

He watched as a local artist sketched an image of Buddha holding Santo on the wall across the street, finally writing beneath it: "*Friends of Man*." Behind him a door squeaked open, and several men walked into the cell. They pulled him from the window and sat him in a chair.

"We wish to see a smooth resolution to this problem," the police chief said.

"Then let me go back to my land. I just want to be left alone."

A flurry of fists beat Zhuang about the head and chest, but he managed to stand and break away from the men who were pounding him, and run to the window.

"Stand strong!" he yelled to the crowd below, before the men pulled him back.

The men set upon him with a vengeance, kicking him and stomping him as he fell on the floor. They kept at it until they lost all their anger, but by then Zhuang was gone. Only his body was left, and that would be dumped outside of town that night. A homeless man, sleeping in the woods by the roadside would witness the event, and tell about it, and the murder of Zhang Zhuang would be recorded as the flashpoint of the People's Revolt in Guangdong that spread like fire across China.

****

The next day, Matt completed his change of residence to the guest quarters in the penthouse, just as Jesus completed his arrangements to sleep at the lab during the research on Santo. Along the way to the lab, Matt heard a news story about a large asteroid that had broken up the previous evening as it had entered the atmosphere, yielding multiple fireballs across an east-west trajectory. The story had no effect on him, except to make him wonder, as he often did, whether such asteroids and comets were not actually the sperm of space, having fertilized the egg called Earth many times over billions of years.

In his mind he visualized the possibilities and imagined primal seas teeming with organic compounds, and he wondered dreamily how the first cell might have ever formed, how physical processes might have become life. More than anything else, he thought about cells, and how some unicellular creatures were effectively immortal, constantly dividing throughout history.

Matt pulled up and parked at the lab. He thought of the cellular regeneration that he had witnessed in Santo and became so excited that he could barely think. There were a thousand questions in his mind all simultaneously crying to be answered, but he had to focus more narrowly and map a course of action. He needed to figure out how to assemble the research team, and design it so no one actually knew exactly what was going on. The team would consist of cells, each working on a different aspect of the project, with no one except himself and Bigelow knowing the entire scope of the project.

The day passed in a blur, and when Matt looked at his wall clock before turning off the office light, he was shocked to see that twelve hours had passed and he hadn't even eaten. He locked the office door and trudged wearily down the hall to where Jesus and Santo were preparing for bed. The door was open, and he knocked lightly on the frame before jutting his head through the doorway.

"Everything okay?" he asked Jesus, who was seated on a cot brushing Santo.

"Magnificent," Jesus said, as he looked up at Matt.

"That beats okay," Matt said with a laugh.

"Just one question, Matthew. A woman on the floor below us told me today that she slices rat's brains into very thin slices to make microscope slides for her research. I am wondering, since I saw some dogs in cages on that floor, along with other animals, are they to suffer such experimentation also?"

Matt frowned.

"I don't know."

"This concerns me greatly, and I think that Santo senses that there is something wrong here, because he has been quivering all day."

"I try not to think about it, because I know that a lot of valuable work is going on here, and sometimes animals do undergo tests of drugs and other things."

"Other things? Yes, which is what I fear, those other things. Have you ever experimented on innocent animals, Matthew?"

"No. My work is with cells. We grow cultures as are needed, and we test various cell functions as our research requires."

"That is good, Matthew. I would not wish to think of you as one who mistreats animals. Nothing can justify cruelty to animals."

Matt stood silent for several seconds watching Santo as Jesus brushed him. The dog seemed to be smiling.

"Okay," Matt finally said. "I am going to go home now."

"Give my love to Pilar," Jesus said innocently.

"If I see her. It's late."

Matt closed the door and walked slowly towards the elevator. He wondered about the dogs on the lower floor, and what they were actually subjected to, but then pushed all such thoughts aside, since they could do him no good.

The new security guard bid him goodnight at the elevator, calling him Doctor West. It was the first time anyone had mistakenly addressed him as a doctor and it made him uncomfortable. During his ride to the ground floor, Matt replayed his top choices for some of the team leaders of the seven research cells that he had designed that day. He wondered how Big would react to his choices, since some would require large stipends to secure their team presence.

Twenty minutes later, Matt was in his new apartment, relaxed in a chair by the window eating hot noodles, when the phone sounded. He lifted it to his ear and said hello, and at first heard nothing.

"Hello?" Matt repeated.

"I'm lonely," came Pilar's voice from the phone.

Minutes later, the apartment door lock clicked open, and Pilar floated quietly in across the living room and sat on the floor, leaning against Matt's leg. She looked out at the rising moon, whose face wore the same surprised expression as the previous night, and pictured it rising over the mountains in Pueblo del Cielo.

"I miss the smell of the mountain air...the clean breeze that accompanies each evening, and the smell of sage," she sighed.

Matt slurped down the last of the noodles and sat his bowl on the table next to the chair without comment.

"What are you thinking?" Pilar asked.

"I was wondering why man seems to have evolved faster than dogs, even though dogs existed in a similar form almost forty million years ago. It seems counter-intuitive since dogs live much shorter lives, and have therefore experienced many more generations than modern man, who dates back a much shorter time. They both hunted in packs, so what made man evolve a much larger brain, and so quickly?"

Pilar turned from the window and stared at Matt.

"That is what you were thinking?"

"Yes," Matt replied, while staring at the moon.

"Look at me."

Matt looked down at Pilar, and she slinked up his leg towards him and handed him a hairbrush.

"I'll tell you the answer if you brush my hair."

She slid back down across him and nestled in between his legs with her back toward him. Matt gently hooked the brush in her hair and dragged it from front to back across her head, resting the shiny locks in his left palm at the end of each stroke.

"I'm waiting," Matt said after several minutes of brushing.

"God. God made man in his image."

"That's your answer?"

"Not my answer. The answer."

"Maybc you'rc right," Matt said, and kissed her on top the head, while continuing to brush. "Something caused it. The dinosaurs had over a hundred million years, but they never grew more than walnut-sized brains. Why man, and not dog?"

"God," said Pilar. "God chose man."

Chapter 25

Science Attempts to Decode Santo

Philip Bigelow was as good as his word, and he met every request that Matt made, including unrestricted funding in order to secure the best personnel for the project. In some cases, he made suggestions to Matt, since his experience and resources were much broader in the business world, but in general, he gave complete control of the management of the Santo project to Matt. At the end of the first month, they had made great progress, which really amounted to no progress at all.

Hundreds of tests had proven that in most ways, Santo was a very common dog. DNA testing revealed his heritage was that of a mongrel traced to several Asian breeds, and he was largely related to an Indian Pariah. It was established that his visual cortex was enlarged, and that his eyesight had an expanded bandwidth that allowed him to see both higher and lower frequencies of light that were invisible to most species.

The photographic team discovered a curious anomaly almost by accident as they were taking spectral photographs using filters and a wideband charge-coupled device. Several photos showed what appeared to be a faint halo surrounding the head of Santo. This halo was brought into clearer view through a combination of time-lapse photography and electronic amplification and it seemed to be eerily reminiscent of the halos painted around saints by renaissance painters. Some thought it was a false find, a mere ghost in the electronics caused by an undetected feedback loop. But an older engineer on the electronics team, who had a strong background in electromagnetic theory, assured Matt that the photographs were accurate, and that they represented a standing wave pattern of narrow-band electromagnetic radiation. He theorized that Santo was acting as a sort of antenna, and was both receiving and transmitting radiation on those frequencies. Unfortunately, he had no theory to explain the process, or what it meant, if anything at all. It was a completely unexplained anomaly, requiring more tests.

However, the ability to see electromagnetic radiation that was invisible to the human eye might explain why Santo had a complete aversion to magnets and magnetic fields. Even after his operation, they dared not let him near the magnetic resonance imaging lab, as it produced horrific results in his demeanor, which resulted in convulsions and near seizures. Instead, thermal imaging and other tests had to be used to gather information.

The second month showed good progress by the cellular team in growing cell cultures, but all tests performed on Santo to ascertain his age showed that he was just a normal dog of approximately one year of age. There seemed to be no abnormalities in telomeric structuring or enzyme balances, and all cell chemistry tests revealed nothing out of the ordinary.

There were however, two very startling results obtained by independent innovations of two of the staff. One younger researcher on the cellular team had generated a bacterial culture from the saliva of Santo. Nothing seemed unusual about it, but one night, on a lunch, he had left one of the cultures next to a small neodymium magnet. In the morning, the culture showed clumping at the side nearest the magnet. After considerable tests and discussion, it was theorized that it might be the result of some sort of magnetotactic nano bacteria that were too small to be detected, so arrangements were made to use an atomic force microscope housed at the University of Maryland nearby. When the photos came back, the images showed what appeared to be some sort of multi-legged creatures that looked like crawler robots equipped with claw-like hands.

One peculiarity was that the bodies of the crawlers seemed to have some sort of symbols along their length. The young researcher immediately dubbed the crawler-like creatures nanites and launched into wild speculation as to their origins. The team opinion was that like the face on Mars, the human mind tended to find recognizable patterns even where none actually existed, and that therefore, more detailed photographs were necessary.

The second startling result of the month was due to Ray Hardy, the senior engineer who had theorized that the Santo halo effect was due to standing waves. Thinking that the waves might be related to Gurwitsch radiation, Hardy built a wave-guide antenna system that collected a portion of the halo field near Santo and funneled it to a cell culture, with the astounding result that cell proliferation was accelerated a hundred fold. Hardy's initial calculations showed that the biogenic field emitted by Santo was at least a thousand times greater than the field of a single person. It was also found that this field varied greatly over time. This raised many new questions.

****

Jesus and Matt sat on the office library couch with Santo between them and turned on the news, as Philip Bigelow pored over the latest reports that Matt had just delivered to him.

"This is fantastic!" Bigelow panted, shaking his head in disbelief as he continued reading. "So it's definitely all real! The dog really can cause miracle cures on others, as well as himself?"

"Possibly, we still can't say. I do know that I took him with me to visit my grandmother two months ago, and shortly after, most of the symptoms of her senility disappeared. To me, she looks a decade younger, although it might be the psychology of seeing her completely coherent again. The doctor seems to think she may have had a blood clot or blockage that cleared, and cautions that she might go downhill yet again. There is no proof that it had anything to do with Santo."

Jesus suppressed a smile.

"This biogenic energy that he seems to be channeling, where does it come from?" Bigelow asked.

"We don't know yet, but the senior engineer on the electronics team theorizes that it's everywhere, almost like the background radiation from the Big Bang."

"So maybe we can collect it with a big dish and amplify it? Maybe focus it, just like in this experiment that caused cell proliferation."

"Collect it, maybe. But amplify it? For one thing, it seems coherent and modulated, and consists of bands of frequencies. It seems cyclical, possibly related to the lunar cycle, but we still aren't even sure about that," Matt said with a shrug.

"Do you think that it could be being transmitted from a single source?"

"You mean like from extra-terrestrials?"

"No...Well, yeah, maybe. I don't know. "

"Anything's possible," Matt said. "Who knows?"

"Can you believe, that it might be God?" Jesus asked.

Matt coughed, rose from the couch, and walked to the bookshelves, where he grabbed a volume and began to browse through it.

"You mean that God is sending the energy, or that God is the energy?" Bigelow asked almost whimsically.

"Your choice," Jesus said quietly.

"So this energy is all around us, like background radiation, and it's actually God?"

Bigelow pulled out a picture that showed the enhanced halo surrounding Santo, and held it out towards Matt, who had looked up from his book and was waiting for Big's answer.

"Yes. I could believe that. Maybe this modulated energy is everywhere, and is actually the mind of God. The Bible says God is everywhere, as does the Kabala, and other texts. But we are part of it, aren't we? So wouldn't that make us part of God? What do you think, Matt?"

Matt held the book up that he had been browsing.

"I didn't know you were a fan of Thomas Aquinas." He slid the book back in its place and withdrew another. "This is more to my liking, Marcus Aurelius, lots of good stuff in here. 'Each man is born with a tutelary genius that guides him.' I believe that. But is it God? Maybe. That's what Tolstoy thought."

"What about these magnetic bacteria? Have you ever seen anything like them before? They look like dust mites with hand tools, or some sort of bacteriophage.

"What is that? It looks almost like some kind of raised symbols on their bodies."

"I can't speculate," Matt said, shaking his head. "Maybe a distortion in the protein coat. We need more tests."

"Look!" Jesus exclaimed, pointing to a news clip playing on the wall screen. At a campaign speech being given by Governor Mendoza, who was now the frontrunner in the presidential election, many people in the audience were wearing hats adorned with stuffed replicas of Santo. "The announcer says that the people wear them for good luck, and that Santo has become a symbol of individualism and self-determination, just like Mendy. People everywhere are being inspired to take control of their individual destinies. They say Santo is the new Teddy bear."

"That is weird," said Matt.

"I think it is a very good likeness of Santo," laughed Jesus. "You see that?" he said to Santo, wiggling his ears. "That's you!"

Santo smiled, and watched the wall screen as if he understood.

"That dog has changed history," said Bigelow.

Jesus smiled as he stood up from the couch, and Santo jumped to the floor excitedly, hoping they were going for a walk.

"Only man changes history, under the auspices of God," Jesus commented flatly. "Animals are under our dominion, and as such, deserve our protection and our love."

He started for the door, and waved goodbye.

"My friends, I bid you goodnight, as I promised to spend some time with my granddaughter on this two-month anniversary of our arrival here."

Jesus turned towards Matt. "She has been lonely, not seeing enough of those she cares about."

Bigelow cast a stern look at Matt, and he turned and looked out the window, as if he had just noticed something of interest. Jesus smiled and exited, and the distant sound of the closing door soon reached the library office.

"You know, Matt, for what it's worth, I'd like to caution you about ambition and drive. At your age, making a mark in the world, staking out a claim on history, sometimes seems very important. But when you get to be my age, and you look back, achievements don't seem to matter very much if they were made at the expense of things that you loved."

"There's only so much time in a day!" Matt retorted. "And life is short...you have to make hay while the sun shines!"

"I believe that is exactly my point," returned Bigelow. "Knowing when the sun shines, and recognizing all that it illuminates. The blinders of ambition can cause us to run past things of great importance, and having once done so, sometimes there is no going back. 'Walk the middle path.' You may be surprised to find that in the long run, you still arrive at the same place, and you will be much happier."

Matt turned from the window and stood in silence, staring at Bigelow for several seconds.

"You're right," he finally said. "I'll see you later."

Matt grabbed up all his things, and headed for the door.

In a few seconds, the penthouse door closed, leaving Bigelow alone. He poured himself a brandy and swirled it around in the glass before drinking it down. "A wise young man," he whispered. "Much wiser than myself."

Chapter 26

The Mark of the Three-One God?

Pilar watched the news channel as she worked on a biology paper. Since the research had started, she was left largely alone with her studies. At school, she had met no one with whom she resonated. The girls were either absorbed by fashion, talking about boys, or mindlessly texting their contemporaries, and the boys were either oblivious to her presence or entirely too aware of it. She enjoyed talking to Santiago on the telephone and raptly listened to stories he told about her village and how the crowds had grown again. Only this time, instead of miracle seekers, they were like people awoke from a sleep that came to see what had awoken them. They were quiet, respectful, and reverent, an entirely different atmosphere than months ago.

Pilar missed Santiago, Alita, and her village very much. Everything in the world at Johns Hopkins seemed meaningless to her now that the novelty had worn off. Only Matt seemed worthy of her consideration, and he was mostly removed by his researches. It was in such social solitude that she had realized in a quiet moment that all current events, no matter how engrossing, were as ephemeral as the morning fog. She decided that she had erred in her course of studies, and that she wanted to help people. She no longer craved science and technology. It had become as empty as the consumables that her classmates raved about, and it seemed like just a type of self-indulgence to chase such things.

It was in that context and thinking about her past life that Pilar entered upon a line of thought about Santo. She remembered the many times since her childhood that Santiago and Jesus had gone on trips to sell vegetables, and she remembered some of the excursions that she was finally allowed to share as she had grown older. Never in all those years, did it occur to her that Santo hadn't aged. He never seemed to change at all, but then neither did Jesus or Santiago.

She wasn't occupied with death or aging in her isolated village existence, and Santo was just a playmate and companion for whom she never saw an end. She wondered about her grandfather and Santiago, and abruptly realized that they had to have known that Santo was youthful beyond his years. She wondered how much they had actually known about his special abilities, and that is when it dawned on her that they might have known all along that he was not just a normal dog.

The phone rang, and Pilar chased its sound until she finally grabbed it from beneath a pile of books that were opened on the couch where she was sitting. It was Santiago, calling for a chat.

He asked her the same types of questions as always; how was school, did she make any new friends, and how was life treating her? She mentioned that she was changing her course of studies and then she said:

"Tell me about Santo?"

There was a pause.

"Oh," Santiago eventually replied, "your grandfather can tell you all about that."

At that moment, the door opened, and Jesus smiled warmly as he saw her occupying the living room, spread out with all her studies and tablets, while watching the TV and talking on the phone. Santo bounded in and jumped up on the couch and Pilar chased him from stepping all over her books. She said goodbye to Santiago, and picked up her books before Santo could lick them, drool on them, or tear out the pages as he walked all over them. Santo took that as an invitation and jumped on her lap, licking her face. Pilar stopped him by scratching behind his ears, and he leaned in against her in tranquil happiness, lulled to stillness by an ear massage.

"Tell me about Santo," Pilar said innocently to Jesus.

"The tests are progressing very well. Matthew and the teams have learned a great many new things—"

"No, I mean tell me his complete history. You told me he was my father's dog. When did he get Santo?"

Jesus gave Pilar a measured stare before answering.

"No, I never said Santo was your father's dog. I said that your father played with Santo, just as you did, growing up. Santo has always been my dog, ever since my friend, Sailor, an old man from Spain, gave him to me when I was twelve. I never knew Sailor's real name. Everyone called him Sailor."

Pilar sat frozen.

"I guess he was the only sailor to ever live in Del Cielo, so that is why the name stuck."

"You had Santo since you were twelve?"

"I used to play with him since I was six. That was when I first became friends with Sailor. I offered to help him with his garden, just so I could get to play with his dog. We became good friends, and he taught me many things about plants and gardening."

Knock-knock-knock came from the door behind Jesus, and he jumped.

"Who is it?" asked Jesus.

"It's Matt," came from outside the door.

"I will tell you the rest later," Jesus said softly, "But say nothing for now."

Jesus opened the door and Matt walked in. He cast a searching look at Pilar and she smiled warmly, putting him at ease. Jesus excused himself and took Santo with him into the next room and closed the door, leaving Matt and Pilar to chat alone.

Jesus bent down and scratched Santo's head while whispering to him.

"I expect that right now, Mr. Matthew is apologizing for spending too much time with you, my friend."

Santo raised his ears and tilted his head to one side as if confused, and Jesus stifled a laugh.

****

Matt switched on the projector and turned off the office lights. On the projector screen were about a dozen fuzzy images of what looked like alien landscapes bisected by cylinders with strange symbols spaced longitudinally along them.

"What do you think, Kyle? Do you recognize any of those markings?"

"Maybe. The symbols that look like three little flags on sticks at the end of each row may be a variant of ancient Thracian, but the others, I don't recognize."

"Thracian?" Matt intoned.

"From Thrace, which later became Bulgaria. Some variants of Thracian hieroglyphs are known to predate Egyptian symbols by two thousand years. They were only used by the initiated elite, but the later Egyptian symbols were the same."

Kyle walked up to the screen and pointed to several photos.

"Can you rearrange these photographs so they go one, two, three?"

Matt dragged and dropped the photos using his tablet as Kyle instructed.

"You'll notice," Kyle said, pointing to the screen, "that the symbols grouped here are the same in these three photos?"

"Yes."

"It looks indicative of a number series to me. I would say that whatever these cylinders are, they have been labeled as part of a production series."

"What?"

"Like model numbers in a series. Or serial numbers."

"Jesus."

"Fitting," said Kyle.

"What?"

"Fitting that you should say that. The symbols at the end of each row mean the *Three-One God,* or *Trinity*. The symbols are read right to left," Kyle said, as he traced his index finger along the cylinders in question. "What are these things from?"

"They're part of a project we're working on," Matt said emptily.

"Can't say, eh? Well, if it's anything juicy, keep me in the loop. I dare say I'd like to know more."

Matt turned on the lights and switched off the projector lamp.

"Thanks," he said, as he shook hands with Kyle. "I will, when I can. Thanks for coming over."

"What's a *pal*--eographer for?"

Matt didn't catch the joke, and Kyle shrugged his shoulders and laughed to himself as he went out the office door. Matt sat down slowly at his desk as the cooling fan of the projector whirred quietly in the background. In his ears, another sound was growing, like the whine of locusts on an August evening. His heart was pounding and he felt light-headed. The projector finally cooled sufficiently, and the automatic fan cut off, leaving just the whine of the ghost locusts and his thumping heart. He collected his notes and tablet, switched off the office lights and left, locking the door behind him.

Jesus met Matt at the end of the hall, as he was leaving for dinner.

"Santo safely locked away?" asked Matt.

"Until I return," replied Jesus. "Philip asked me to drop by this evening before I visit Pilar."

"Philip? You and Mr. Big have gotten quite chummy over the last months."

"Men of age like to compare notes sometimes. I find that we share many common interests, your employer and myself."

"Really? I would never have guessed that."

They reached the elevator and a new guard asked them for their ID's. They obliged mindlessly and he thanked them, and unlocked the elevator.

"Have a nice night, Doctors," the guard said as they went into the open elevator.

"We're not doctors," said Matt, as the doors closed.

"You and Pilar are okay?"

"Yes. Yes, she's changed her courses."

"I know."

The elevator doors opened, and a guard asked for their identification.

"Another new face," Matt said to the man.

"Yes, Sir," the guard responded.

"Something's not right," Matt said to Jesus as they crossed the lobby. That security guard wasn't in uniform, he was wearing a suit."

Matt flipped out his phone and speed dialed Bigelow.

"Big," he whispered, as he eyed the front door, where two more men in suits stood sentry, "something's up, our security men at the lab have disappeared, and there are a bunch of strangers here in suits. What should we do?"

"Relax," said Bigelow through the phone. "They're NSA."

"What?"

"National Security Agency, has taken over. I just found out myself. I'll explain when you get here. There's nothing to worry about."

The ghost locusts had returned to whine in Matt's head, their amplitude, modulated by his heartbeat. He stopped at the water fountain and took a long drink.

"Is everything okay?" asked Jesus.

"Big says it is, but I'm not so sure."

They walked slowly to the front door, where they were again asked for their ID's.

"Could I see your ID?" Matt said to one of the sentries.

"Yes, Sir," the man said, and handed Matt his identification for inspection.

Matt examined it closely.

"Thank you," he said, as he finally handed it back.

"Yes, Sir. My pleasure. Have a nice night."

They walked out to the parking lot, where they were less surprised to find the lot's key pass gate now manned by two armed Army personnel. Without their having to ask, Matt showed them his ID, and they passed the car through.

It was much the same at the Bigelow Building, with all new security people and armed army personnel at the front entrance. When they arrived at the penthouse, several men were on their way downstairs. The men all nodded politely as they passed in the elevator and Bigelow, who had walked them out, met Matt and Jesus in the penthouse atrium.

"What's going on?" Matt asked, as Bigelow guided them in towards the library office.

"At first, I thought we had a mole in our midst, when they swept into the building this afternoon. But those gentlemen who just left were kind enough to inform me of the real reasons that we have just been deemed a national security issue, and it has nothing directly to do with our research. It's all about Santo."

"They know he's here?" asked Matt.

"Don't be naïve," Bigelow scoffed. "Of course they do."

They reached the library and Bigelow went to his desk and switched on the wall screen. The banner across the bottom of the screen read: "*Live from Guangdong, China*." A mob of people was in the street and soldiers were pushing them back. Suddenly the transmission was disrupted and the announcers came on screen to explain what had been happening.

"That's China," Bigelow said as he switched the channel. The next channel showed images from Red Square, where throngs of demonstrators were protesting the most recent election and calling for overthrow of the existing government.

"Moscow."

Bigelow switched the channel again, and rioters in Egypt filled the screen. "This is the real problem."

The rioters held an effigy of Santo hung by his neck, which they had set on fire and were beating with sticks. Some held signs written in English that read: "Kill the Christ Dog," and "Die Santo, Die!"

"Yeah, so they're nuts," Matt said. "Everybody knows that. So what?"

"Apparently, NSA intercepted messages that have led them to believe that a real and current threat exists with respect to Santo. Acting under National Security Directive Forty-two, President Mendoza ordered NSA and the Central Intelligence Service to take over security for our project. It seems that Santo is now not only a Mexican national treasure, but has become indispensable to American national security as both a symbol of the Individualist Movement, and a sacred symbol of the Christian faith the world over. Our new president feels a personal connection, and has vowed not to let anything happen to Santo on his watch."

"How is this going to affect our project?"

"Actually, it helps. We are no longer footing all the bills, and we have a much higher security presence."

"Yeah, but how will they explain all the extra guards and military? Doesn't this just paint a target on us?"

"Not really. Nobody knows why they are here. They will probably float some kind of story to satisfy the public."

"I'm still not convinced that we don't have a mole, or at the very least that we haven't been hacked by government spies. This is all just too coincidental, coming now."

"What do you mean," asked Bigelow.

Matt carried his tablet over to Bigelow's desk, set it down, and logged on to Bigelow's local network. He picked up Big's remote and switched the video to the wall display, where an image of a mangnetotactic bacteriophage filled the screen.

"We've had a break-through."

Bigelow moaned with approval as he and Jesus both sat down on a couch in front of the screen.

"That's a fantastic image. Almost like a lunar-lander or robot"

"The best is yet to come."

Matt rotated the image to a horizontal position and zoomed in on the cylindrical mid-section.

"Remember what I theorized were folds in the protein coils that looked like symbols? This is what our newest photos show after computer enhancement and filtering." Matt clicked through several views, each one larger than the last, until the cylinder filled the screen from left to right.

Bigelow floated from his seat on the couch to the front of the screen, and Jesus was sitting so erect he looked like he was just about to join him.

"That's incredible," whispered Bigelow. "It looks almost like hieroglyphs."

"Si," whispered Jesus, forgetting his English.

"That's what I thought, too," said Matt, as he brought up another screen that showed a dozen cropped images of the bacteriophages. "So I called in an expert paleographer I know from

Hopkins to have a look at them, and he pretty-much confirmed it."

"No way," Bigelow sighed. "What does it say?"

"If you take note of the first three images, you will see there is a similarity in their groupings and sequences. The paleographer couldn't identify all of the symbols, but he said he thinks the grouped ones to the left represent numbers. He didn't know what he was looking at and thought it was a manufactured artifact, so he theorized that they might be like model numbers.

Bigelow's arms fell to his side and he stood silent.

"What about the three symbols that are on the far right in each image that look like little flags?" asked Jesus. "What do they mean?"

Matt paused before answering, and both Bigelow and Jesus turned toward him in anticipation.

"The Three-One God," Matt finally said. "Or the Divinity."

"Holy shit!" erupted Bigelow. He looked toward Jesus and they shared a look of commonality.

"There's more," continued Matt. "The script is a Thracian variant that dates back to five thousand B.C. Furthermore, these things are not bacteriophages. They aren't limited to what they can attack and are multifunctional. They are magnetically mobile, and seem to be affected by local cellular fields. That is apparently why magnetic fields play havoc with Santo.

"This is phenomenal. You're doing a great job, Matt."

"No, I'm not. I am completely at a loss to explain any of this. It's all nuts."

Matt collapsed in a chair with a sigh and rested his chin on his chest.

Bigelow sent a searching glance to Jesus and he nodded. He

then walked to a wing chair that cornered with Matt's and sat down.

"Matt, I'm afraid I haven't been completely open with you."

"What do you mean?" Matt said, looking up from a spot on the floor.

"I've withheld information that Jesus told me about the true origin of Santo, because I didn't want to taint your researches with any preconceived notions."

"What is it, that he came from another planet? Because that would explain a lot."

Bigelow laughed.

"Nothing so simple as that, I'm afraid." Bigelow went on to tell the whole story and Matt listened intently till the end.

"Are you drunk?" Matt said flatly. "Or crazy?"

Bigelow chuckled, got up and walked to his desk and retrieved a box and opened it. He removed a sealed, cube-shaped display case that held something inside.

"This is the object that you had removed from Santo. With the permission of Jesus, I sent it out and had it analyzed and dated. The world's best antiquities expert confirmed that it is a Roman spear point from around the time of Christ."

Matt rose from his chair with a growl.

"You expect me to believe that Santo is two thousand years old! I could more easily believe he *was* from another planet."

Bigelow laughed sardonically.

"Yes. Funny isn't it, how much easier it would be to believe that, because it wouldn't upend our most solid beliefs, namely that miracles don't really happen.

"In a way, maybe Santo is partly from another world… infected with the blood of Christ, maybe he is almost like Christ, reborn. All these years he has been helping and healing people, just as Christ did."

"I think you need another drink," Matt sneered.

"Actually, I haven't had one in months."

"Well maybe you should."

"Don't be disrespectful, Matthew," Jesus said. You arc still a baby, a child. You have filled your head with science and mathematics and biology, and in that respect your mind is still profane. What do you know of suffering? Not just physical, but emotional. You cannot possibly understand what it is like to have a child and to raise that child to adulthood, and then to have that child and his young wife blown to bits by terrorists in the name of Allah.

"You cannot know what it is like to feel all-encompassing hate that closes in on you from all sides like a malevolent disease, until all you can think of is killing, and wanting to kill those that killed yours…blood for blood.

"And yet, through a miraculous chain of events, God in his infinite wisdom, removed the sword from my hand and brought us all here together, perhaps, to do his work."

"By all that's sacred, I think you are right, Jesus! I have to believe it," Bigelow said sincerely. "As I look around and see the events unfolding in the world, many largely due to Santo, how can I not believe that it is God's work we are doing here?

"And, not to be disrespectful to anyone's beliefs, but I cannot also help but wonder so many other things, like…who Christ was, and where did he really come from? I've read that just from a probability standpoint, that there probably exist over a thousand technical civilizations in our own galaxy that are far in advance of our own. Imagine a society a million years more advanced that our own. Wouldn't they all seem like gods to us?

"Or perhaps all life is equal! Perhaps left alone, any life form would evolve towards the highest plane of consciousness. What chose man over other species, with almost nothing in between? Or is it that we just refuse to see the facts in front of us, that all animals are individuals just like us, that they all have emotions and feelings just like us, but are just on different planes of consciousness?

"In fact, where do you stop with that line of reasoning? Maybe every cell is a primordial precursor to God. Then every cell, no matter where, is holy, and should be treated with reverence, both plant and animal."

Matt suddenly became animated, his imagination tweaked by the conversation, and he started to pace.

"Or maybe this universe was made just for us, and we are all alone here. In fact, maybe the whole universe is like one big cell culture, and we are all embryonic gods, evolving to a higher state of consciousness."

"That," said Jesus, "is the height of hubris and egotism, but understandable from a young mind with great aspirations."

Bigelow laughed heartily.

"Gentlemen, I think that we are all three on the same page, and perhaps we can agree that we know almost nothing. However, I hope we can also agree that we are at a great point in history, and that what we are doing here is very worthwhile, and it may change the world for the better. Certainly, the world is changing now faster than it ever has, and some of it has been caused by Santo."

Bigelow looked to Jesus. "Or by God...you choose." He turned and walked to the bar and pulled out some ginger ales and poured them over ice into three glasses. Then he handed a glass to Jesus and another to Matt, and raised his in a toast: "All for one, and one for all, and to the success of our endeavor!"

They clinked their glasses together in unison.

"To the Three-One God!" Matt said, and smiled.

"We humbly ask his aegis and guidance," added Jesus.

They sipped the golden ale and smiled, united as one.

Chapter 27

Hell at Hopkins Campus

Pilar dreamed that she was back in Pueblo del Cielo and it was New Years. Horns were blowing, drums were beating, and people were chanting out salutations: "Santo," **bum-bum-bum**, "Santo," **bum-bum-bum**.

Suddenly, she awoke, but the noise of the crowd did not fade. In fact, it seemed to grow louder. At first, she was confused, and wondered if it was a dream within a dream, but then she realized that she was awake, and she sprang from her bed and ran to the window. The street below that wove through Wyman Park was clogged with cars and people, all headed towards the lab. This had to be a dream after all, she thought.

The phone rang, and it was Bigelow, and he advised her that a driver and a guard would take her to class via the back service entrance to the building.

"What is happening?" Pilar asked.

"The word got out that Santo is here."

"How?"

"We still don't know."

"Are Grandfather and Matthew safe?"

"Very safe, but this is going to make getting around more

difficult until the news wears off."

She thanked him for calling and hung up. The horns and constant drumbeats were annoying, and she was anxious to leave them behind, so she dressed and left for classes ahead of schedule. It recalled the hysteria of her village that had forced them to leave. To see it repeated here in this foreign land seemed so strange that it again made her question reality.

Shortly after, a car whisked Pilar along Carnegie Way, back onto Wyman Drive, and then circled the campus counter-clockwise, until it finally re-entered and deposited her in the circle in front of the Milton S. Eisenhower Library. The pulsing drumbeats met her there, but the trees had blocked the noise of the horns from the far side of the campus.

Spring was in full bloom and an early warm spell had brought sun-seekers out from the shadows to read and bask in the rays. They seemed oblivious to the distant drumbeats, and that fact and the warm sun began to relax her, until a headline across a Baltimore Sun newspaper sprang up like a cobra in front of her: *"Miracle Dog Found in Baltimore."*

It shouted her identity like a bullhorn; a group photo of her and Jesus and Santiago with Mendy, circled around Santo, just after the El Paso tragedy. She walked quickly past the person reading the paper and started into the library but overheard someone talking about Santo, so she changed course and proceeded across the upper quad to her class.

The drumbeats grew louder, and her heart began racing. No more anonymity, she thought, but maybe it wouldn't matter so much here, as back home. At her classroom, fellow students thronged her, bombarding her with questions about Santo, and she left on the pretense of having forgotten her tablet. Once outside, she felt a wave of panic and an overpowering impulse to escape, so she phoned for the car to come and get her.

It was happening again, just like before. There would soon be a frenzied crowd of reporters and pilgrims wherever she went, and her life would no longer be her own. Only here it was worse, because this place wasn't home. She suddenly missed Santiago and Alita, Aunt Maria and her village, and all the life that she had left behind very much. At least there, the people of the village protected her privacy from the mobs when they became too enraptured. She longed to be back in the mountains where the clouds kissed the hills and her life seemed bigger. She was nothing here and like a fish out of water, she gasped for air. Every stranger's face that passed held a new threat of recognition. She put her kerchief on, kept her eyes to the ground, and waited for the car.

Once safely entombed in the Bigelow Building, she worried about her grandfather, and called Jesus to check on his status.

"Someone needs to tell the merry-makers outside the building that Carnival is over," Jesus said through the phone.

"Yes," replied Pilar. "But what is their purpose?"

"Self-gratification through anarchy is the goal of any mob. They have no purpose, other than that. Once their emotions are sated they will disperse."

"I feel so empty and lonely," sighed Pilar. "Our pictures are all over the local news. I want to go home."

"It would be the same there, Nieta."

"But at least we would be home."

"I understand," Jesus said sympathetically. "Just try to last a little longer. Things will soon be better. Try to think of the greater good that may be accomplished here. Trust God."

"I do," sighed Pilar. "But sometimes I am weak."

"As are we all, and that is why we pray."

A siren wailed in the background amongst the blare of horns.

"Will you be home tonight?"

"It may be wiser for me to stay here with Santo. The noise is upsetting him. I will ask Matthew to stop by and check on you."

"No," said Pilar. "I'm okay now. I'm going to watch the news."

She said goodbye, and hung up with a kiss, and Jesus knew that she was better. For she was stronger than he, and had a natural strength beyond anyone that he knew. She got that from her father, he thought. His son lived in her.

****

Matt shuffled through the papers on his desk, results from the various research teams, trying to make sense of it all. He turned on his radio to WBJC in the vain hope that some classical music would blanket the cacophony from the street outside. In final desperation, he donned earplugs for a welcome amplitude reduction of chaos.

The cell cultures showed that all harmful bacteria were reduced to harmless levels when exposed to the blood of Santo. Neither did any harmful virus withstand exposure to the blood. More exciting to Matt, was that no sign of cell senescence could be found in any culture from Santo. The answers to all his dreams were in Santo. It would just take time and perseverance to decode them. Hours had passed, and the sounds from the street had faded with the evening sun. He removed his earplugs and gathered up the papers and locked them in his file.

Jesus had called him earlier and asked him to look in on Pilar. He wondered as he started off for her place, if he could save her body from the ravages of time. Or at the very least, lengthen the bloom of the flower. How wonderful it would be if we could all spend more time with those we love. What better gift could God give than that, he thought.

Matt left the lab and worked his way through several hundred pilgrims with no difficulty. The driveway in front of the lab building was adorned with thousands of flowers placed by believers and several small shrines dotted the road. One in particular he found amusing, since it looked like a manger scene with what he guessed was supposed to be Santo looking at the Christ child, but the dog looked more like the old RCA Nipper dog than it did Santo.

It was a beautiful spring evening and the moon was just rising beyond Gilman Hall as he made his way past the guards and into the Bigelow Building. He decided to drop by and see Big before visiting Pilar, and make his weekly update in person, rather than by phone.

Bigelow had become a much warmer, friendlier, person in the past few months, even to the point of joking around and coining the term the "Big Three" as applied to himself, Jesus, and Matt. They were, as Big had intimated in a previous toast, like the Musketeers, serving a higher purpose, undaunted at the odds against their quest. Matt believed it was due to the influence of Jesus who had become good friends with Big, and seemed to have given him a new perspective on life. Big no longer seemed the hard-line capitalist that he used to be, even scoffing at the idea of costs being important, insofar as they pertained to the Santo project. No expense was spared, no line of inquiry stifled. Bigelow was a new man.

Matt was in and out from the penthouse in less than an hour, and was knocking on Pilar's door moments later. She answered the door wearing a white terrycloth bathrobe with her hair wrapped up in a towel. As always, she greeted Matt with a warm smile, and soft eyes that seemed pleased but curious.

"I'm sorry, did I come at a bad time."

She stepped aside from the door.

"Is a good time."

Matt walked in past her and she locked the door and followed him slowly into the living room. The opened curtains yielded a spectacular view of the campus through the window wall, and Matt stood silent for a moment admiring the view.

"Jesus asked me to stop by and check on you. He said—"

"So you only stopped by because of my grandfather?"

"No," Matt said defensively as he turned from the window. "I was going to stop by anyway."

Pilar laughed, took the towel off her head with a shake, and her hair bounced off her shoulders.

"Then why mention my grandfather?"

Matt's throat tightened as she moved close against him.

"Are you afraid to say you missed me?"

"No."

"Then say it."

Pilar pushed into him, her palms against his chest and backed him up against a support column in the living room. She could feel his heart thumping against her palms.

"Say it," she whispered.

He combed his fingers through her hair, pulled her closer and kissed her.

"I missed you," he said with a sigh, as their mouths parted.

"You invade my thoughts, constantly."

"That's progress." She smiled mischievously and pinched his cheek.

She laughed, and he pulled her towards him and kissed her through her laughter until she stopped. Then he kissed her again, until her knees felt weak, and she pulled away from him.

"That's definitely progress," Pilar said as she walked to the window, fanning herself.

Matt followed her to the window and gently hugged her from behind as they stood looking out across Hopkins' upper quad, where a warm yellow moon was rising next to a cloud over the Eisenhower Library. The lights of East Baltimore twinkled in the distance.

****

A young man of about twenty-two years of age walked up the curved cobblestone driveway toward Eisenhower Library. He shivered as he looked at his watch and turned up the collar of his bulky tan trench coat. The night was quiet with few cars left on Charles Street but the conversations of passing students went unnoticed by the young man. A young Asian girl smiled as he passed her, but he clutched the book he held in his left hand tighter, and didn't return her smile. He could see the clock tower of Gilman Hall through the widowed walls of the library and its clock agreed with his watch. It was ten minutes before nine.

He opened the door of the library and walked into quiet warmth and the smell of fresh-brewed coffee from the upstairs lobby. In the lower lobby, several pairs of students sat on couches whispering, and he walked down the stairs towards them. He started through the entrance turnstile and it beeped, and a fat guard behind the desk next to the turnstile spun around in the swivel chair from which he rarely emerged, met eyes with him, and smiled.

"Do you have your student ID?" the guard said cheerily.

The young man smiled with white teeth that glowed against his dark complexion.

"Here is my ID," he said as he tossed his book on the desk towards the guard.

The bewildered guard opened the book but couldn't read the symbols of "*The Holy Quran*."

"What's this?" he said, looking up.

The young man opened his trench coat like a proud peacock spreading its plumage and the smiling guard's face turned to a grimace of horror as he glimpsed three rows of dynamite sticks completely surrounding the young man's torso and even more stitched into the interior of the coat.

"Allahu Akbar" the man said very softly, as he released his thumb from the pressure-switch in his right hand.

A great white flash of light and an exploding ball of fire vaporized all the people in both the lower and upper lobbies and continued outward and upward blowing out both window walls of the library. A group of about six students chatting outside the Keyser Quad entrance were blown fifty feet across the quad, their hair and clothes set on fire, and several bones broken. Flying debris killed several more, as the entrance doors to the library became deadly projectiles.

****

"Oh! What is that?" said Pilar, as the flash lit the living room.

Twin fireballs flew simultaneously from the east and west sides of the library in the distance below them, rising towards a surprised man in the moon.

"My God!" said Matt. "That's the Eisenhower Library!"

Seconds later, a colossal boom shook the building, and Pilar grabbed Matt tightly.

"What's happening?"

Matt's phone beeped and he looked down at a text message.

"The campus has gone to lock-down," he said to Pilar.

"There's nothing in that library that I know of that could explode like that. I wonder."

Matt called Jesus at the lab and verified that everything was okay there. He explained that the jolt Jesus felt was an explosion, but couldn't answer what caused it, other than to say that it originated at the library.

By the time Matt hung up with Jesus, flames had fully engulfed the roof of the library and it was burning out of control. A crowd of onlookers had formed, and at its edge nearest the library, people were trying to help some of the victims away from the inferno. A young Asian man tried to console a hysterical library worker who had escaped from one of the lower levels. Her broken glasses still hung from a chain around her neck and her face was blackened by smoke.

"For the love of God, who could have done this!" she kept repeating. "Why, oh why."

The same level of shock was everywhere as emergency vehicles began pouring into the area, and despite the terrible heat from the flames, spectators to the disaster continued to crowd in from the surrounding city streets, making it more difficult for rescuers to perform their jobs. Across the campus, the last remnants of pilgrims seeking Santo trickled through Wyman Park, drawn like moths toward the flames of the library.

Suddenly, the blowing horn of a speeding small sports car chased startled pedestrians from the drive, as it rapidly accelerated past them. It was almost silent as it passed, the slight squeal of its tires on the bend being far louder than the whir of its electric motor. It shot past them too fast for the driver to hear the obscenities hurled after him by the frightened crowd.

Matt watched the flames with lurid curiosity and a wistful sadness at the demise of so many books.

"Those poor people," Pilar whispered. Tears glistened on her cheeks in the flickering light from the flames. "I've never seen anything so terrible."

Matt felt her shivering and hugged her closer from behind.

"I wonder what caused it," he said.

****

The NSA guards at the lab entrance looked up in surprise as the narrow headlights of the sports car passed between two of the many large concrete spheres that formed a circle around the lab to protect it from vehicles. They jumped in opposite directions perpendicular to its path as it crashed through the front doors of the building and exploded, sending glass and metal fragments back out through the front of the building in a wall of flame and noise. The fire alarm sounded and the sprinkler system activated, and the few remaining nighttime occupants of the building made their way down the stairwells as the elevators locked off.

Jesus stood momentarily frozen as the explosion shook the building. He attached Santo's leash when the fire alarm sounded and they went down the hall to the elevator. He quickly realized that it had locked out, so he turned to the stairwell and opened its door, and immediately smelled smoke. He started down the stairs with Santo.

A loud boom shook the Bigelow Building, and Matt's phone simultaneously sounded the arrival of a text message and he grabbed the phone off his belt and read it.

"It's the lab! Stay here!" he said to Pilar as he broke for the door in a run.

"No, wait!" she said crying.

"Stay! I've got to go."

He was out the door and gone before she could say more.

Pilar searched frantically through her purse for her phone, finally found it, and called Jesus. He answered immediately and assured her calmly that he and Santo were both fine, and that they were about to exit the building. He had no idea what had happened, and told her not to worry.

****

Pop!

The back door of the lab building broke open easily under the onslaught of the pry bar, and the four men clad in black went stealthily in and up the stairwell.

They met Jesus descending at the second level and two of the men tackled him to the ground, while a third placed an object to his neck. Jesus felt something stick him and an electrical current surged through his neck. He saw a flash like a thousand stars in front of his eyes and faintly heard one of the men bark a command and Santo growling as he slipped into unconsciousness. They quickly slipped a canvas capture bag over Santo, pulled it closed, and took off back down the stairs and out the back door.

Outside, the men ran past the dumpsters and down the hill through the woods to Beech Avenue where they entered a parked, waiting van. It drove slowly off through the quiet residential neighborhood, unnoticed.

****

Matt ran full speed towards the burning lab building, dodging disoriented people along the way. He met up with some Army guards at the front of the building and he guided them to the rear lower entrance, since the first floor was an unapproachable flaming inferno.

They entered through the jimmied door, climbed the stairwell, and found Jesus lying on the stairs. Two of the guards helped Jesus outside and Matt and another climbed the stairs to his floor, where they searched in vain for Santo. Finding no one, and nothing amiss, they went back downstairs and outside where Jesus was now conscious and recovering from his stun.

"They took Santo," Jesus said, upon seeing Matt.

Matt scanned the immediate area and saw nothing.

"Four men, and they were wearing masks."

"Okay," said Matt. "We'll get him back. Don't worry."

Less than two hours later, at about eleven p.m., a white van struggled to climb the incline of Sideling Hill Mountain in Western Maryland. It passed through the Sideling Hill Road Cut and the temperature dropped ten degrees in blowing snow on the west side of the mountain, squalls from a spring storm. The headlights bounced back from the blowing snow, cutting visibility in half, and the driver strained his tired eyes to see the road.

Suddenly, a twelve-point buck jumped into the light conc just beyond the van. A fraction of a second later, it crashed through the windshield at sixty miles an hour, instantly killing the driver. The van careened off Interstate 68 and rolled sideways down the embankment into the valley below.

****

At two a.m. a very somber group consisting of Pilar, Matt, Jesus, and Phillip Bigelow sat in the penthouse of the Bigelow Building, watching the late night WBAL news on the wall screen of the living room. Far below them they could see it live, but they were hoping for news about Santo, since a statewide search had been instigated for his kidnappers.

"I did this," sighed Jesus. "We should have never come here."

"It would have happened anyway," said Bigelow. "Perhaps sooner, had you stayed in your village. You can't blame yourself for the evil others do."

"Old Sailor warned us to keep Santo secret. He knew."

"But you did keep him secret," added Matt. "It was fate that outdid your efforts."

"You are right, Matthew, of course. It was that."

“Yes,” said Bigelow. “Millions of people’s lives have been uplifted world-wide by Santo. What happened here tonight can’t change that.”

The local news of the John Hopkins campus explosion ended, and the screen cut to the crash scene of a mangled van. The news banner below a reporter read: “*Live at I68*.” Spotlights glared at the crash scene, illuminating the van, and showed workers lifting it onto a flatbed truck, while the reporter droned on, emotionless.

“In yet another tragedy on Maryland highways, two men were killed here tonight, and two more were critically injured as their van collided with a deer on Interstate 68, seven miles west of Hancock.

“The four young men, all Asian, were originally thought to have possibly been divinity students, since they were all dressed in black uniforms. Since then however, tools and weapons found in their vehicle, along with a GPS unit, have caused police to believe that these may be the same men that have been the subject of a statewide manhunt related to an incident on the Johns Hopkins Homewood campus yesterday evening, in Baltimore. Maryland State Police are asking the public for their help in identifying the four men.”

Bigelow snatched up the phone and dialed the police, as Jesus stared emptily at the image of the crumpled van. The report ended with no word of Santo.

Matt sat down on the couch with Pilar, and gently wiped tears from her face. He pressed her head to his shoulder and hugged her tightly as she shivered in his arms.

“So much for great dreams,” he whispered.

Chapter 28

The World Seeks Santo

President Mendoza walked into the cabinet room and tossed the newspaper he was carrying onto the mahogany table. Its headline read: *"Santo Stolen."*

"Gentlemen, we have a newly re-prioritized agenda…Finding Santo! This dog has become more than a major symbol of faith to modern Christians everywhere; he has become a national symbol of pride and the individualist movement. I share a personal attachment to this animal, since as many of you would readily admit, I may not have been elected if not for the increased notoriety and friendly press afforded me during my campaign due to my own incredible experience involving Santo."

Some murmuring and laughter erupted around the oval table and Mendy accepted it in good humor.

"Beyond that, the most recent report from the Joint Chiefs affirms that Santo is a matter of national security due to the catalytic effect he has had on uprisings around the globe. The proof of that is the confessions we have received from the survivors that kidnapped him, two Chinese nationals, who under orders from a rogue faction of their government, orchestrated diversionary terrorist attacks at the Hopkins campus in Baltimore yesterday, recruiting radicalized

Muslims, to help them capture Santo.

"This won't go public, nor will the identities of the survivors, since it would be too detrimental to our international relations, but we need to get ahead of this thing now, and put a lid on it."

General Littlejohn stood, and walked to the viewer that had been set up on a tripod next to the table at the north end of the room.

"We have established a possible search area of fifty miles radius, figuring that the dog wouldn't run more than about five miles an hour in an extended period, similar to a wolf on the move."

He drew a yellow circle on the map image on the screen, and then switched to a satellite photo of the area.

"We have a volunteer pack of Shadow Wolves from ICE leading the hunt, which started here, on the south side of I68, where they found some blood trails and dog tracks in snow that had not yet melted. The dog appeared to have been following the ridge to the southwest, and we have some choppers with thermal imagers searching a broad path in that direction. The Potomac, will block him to the east, so we feel pretty sure that he is in this pie-shaped area that opens to the southwest away from the accident scene.

"We should find him by tonight."

"Very good, General," said Mendy, and a general nod of approval went around the table.

****

Matt pulled up in front of the damaged guardrail on I68, parked, and exited the car, along with Jesus and Bigelow.

"This is a bad place to park," he said, as a tractor-trailer roared past.

They followed the skid marks in the grass down the hill and spread out in different directions searching.

"Look at this!" Bigelow said almost immediately, holding up a torn canvas bag stained with blood.

"That's what they put him in," said Jesus. "I saw them as I was being electrocuted."

"So we know he was here," said Matt, "or that bag would not have been in the truck. They still had him when they crashed."

Jesus began to whistle for Santo as they spread out in different directions searching.

"Over here!" Matt hollered.

Jesus and Bigelow ran to Matt and the three of them followed dog tracks in the snow that ran in an arc through some small pine trees, and back towards I68.

"He was here, he's alive! Bigelow panted, as they ran up the embankment towards the interstate.

They crossed the highway, and quickly picked up the tracks on the far side.

"He's hurt, said Jesus, pointing to a blood trail in the tracks.

"But the tracks are steady and straight," added Matt.

"Yes, the old boy is okay!" Bigelow said through heavy breaths. But look here, someone else is tracking him," he said, pointing to two pairs of boot prints parallel to the tracks.

They followed the tracks in and out of thinning patchy snow until there were none left. They were high on the ridge of a mountain when the footprints finally disappeared into rocks and pine needles.

"What do we do now?" Matt asked.

"We send for help," said Bigelow. He took out his phone, but there was no repeater signal, so they marked their trail end and headed back to the car.

They got a signal at the interstate and Bigelow ordered up hiking clothes, supplies, and even a tracker through his office in Baltimore. Then they found a diner off the interstate and took a slow lunch while they waited for supplies and reinforcements.

Within several hours, they had donned hiking clothes and outfitted themselves with backpacks, and accompanied by a professional hunter hired by Bigelow, they had retraced their tracks and gone onward in search of Santo. They picked up his tracks at several places along the ridge as they followed it south-by-southwest, and after about five and a half miles, they found his tracks on both banks of a creek. He turned west at the Potomac and roughly followed it as it snaked southwest.

They found his tracks again in the mud at the canoe put-in where Fifteen Mile Creek met the Potomac, but then burnt an entire hour trying to find them again on either side of the aqueduct or railroad bridge. He seemed to have doubled back toward Little Orleans, possibly smelling food from the local bar/restaurant, but they could find no trace of him there. So they stopped at Bill's Place for a rest, and Matt told some fellow customers that they were camping and had misplaced their dog, but no one had seen any stray dogs around.

Finally, the tracker picked up some blurred paw prints that took them westward into the Green Ridge State Forest. It was getting dark, so they made camp on a high ridge overlooking the river. Matt's legs were like rubber, and he collapsed against a log on some dry leaves, while the others unpacked their gear.

"Aren't you tired?" Matt asked Jesus.

"No, I am used to the mountains. These are hills."

"How about you, Big? Why aren't you tired? "

"You've seen that climber in my office. I read while hiking, every day. You need to get out of the lab more often."

Matt groaned as he folded his legs, and then looked towards their guide.

"Pete, how much farther ahead of us do you think he might be?"

Pete stopped digging the fire pit and looked like he smelled the air for Santo.

"No way to say. He might have found himself a meal…maybe killed a rabbit or a grouse, and he might be resting now."

Matt, Bigelow, and Jesus broke into laughter, and Pete looked perplexed.

"He's a vegetarian," Matt said laughing.

"Not anymore, he's not," Pete said with confidence. "He's gone wild and he'll live by the law of the wild. A dog is part wolf and it's in his genes to eat meat, and that's what he'll do in the wild."

"I guess you're right," Matt replied, the smile fading from his face.

"I don't know," Jesus said quietly. "I have had Santo a long time. I don't think he has the instinct to kill, except perhaps in self-defense."

Pete reached into his sack and pulled out a block of cheese, and held it up and admired it as if it were a shining apple.

"Out here, it's the 'law of fang and claw'. Sharp teeth and an empty belly have no conscience." Pete bit into the block of cheese like a savage, growled, and laughed. "That's what your dog will do to the first mouse or rabbit he encounters. If we're lucky, he already has, and now he's sleeping somewhere. He'll stop when he finds food."

Pete chewed his cheese as he started the fire and prepared a coffee pot with some water and grounds, while Jesus and Bigelow scouted nearby for more firewood. He placed two large rocks in the fire pit on either side, and when the wood burned down to fiery coals, he straddled the coffee pot across the tops of the two rocks and waited for it to percolate. He offered some cheese to Matt, and when he refused, instead tossed him a wrapped ham sandwich, a box of raisins, and a Hershey bar for desert.

Bigelow and Jesus came back with enough firewood to last them into the night, and the men settled down around the warm glow as darkness fell. Pete entertained them with a story of a black bear that had extracted revenge for the killing of its brother, and then watched Matt squirm nervously when he said that many bears traveled the woods nearby. "You've been awfully quiet, Big," Matt said, in hopes of changing the subject.

"I was just remembering how I used to go camping in the woods with my father as a boy…just remembering how he used to tell me stories across the campfire. It seems not long ago."

"It's not long ago," said Pete. "Life is like this campfire. It starts from nothing, grows to a peak, and then quickly burns to nothing, leaving only ashes."

"Well put," Matt said solemnly.

"Out here, in the forest, this is what's real. The world you boys come from is all an illusion. Take away man, and this is what's left. No news headlines to confuse you here."

"The stars are different here," Jesus said softly. "I miss my village and my friends. Not that this is not good company, but I miss the drier mountain air of Pueblo del Cielo and the people I love there."

A distant helicopter hovered over the next mountaintop scanning the forest, but no one took notice.

"I can't help but wonder," continued Jesus, "if Santo is feeling much the same as me. Only he has no one to keep him company, and no fire to give him warmth in the cold night."

****

Santo had run down a hill to the canoe launch point, where Fifteen Mile Creek meets the Potomac. Not wanting to swim the cold creek, he started west, but turned abruptly at the smell of food wafted on a breeze from a nearby bar and grill. He recognized the familiar scent of potato cakes as he approached a parked pickup truck outside the bar, and he jumped up into the truck and quickly ferreted out the cakes from inside a brown paper lunch bag and wolfed them down.

Inside the bar, David Watson was with the four amigos that had helped him build his new barn the past two weeks. He had given them their final pay and they were all celebrating a job well done. They all signed their names to a dollar bill and added it to the collection of bills signed by previous visitors to the bar that papered the walls and ceiling. Watson bought a round of beers for a final toast, before the ride south to his brother's home.

Santo felt safe in the bed of the pickup truck. It reminded him of the truck he used to ride in with Santiago and Jesus. He found some chocolate chip cookies in the bag, ate them, and curled up on a tarp next to several backpacks. His side still hurt from where the deer antler had gouged him as it ripped through the canvas bag he had been trapped in. He slept deeply and dreamed he was back in Pueblo del Cielo with his friends and family.

A little while later, David Watson and his four passengers spilled out of the bar and got into the truck, filling both front and back seats. The amigos spoke Spanish at times, and Santo heard it in his sleep, and it made him happy. He dreamed he and Jesus were driving with Santiago on one of their many journeys.

He liked meeting the many friendly people at all the villages and towns to which they traveled. They all smiled and made friends with him. He had more friends than any dog he thought. So many happy memories and such a good life he had with Jesus. He remembered Sailor and the journey across the big water, and in one dream he was with Sailor and the young boy, Jesus, who threw the stick for him, as Sailor laughed and smoked his pipe.

David Watson exited the interstate just before the 24-59 split west of Chattanooga and turned into a gas station. The men stepped stiffly from the truck, and squinted in the bright morning sunlight. When the doors of the truck slammed Santo awoke from his dream, and sprang from the back of the truck, expecting to be greeted by young Jesus.

"Is that your dog, David?" asked one of the men.

"No."

"He was in the back of the truck," said the same man.

"Come here, boy," Watson said cheerily.

He reached for Santo, but he bolted and ran, into the safety of the nearby woods.

"I hope that wasn't somebody's dog from back home," Watson said, as he watched Santo disappear into the woods.

Santo ran across the interstate and kept running until he came to a natural path southwest that followed high-tension towers. He kept a brisk pace throughout the day, always moving southwest, and at nightfall, he found a secluded safe spot in Buck's Pocket State Park where he slept soundly, having found the discarded remnants of picnic lunches along the way.

****

Matt awoke to find Jesus staring eastward from their hilltop toward the rising sun. A heavy fog blanketed the valley below them, hiding the Potomac and making the distant hilltops look like islands floating in a sea of shimmering light. Pete arose behind them and threw some branches on the coals from last night's fire and within a few minutes flames were once again dancing in the fire pit.

Bigelow was snoring with just the top of his head protruding from his sleeping bag, but the crackling of the fire soon woke him and he joined Jesus and Matt at the precipice to watch the sun rise.

"Wow," Bigelow said, watching the glowing fog burn off from the valley in front of them, "that sight alone is worth the hike to get here."

"My legs are so sore, I can hardly walk," Matt replied.

"You'll be fine once we start walking," Pete said from the fire.

Voices and laughter echoed up from the valley below them rupturing the serenity of the scene.

"Early risers, or late partiers?" Matt asked sarcastically.

They turned away from the glowing ocean of fog, and joined Pete at the fire and steam soon rose from their damp clothes as the fire warmed them.

"After breakfast, we'll split up to save time. Jesus and Mr. Bigelow can search along the river bank, and Matt and I will follow the ridge to try to pick up a trail."

They searched the ridge, and along the river for over a mile with no luck, and by mid afternoon, all were in agreement that they had lost the trail completely and it was pointless to continue. So they followed the road north to the interstate and picked up their vehicles, where they bid goodbye to Pete, and set off for home.

The three men were mostly quiet as Matt piloted them home in dead-tired, despondent silence. They didn't stop to eat along the way, and each retired to their own apartment when they finally reached the Bigelow Building in the evening. Matt showered, shaved, and ate dinner, then couldn't stand the seclusion, so he wandered up to the penthouse to visit with Big. Jesus and Pilar were already there. Everyone seemed delighted to see him and welcomed him warmly.

"We were just talking about you," said Pilar as she pulled him onto the living room couch next to her. "We were going to call you, but were afraid you might have gone to sleep."

"I can't sleep. I keep thinking about Santo."

"Look at this," Big said, as he passed a newspaper to Matt.

Matt looked at it and slowly shook his head. The headline read: *"Seeking Santo."* A photo spread showed hundreds of people searching the woods of Western Maryland and the surrounding area.

"Someone has offered a ten-million dollar reward!" Matt said with disbelief. "Who would do that?"

"I'll never tell," Big said with a smile.

"You? When did you do that?" Matt said with disbelief.

"As soon as I learned he'd been taken. I did it through a non-profit corporation I have, so no one will know it was me. It looks like it's having the desired effect."

"That was so good of you Mr. Big," Pilar said with sincere innocence. Grandfather has always said that you are a good man."

Bigelow smiled sheepishly.

"There is a large profit motive, Pilar. I'm not that good."

"I still think it is a wonderful gesture, don't you Matthew."

Matt smiled at her warmly and then looked at Big.

"Yes, I do. And I think it's more than just profit, too. I think you really care, Big."

Bigelow's face flushed and he started to pace, not seeming to know in which direction he wanted to walk. Jesus reached out and grabbed him by the arm and stopped him, smiling.

"We have become a family," said Jesus. "Nothing can change that now. Bonds have formed between us that will never be broken."

Bigelow's eyes filled. Matt smiled and hugged Pilar as they both watched Bigelow in a rare moment of genuine emotion.

"I'm going to go check out the clean-up at the lab," Matt said, as he stood up from the couch. He turned back to Pilar and put out his hand. "Want to come with me?"

"Yes."

They bid their goodbyes and left.

"I think they might share a future," said Jesus.

"I hope so," returned Bigelow. "They're both great kids."

****

The restoration of the lab building was well under way, and the glass front entrance wall and doors had already been replaced. New guards met them at the entrance and checked their identification before passing them through. Only a faint smell of fuel tinged with smoke gave any hint of the fireball that had consumed the lobby two nights previous. One elevator was out of service for renovation, and the other was already on its way up, so they took the stairs. When they came out of the stairwell into the upstairs hallway, Matt noticed a man dressed all in white loading a cart with things from inside the pathology lab.

The man paused when he saw them, and smiled. He was tall, with golden hair and lean, like a Viking. He turned back to the cart and started to push it towards the open elevator and Matt called out to him.

"Hold up there, just a minute."

The man kept walking and didn't look back.

"Hey!" Matt yelled, and ran down the hall, pulling Pilar with him as he held her hand.

The man pushed the cart into the elevator and turned back towards Matt and Pilar and paused. Then he smiled a broad warm smile that revealed a perfect set of teeth, so white that they almost glowed beneath his pale blue eyes. He held up three fingers and waved like a Boy Scout pledging, as the elevator doors began to close, still smiling silently.

Matt extended his arm to block the elevator doors from closing and hit an invisible wall of cold jello. He recoiled in stunned surprise and the elevator doors closed shut.

"Did you see that?"

"What?"

"Something stopped my hand from blocking the elevator doors. Come on."

They walked quickly back to the pathology lab. The door was locked, so Matt used his keycard and walked inside with Pilar. Nothing seemed amiss at first glance.

"What was that guy taking out of here at this time of night?" Matt said aloud, not expecting an answer.

"Was he a clean-up man?" asked Pilar.

Matt unlocked several of the incubation chambers and checked their contents.

"No cleaning personnel currently have access to this room," he said, as he unlocked the refrigerator.

He opened the door and his face froze.

"Shit!"

Matt rooted feverishly through the refrigerator.

"Shit, shit, shit, shit, shit!"

"What's wrong?"

"Everything," Matt replied, as he keyed his phone.

"Stop that guy leaving the building!"

"What guy?" replied a voice through the phone.

"Did the elevator come down?"

"Yeah, I'm looking at it. It's empty."

"Okay," Matt said breathlessly. "He must have got off on a different floor."

"You and the lady are the only two visitors, Doctor West. The last of the staff checked out at 6:00 p.m."

"Somebody's here...an intruder, I saw him…a tall guy with

blonde hair. He left pathology when we got here."

"Nope. No movement anywhere, and the cameras are all clear. Just you two, Doc."

"I'm not a doctor!"

"What?"

"Look at the DVR, we're coming right down."

They locked the lab and hurried to the elevator. Matt pounded the thumb pad repeatedly until he saw the elevator indicator moving up. The doors opened and he started to walk in, but stopped short, and extended his arm slowly through the doors to test the opening. All seemed normal so they got in and proceeded to the downstairs security station.

Once at the security station, Matt viewed the pathology lab recordings repeatedly in disbelief.

"Okay," Matt finally said, "how did you do it?"

"Do what?" the guard replied.

"Someone modified these recordings! They show no one. Not in the lab, not in the hall, nor in the elevator. But we both saw a man take a cart from the pathology lab into the elevator, so someone had to modify these recordings."

"That's crazy. These recordings were just made a few minutes ago. No one could have accessed them. The building's empty."

"It was not empty! There was someone here. We both saw him."

"I didn't see anyone," said Pilar.

Matt's mouth dropped open.

"What are you saying? You had to see him!"

Pilar looked at him in wide-eyed innocence for several seconds before bursting into laughter.

"Got you!" she said, laughing heartily. "Of course, I saw him."

"This is not funny! You don't know what has happened. The blood samples are all gone. All of Santo's blood samples have vanished."

Matt had security make a copy of the video file that showed their time in the lab building and took it with them. He and Pilar exited the lab building and walked slowly back along the drive to the condo. Matt was pensive and said nothing, even as Pilar tried to be playful with him.

"I don't get it," said Matt. "How can you be so cheerful, after all that's happened?"

"This is life." Pilar smiled, and hugged him as they continued to walk. "I think you are harder to understand. You are always saying how short life is, and yet in the spare moments you do have, you choose to be sad, instead of being happy."

"I don't choose. This is the result of events! It's perfectly logical."

Pilar laughed.

"Logical? It is completely illogical. What if someone finds Santo and returns him tomorrow to get the reward? Then all of the past three days won't matter, and it will be back to business as usual."

"And if they don't? What if we never see Santo again?"

"But you don't know that will happen, Matthew. So it is foolish to not be happy here with me, while we share this time together."

"No. If your car is out of control and you're headed for a brick wall, you wouldn't be happy!"

"But there is no brick wall. Do you see a brick wall?"

"Maybe."

Pilar laughed, then jumped up and kissed him on the cheek.

"In your example, Matthew, if we were about to hit a brick wall, would you be sad and gloomy, or would you kiss me goodbye and be happy in the few moments we had left?"

Matt stopped walking, and looked down at Pilar, standing directly in front of him smiling. For a moment, he stubbornly tried to hold on to his fears and grim mood, but that smiling face, so filled with life and energy, blew it all away, and he finally laughed, reached down and pulled her toward him and kissed her gently. Then he growled and gave her a bear hug and they both laughed at life.

"I think there is hope for you," Pilar said, as she squeezed him back. May I be serious for a moment?"

"Definitely."

Pilar slipped her arm into Matt's, and they began walking.

"What do you think happened tonight?"

Matt sighed.

"I don't know...we seem to have been robbed."

"But how would you explain it, the way that man disappeared, and then he and the cart did not appear on the recordings."

Matt reached into his pocket and made sure that the memory stick was still there and his eyes went glassy.

"Tomorrow, I will have our engineering team analyze this recording, and then maybe I will be able to explain it."

"I think that man was an angel."

Matt stiffened.

"What makes you say that?"

"It was a feeling I got when he looked at us and smiled and waved, like he knew us, and was our friend."

"More likely, is that he was an industrial saboteur, who was contemplating how much money he is going to make selling those stolen blood samples."

They stopped speaking, but continued to hold each other tightly and Pilar didn't release Matt's arm until he left her at her door. He walked back to his room slowly, feeling the empty spot on his arm where her hands had been. He was giddy. His stomach muscles ached from an adrenalin-induced crunch and his legs were still sore from hiking. He made coffee, then sat down in the living room with a tablet, and watched the recording again and again, until he nodded off to sleep.

The next day, the engineering team analyzed the recordings using pixel analysis, but could find no signs of tampering. Ray Hardy suggested that Matt and Pilar might have hallucinated the strange man, but that did not answer how the blood samples went missing. Nor could it answer how every cell culture in the pathology lab had suddenly become dormant. All research on the Santo project was at an end. Without Santo acting as a collector and modulator-transmitter, even the Gurwitsch radiation experiments that seemed so promising were no longer possible. They combed the lab for DNA evidence of the intruder, but it was as if the entire lab had been sanitized, and not one hair or shred of evidence was found. It was as if Santo had never existed.

Chapter 29

Santo Returns Home

"Santo! Come here, boy. Chase the stick!"

Santo heard Sailor's voice loud and clear, and awoke with a start. He must get home. His friend, Sailor, was there waiting for him to play. The night sky painted his path in dancing colors from green to pale pink and red, north to south, back to his home latitude. Santo did not know the word latitude, but to him the night sky was a map of colors and sparkling diamonds that he knew well. He stopped at a creek to quench his thirst, and then took off at a trot. He passed to the northwest of Birmingham, ever southwest, following a path parallel to Interstate 20. He stayed clear of people, except when he became hungry, since they always left meals behind for him that suited his taste.

In a few days, Santo found himself in familiar territory, near Moundville. The surface land was different now, but the colors that emanated from the mounds at night were much the same as when he and Sailor had visited there many years ago on trips they took to where the Carolinas are today. Back then, there were no Anglos, but the area was a busy trade center, and the local river people revered his body style and treated him and Sailor with great respect.

The next night, beneath a crescent moon, Santo emerged from

the woods onto a wide prairie that smelled sweet from grass, flowering wild geraniums, and buttercups. He waded out into a soft red glow that hovered over the plants like a luminescent evening mist. It was the radiation from many billions of plant cells dividing that only his eyes could see. Above him the glistening stars peppered the sky over the Alabama prairie, just as they had a thousand years past, and as they still would a thousand years hence. But he had no sense of time, except to hurry back to Sailor, who waited for him under a more southern sky.

Suddenly, a musical howl reached his ears from far across the prairie. His neck hairs stood on end, and he instinctively sung back to it, and began trotting in the direction from which it came. His tall pointed ears pivoted forward like two microwave horns searching for a signal, and his head scanned side to side as he trotted.

"Ooooo-wooo-wooo," came the baleful wail again. Only it was beautiful music to the ears of Santo, like none he'd heard for many years. It called to him in a primordial voice that resonated deep inside him and was irresistible in its beckoning. He answered back without thinking, and ran in the direction of the song. The bands of frequencies and their modulation envelopes were unique, and as distinctly recognizable to Santo as a human female voice is to a man.

He found her on the far side of the prairie in a wooded grove, beside a log cabin. She was tethered to a wooden stake driven into the ground and her radius of freedom was worn to bare earth, a brown circle of dirt surrounded by grass. Her eyes caught the light from the cabin window and glowed at him, and she stood in silence as he approached. He saw her aura and recognized her status before he was close enough to catch her scent.

She was a beautiful Carolina Dog with rusty red atop her head and the back of her ears, which rose to parabolic tips much like his, and a clean white throat that contrasted against the black lips and nose above it. Her forehead had the same thoughtful furrows as Santo, but her eyes were a rich soft brown surrounded by black eyelids, and the rusty fur of her forehead was split by a deep wrinkle that smoothed out into the bridge of her nose. The white inside horns of her ears tracked his approach as he emitted a subsonic growl of approval.

They met with sniffs and circled one another as she fought the restraint of the rope and moved around its limit, so Santo's motion was like the moon circling the earth as the earth orbits the sun. She nipped at him, but not severely, and they played like two long-lost friends in bliss before he mounted her and they united. Unknown to Santo was that she was his distant granddaughter carrying his DNA, a descendant from his encounter with one of her great-grandmothers on a voyage with Sailor, long ago.

In a few hours, the crickets had stopped trilling and Santo lay on the ground a few lengths from his new friend with his paws crossed in front of him, relaxing. The door of the cabin opened and a rectangle of gold light lit the ground below the several stairs up to the porch. A man appeared in the doorway with a bag. He set the bag down, lit a match, and held it up to something in his mouth, and in a few seconds the familiar smell of pipe tobacco reached Santo.

The man picked up the bag, closed the door, and stepped forward into darkness at the porch front. He felt for the handrail, and having found it, stepped slowly down the stairs.

"I got somethin' for ya, Belle."

Belle strained at the rope that held her in her circle, as she smelled the ham bone in the bag.

"You already smell it, don't you," the man said with a laugh. "Here ya go."

He stretched his arm out with the bone, and Belle took it gently from his hand and began gnawing on it.

"That's a good girl," he said, as he stooped and patted her head.

Suddenly, he froze, then stood up and turned around.

"Who's there?"

Santo moved into a shaft of light from the cabin window and stood in front of the man.

"I know you're there, I can smell your aftershave. Come on out!"

The man turned his head from side-to-side but never looked at Santo. Finally, Santo walked up to the man and began licking his hand. The man jumped in surprise and then laughed.

"So, Belle has a new friend! That's good."

He bent down and patted Santo on the head.

"Dogged if you don't smell sweet. What you been eatin'? Ya hungry?" The man stood, then started back to the cabin. He came back shortly with a bowl of meat scraps and set it down on the ground for Santo, before going back inside.

The next morning when the man went outside, he bent down to collect the bowl, and was surprised when his hand felt the untouched scraps. He guessed that Belle's nighttime visitor had been a pet that had wandered from a nearby campground. Why else would a dog leave a full bowl of food? By then, Santo had crossed into Mississippi, and was sleeping on a bed of pine needles in Bonita Lakes Park, southwest of Meridian.

****

Weeks went by and became months, and no credible word of Santo surfaced. Santo was everywhere, seen on street corners in every city in America, and even in other countries. His fame seemed to grow, accelerated by the vacuum of any real news. Wherever a miracle cure was claimed, there was often an accompanying claim of a Santo sighting. It was a good time for vagrant mongrel dogs, which were now treated with the love and reverent care previously awarded them mainly by Buddhist monks. Whether it was because people hoped that the dog they fed or cared for was Santo, or whether it was just a renewed love for animals that inspired people to do so, was unknown.

The New Christian Revolution that had swept Mexico had in some ways done the same in the United States and elsewhere, as it morphed into a wave of worldwide individualism, threatening to overturn established institutions and governments, and reinvigorating humanity with hope, and a rediscovered sense of individual greatness.

Pilar continued the semester at Hopkins without incident, since her notoriety vanished with Santo. The events of the bombing and destruction of the Eisenhower Library and the loss of innocent lives were what dominated most news and memories there. Their contractual obligations having been fulfilled with Bigelow Pharmaceuticals, and with the end of the semester near at hand, she and Jesus made plans to return to Pueblo del Cielo.

Matt compiled his complete notes on the Santo project and received permission to use them as part of his doctor's thesis, although with no proof except the previously obtained supporting data, much of it was now deemed a work of fiction. Photographic evidence of what appeared to be some sort of unknown bacteriophages and impressive test results of Gurwitsch radiation experiments that could not be duplicated, were thought fascinating, but not to be believed by most factions.

Bigelow seemed most changed by the events. He laughed at their travails and said it was a great joke played on him by God, but he also had a new warmth and compassion that most people noticed. He made plans with Jesus to build a new school that would serve the people of the rural areas around Pueblo del Cielo, and which would also house a free clinic.

He had sold millions of shares of Bigelow Pharmaceuticals as soon as the news of the Santo Project and subsequent kidnapping had become public knowledge, and he bought back many times that much at the lows that followed the panic selling that had soon ensued. Then he sold half of all he owned at the peak of a massive dead-cat bounce. All told, he had doubled his net worth. Many complained that the Santo rumors were being used to fuel speculation in the stock, but you can't stop people from talking, and the rumors were clearly organic and could not be tied to any company insiders.

For weeks, Matt and Bigelow had waited for some news on the missing blood samples, and searched the headlines daily, hoping for any clues that might carry the project forward, but there were none, and eventually they came to the final acceptance that it was over. Life hurried them on to new plans and goals.

On the anniversary of the El Paso Tragedy, Matt and Pilar, and Jesus and Bigelow, gathered at the penthouse for a farewell dinner. The spring semester would be over in a few days and Pilar and Jesus were slated to return home. The occasion was at once, both happy and sad, and that dichotomy ruled all their emotions as they recalled some of the fantastic events that had occurred in their lives and the world in one short year.

After dinner, they retired to the office library, where Big acted as bartender dispersing golden ginger ale for himself and Jesus, and wine for Matt and Pilar. They made several rounds of toasts to one another, and then toasted President Mendoza, who was on the wall screen, live from El Paso, beginning a commemorative speech.

"A year ago, a senseless act killed many of our friends, right here, in what has since become the International Zone at Chamizal," began the president.

"He is a great man," said Jesus. "A very great man."

"And very kind," added Pilar. She turned to Matt who nodded agreement as he sipped some wine.

"Such acts," continued Mendy, "are meant to frighten us and make us lose faith. That is the goal of all terror. But that didn't happen..."

Mendy paused, and scanned the audience, making eye contact with several people. "No. Something else happened."

Hundreds of heads nodded in the audience amid a mumbled chorus of yeses. The cameras pulled in close on Mendy.

"We got angry. We said ENOUGH! We kept our faith!" Mendy held out the palm of his hand to the audience, and they roared their approval. Camera flashes reflected off his hand as he slowly waved it from left to right across the crowd and back again, and the roar grew, as many chanted his name over and over in a crescendo, until it was deafening. He finally lowered his hand and waited several seconds for the chants to fade, and then continued.

Bigelow laughed.

"Talk about having the crowd in the palm of your hand."

An aerial shot from a news helicopter showed a view from above the stage, and the crowd was enormous, spilling across both sides of the border, spanning the new footbridge and the International Bridge, one half of which was temporarily closed to motor vehicle traffic.

"There must be a million people there," Matt observed.

Big turned the volume lower, because the chanting was annoying him, and Mendy's words were starting to sound more political as he continued on about all the progress that had been made since prohibition was ended, and then went on to list a litany of new cooperative programs with Mexico.

"This man was spared for good reason," Jesus whispered.

Mendy finished his speech, and he and some of the other dignitaries started making their way through the crowd, ringed by secret service men, shaking hands as they moved towards the new footbridge that connected both sides of the International Zone. The plan was to hang flags of the U.S. and Mexico beside one another from the center of the span.

Bang-Bang-Bang...**Bang**...**Bang**...

"Oh!" Pilar whined, as screams and mass confusion erupted on the wall screen.

"No," gasped Jesus.

"Not again," moaned Big.

A man had shot point blank at Mendy, who was knocked to the ground by the impact of the volley of bullets. One secret service agent was also wounded as he jumped between the gun and the assassin, and one woman from the audience had been shot.

President Mendoza lay face up on the ground inside a small circle in the crowd that had cleared around him. Turmoil could be seen from an overhead shot, as agents tried to rescue the assassin from the crowd, which was trying to tear him to shreds. He was pulled up onto the footbridge where Texas Rangers and government agents ringed him, as the crowd pushed in from both sides trying to get at him.

An audibly shaken TV network news announcer tried to describe the events, but the camera shots revealed more than his words. After a long minute, agents were seen helping the president to his feet and he raised a defiant hand in the air and waved to the crowd, and cheers filled the air.

Agents tried to scurry him away, but he fought them off, and returned to the stage to the microphones.

"No!" he said, pushing the agents away. "I'm alright. Are the others okay?" His would-be handlers advised him that they were being tended and would not die, and he proceeded.

Mendy tapped the microphones until he found one connected to the audience speakers and plucked it from its holder.

"I'm shot, but I'm okay, and I will speak!"

Blood was weeping from his suit jacket at the shoulder, and he looked down at his chest, where a bullet hole showed near the left pocket. He reached inside his jacket and pulled out two small rectangular objects and held one up for the crowd and cameras to inspect. He put his finger through a hole in the object, which proved to be a book on a camera close-up view.

"This copy of the Constitution helped protect me!"

The crowd gasped, and then he held up the second rectangular object and the cameras zoomed in on it. *"Pocket Bible"* showed on the screen, and a squashed bullet was imbedded in it.

"But the Bible saved my life!"

The crowd gasped again, and then gave a wild roar. Mendy swooned and the crowd went silent, as he fought off agents who were trying to talk him off the stage.

"No! I will speak now, just a few minutes more, my friends. Did you hear what the assassin shouted as he let loose with gunfire? He said…'Allahu Akbar!'"

Mendy looked towards the footbridge where the perpetrator was still under siege.

"Yes, God is great...he is also good...and what you did here today, my friend, was neither good, nor anything to do with God. But I forgive you, because your mind is diseased with false truths. I will pray for you.

"Let them pass, please. He is not worthy of your wrath."

Some in the crowd shouted to those closest to the man to clear a path, and it was done, and the Rangers and government agents took the shooter away.

"You know," Mendy continued, "Christ was the ultimate individualist, and his most basic lesson was for us to love one another. For we are all our brothers' keepers, and if we do not watch and guard each other's freedoms then who will be there to guard our own?"

He swooned again, and people on the stage tried to remove him but he fought them off.

"Today, let us celebrate the truths that we have learned since the El Paso Tragedy. They cannot commit acts of evil, without strengthening our resolve for good. For every evil act reveals itself for what it is, a sin against God and man.

"That is why we fight so hard. That is why we revile evil and all its lies. The individual must always fight tyranny, for it is in the nature of man and the heart of man to be free.

"We fight against the collectivists because we are not ants or bees. We are individuals, and as such, each one of us is the most valuable resource on this planet. When we lock arms in the name of freedom, we become what we were born to be.

"Some months ago, I came here and made a statement as an individual. Let me speak again as an individual. We must all stand up against tyranny...When Caesar asks too much, we must say…'Stop! You ask too much.' Or we will no longer be free men.

"The ultimate goal of collectivists is a society of automatons, ruled by oligarchs. Whether such a society is a theocracy or is one ruled by a corrupt government of any name or description, is immaterial. Any government, sect, or religion that unjustly represses any individual, or restricts his or her maximum potential and growth, or challenges that individual's rights of life, liberty, and the pursuit of happiness, is a deceit, and a sin against God and individuals everywhere.

"This is what the world is learning, and this is why across the globe, individuals are uniting and learning to say with one united voice... 'We will not give up our freedom!'

"We must keep fighting, until every individual has been 'conquered into freedom'."

Mendy swooned again and winced in pain, before pointing to a statue of Santo that was part of the memorial constructed along San Marcial Street. The camera showed a quick glimpse of the memorial with Santo, and Pilar sang out: "Ooooh!"

"If you watch the news," Mendy continued, "Santo is everywhere...So is the spirit of what he has come to represent. The individualist movement is unstoppable, and for every one of us that is struck down, many more will rise and follow. This is what we have learned...and we shall not forget. This is the future of mankind.

"Thank you, my friends. I must go now, and have this bullet removed. May God bless you all."

He waved his good arm, upholding the bullet-scarred copies of the Constitution and Pocket Bible, and the crowd was mixed with cheers and tears as he was helped off the stage. Both women and men wept, venting the emotions of the moment.

"Well that's something you don't see every day," Bigelow said half-amused, half-shocked.

"Surely, God protects this man," Jesus whispered.

"Then why did he let him get shot and blown up?" Matt said innocently. "I'll bet he never goes there to give a speech again."

Pilar sighed, and carefully carried her glass of wine up the spiral staircase to the observation deck, as Matt watched her go. Jesus cleared his throat, and when Matt looked over at him, he signaled with his eyes that Matt should follow Pilar, and he did.

Bigelow and Jesus watched Matt leave, and then shared a smile, both remembering being young and in love.

On the observation deck, Matt found Pilar sitting in the shade of a tree staring southward. At first, she pretended not to notice him, as he sat down in silence beside her on the bench seat beneath the tree.

"Tomorrow at this time, I will be two thousand miles that way," she said, pointing southwest. She turned toward Matt and leaned into his discomfort zone, watching him carefully. She saw him stiffen, and watched his mouth draw tight with anxiety. "Will you miss me?" she asked almost whimsically.

Matt reached forward and combed her thick, luxurious black

hair through his fingers, studying it like a hairstylist. It was so rich and radiant, he thought, and yet she never treated it. He squeezed it between his fingers, admiring its texture for several long seconds, before letting it drop to her shoulder.

"What do you think?" he said, pulling Pilar slowly towards him, staring deeply into her inviting eyes. His head slowly drifted towards hers and they kissed softly at first, and then harder as he pushed into the full firmness of her lips.

Pilar felt his body tremble and gently pulled back.

"I think you will miss me more than you know, Matthew."

"Of course I'll miss you."

Pilar smiled in a way that he had not seen her smile before. He couldn't tell if it was confidence or disguised hatred, but it made him uneasy, and he didn't like it. Her eyes narrowed and she looked back at the horizon and turned cold.

"That will be your choice," she said into a sudden gust of wind. "As will what you choose to do about it."

With that she stood, and looked down at Matt. She touched his cheek with the palm of her hand and smiled warmly.

"Adios," she said, still smiling, and she turned and walked away.

Matt watched her go, savoring every step and sway of her walk, and he felt an ache in his chest like his heart was being squeezed in a vise. He wanted her badly, but it was no good, he thought. They were from different worlds, and he had his doctorate to finish, so what could he do? It was all wrong, and everything that had brought them together was gone. They were like a season that was suddenly over, and no amount of desire could hasten its return. So he let her go, and she never looked back.

****

Santo was tired, more tired than he had ever been. Crossing the Chihuahuan Desert had drained the last of his energy. He crawled the last few feet of his journey and came to rest crosswise across Sailor's grave, facing toward the cottage where Jesus and Pilar were sleeping just a few hundred feet beyond.

Sailor had made a will, leaving his house and land to Jesus as soon as he became of a responsible age to manage it on his own. Until then, Santiago had promised to help with the care, which he had done faithfully until Jesus became able. Sailor had donated two gold candlesticks to the church, and he gave a small bag of silver, about two thousand dollars, to Santiago, to help pay for raising Jesus. All his other possessions, which were very few, he had left to Jesus.

Sailor had requested that he be buried on his own land, overlooking the cliff north of the cottage and facing eastward towards Spain. This had been done, and in the intervening years Jesus had adorned the grave with a nautical cross headstone whose bottom was shaped like a two-barbed anchor and whose top was a Spanish cross with three leaved curves at the end of each cross arm and its head.

In later years, Jesus planted hedges that encircled the site, and flowers that were all irrigated in a fashion similar to the vegetable garden. A trellised walkway covered by roses lead to a bench seat near the grave where Jesus spent many hours reading and studying next to his old friend. Several decades after Sailor passed, the site grew to include the graves of Jesus' son Miguel, and Miguel's wife, and in those years Jesus spent many nights bathed in tears at their graveside praying. But in time, visiting their graves became a source of consolation and connection, and Jesus often began and ended his day at the clifftop garden visiting his removed family.

Santo looked south past the cottage and saw the familiar twinkle of village lights coming on from further down the mountain as early-risers prepared for their day. New sage was glowing faintly in the darkness like the red glow of dawn that was growing on his left. He closed his eyes and slept as he waited for the dawn.

****

"You barely touched your food." Jesus gently scolded Pilar as he cleared the breakfast plates. "I guess you miss the excitement of university life, no?"

Pilar seemed to not hear him.

"Pilar?"

She looked up and smiled weakly.

"When your wife left you, did it hurt for very long?"

"It didn't hurt at all. She wasn't happy here, and craved the excitement of the city. And I was a bad husband, often away on trips, or when at home, always working in the garden. We were not right for each other, and I felt a sense of relief that she had the courage to chase her dreams. It was better for both of us."

"Did you ever see her again?"

Jesus placed the last of the dishes in the sink and ran some water over them before answering.

"No. I heard she went to California and remarried."

Jesus bent down and kissed Pilar on top her head.

"You are missing Matthew."

"I am good," Pilar said with a sigh.

"I had an old friend who once told me…'Whatever is for you,

will never miss you.' He was very old, and wise, and I believe he was correct."

"But how can you tell what is really for you?"

"You'll know. If it passes you by, then it wasn't for you."

"Well...no one can argue that!"

Jesus laughed.

"I know."

He put a cinnamon stick in a cup, poured hot black coffee over it, and savored the smell before taking a sip.

"I will be in the cliff garden if you need me," Jesus said, as he tucked a book under his arm holding the coffee and opened the kitchen door with the other.

Pilar watched him walk slowly toward the garden and laughed.

"Of course!" she said aloud to herself. "That could apply to anything! If it misses you, then it wasn't for you."

Jesus stopped first at his son's grave and said some Hail Marys, before turning back up the path toward the bench near Sailor. At first glance, he thought an old rug had blown on top Sailor's grave, for it was covered with dirt and looked very decrepit. His heart stopped, and then pounded hard as a jackhammer, almost jumping right out of his chest when he recognized the lifeless form lying in front of him.

He bent down to Santo and immediately felt the warmth from his body as he touched his head and ears.

"Come quickly, I need you," Jesus said into his phone, as he paged Santiago. "It's Santo! I'm at the cliff garden."

Jesus ran and got the ladle from the garden fountain and dipped some fresh water. He wet Santo's nose and washed the crusted dirt from around his eyes, while speaking gently to him.

"Oh, you are such a good boy, such a brave dog. You have come back to us."

Some minutes later, Pilar saw Father Santiago rush past the kitchen window just as she was finishing the breakfast dishes. The look on his face, as well as his pace, told her something was wrong, and she dried her hands and ran after him.

"It's Santo," he said as she reached him, and she ran on ahead to where Jesus was bending over Sailor's grave.

Pilar saw the shriveled, dusty body of a dog being administered water by hand from Jesus. Except for the shape of the ears and head, Santo was unrecognizable as his former self. He was not only starved and dehydrated, but he looked very aged. His once beautiful blue eyes that sparkled with light were now half-open slits with milky, clouded lenses. His fur was shaggy with many longer strands that extended beyond the shorter coat like so many porcupine quills. He looked like a partially mummified wild dog of great age.

Pilar burst into tears at the sight of him and bent down and kissed his head.

"My poor, Santo," she cried.

Santiago arrived, and immediately made the sign of the cross and began praying.

Pilar talked soothingly to Santo and scratched him behind his ears, the way he always liked it so much, and he wagged his tale feebly in response. He knew he was home with those who loved him. He closed his eyes and drifted into sleep.

"Santo!" Sailor's voice woke him, and he was suddenly alert and not tired. "Come on, boy, you have done well."

Sailor was young and smiling, and with him were a beautiful woman and a man he had seen so very long ago, before he had even met Sailor. They smiled at him and Sailor hugged him and they walked out past the cliff edge across the canyon, which disappeared beneath them in clouds. Santo looked back and saw his former family huddled around Sailor's grave. They were crying, and he barked to let them know he was okay.

Pilar shrieked and jumped back as what appeared to be a luminous mist arose from Santo. Jesus hugged her and Santiago stopped praying as the three of them watched the glowing mist float out over the cliff edge, where it seemed to hover momentarily.

"Grandfather," sighed Pilar.

"I see, Nieta."

In the mist, shimmering like a mirage in heat waves, were three figures and a dog. They were small, as if far away, and yet the mist was only a dozen feet beyond the cliff edge. One man looked at Jesus and waved as he petted the dog, which seemed happy to see him and was jumping up on him. Without thinking, Jesus waved back, and the figures shrank rapidly in size as the mist moved out and up over the canyon, and quickly disappeared in the sky into nothingness.

"Christ is love," whispered Santiago.

Jesus turned towards Santiago. Tears streaked his face and he smiled and laughed and patted Santiago on the back.

"Yes!" Jesus said through laughter. "Yes. Did you see, Pilar? Did you see Sailor wave to me?"

"Yes, Grandfather. Was it Sailor?"

"Yes, I am sure of it."

"What? You say you saw Sailor?" asked Santiago. "I saw the Virgin of Guadalupe. She smiled at me as clear as day, so beautiful, a vision of goodness, and such kind eyes."

"I couldn't see detail," said Pilar, "but I definitely saw a man wave and he was with a dog that looked like Santo, and another man was behind them with a woman. I couldn't make out their faces."

Pilar laughed nervously, still not believing what had just happened. Jesus hugged her to him, and put his other arm around Santiago and pulled him close.

"I think that we witnessed a miracle, and I hope we can agree what to do next," Jesus whispered.

It was agreed to never recount the tale of what happened there, to never tell that Santo had made a two thousand mile journey across a continent to come home. It was best if people still believed him alive and wandering somewhere amongst them. They carefully washed and dried Santo's body, gently wrapped him in a clean white sheet, and buried him atop Sailor where he had finally come to rest.

Jesus and Santiago dug the grave while Pilar kept watch against stray visitors from the village who might wander into the garden before they were finished their task. The hedges shielded them, but no one ventured closer than a quarter mile while they were there.

Jesus paused digging and wiped his brow.

"Near fifty years since we buried Sailor here."

"Yes," huffed Santiago, still digging. "You saw him today?"

"He was young," Jesus said, starting to dig again. "Life is very short."

"Not for him. Not for Santo," mused Santiago.

"Why did Santo die? You think maybe the desert?"

"Perhaps. But I think more than anything, he had fulfilled his mission, and it was his time. His slow miracle continued to flower the world with the love of Christ for many centuries, and came to its fullest bloom just when the world needed it most."

Jesus stopped digging again and looked up at Pilar, who was watching vigilantly the road to the village, and he smiled.

"Yes. Now he will help people remember."

"This is what we must pray," said Santiago. He stopped digging and surveyed the hole. "This is deep enough, let us put his body to rest."

They climbed out of the hole and gently lowered the sheet holding Santo, whereupon they filled in the grave. Then they spread some shovels of dry dirt on top and transplanted a few clumps of grass taken from elsewhere to camouflage their efforts. Completed, the three stood in silence for several minutes, before Pilar finally spoke.

"Nothing will ever be the same again."

Jesus hugged her to his side and kissed the top of her head.

"We have all been blessed greatly," said Jesus. "Perhaps I more than anyone, for I was reborn."

"I was not without sin either," said Santiago, "but I feel I have been forgiven. I saw it, in the Virgin's eyes."

They said a final prayer and started back down the path to the cottage with Pilar in the center, arm-in-arm with Jesus and Santiago.

****

The summer was almost over, and Matt had barely seen the outdoors. The last three months had been spent compiling and organizing the wealth of data from the Santo Project with almost no time taken for rest. He had become a permanent houseguest of Bigelow, who, good to his word, was in Mexico helping Jesus and

Santiago get the new school and hospital started in Pueblo del Cielo. Bigelow called frequently just to see how things were going, and he never failed to mention some small tidbit about Pilar, which always left Matt feeling empty and frustrated. But the last few times Big had called, he never mentioned Pilar at all, and Matt found that far worse than when he spoke of her. He wondered if she thought about him, or if she had already met another.

The telescope of distance narrows one's field of view, and allows close inspection of detail unnoticed in the original moment.

Thus it was, that Matt found himself a few days later nearing the mountain pass that lead to Pilar's home. The sun was near the horizon on the far side of the mountain, making it already much darker and foreboding on the lee side of the light. Matt's thoughts tilted negative and fears of rejection and loss started to seep into his mind.

A sharp rock found a weak spot in the front right tire and it blew. Matt veered off the road and parked just short of the pass between two boulders. He got out, inspected the damage, and opened the trunk, only to find that the jack base was missing. Up ahead, the sun was reflecting off the rocks at the top of the pass. He locked the car and started walking toward the light.

****

Bigelow, Santiago, and Jesus cheered with delight as Aunt Maria set a pitcher of iced lemonade down in front of them on the front porch of the cottage. It had become a fast-forming tradition to gather on the porch after dinner, where they had a strategic view of the new buildings rising at the edge of the village, and to chat about the progress of the workday.

Pilar was slowly rocking on the porch swing, when she spotted someone walking down the north road from the pass. It was strange to see anyone on foot coming from that direction, since there was nothing beyond the pass for many miles, and most travelers used the southern approach to the village. She mindlessly watched the figure grow larger as it approached at a fast pace. It became obvious that it was a man, and at one point he bent down and picked a bouquet of blue sage, which told her immediately that he was not a local since it bloomed everywhere locally in abundance.

Suddenly, Pilar's heart started pounding as she recognized something familiar in the stranger's gait. She jumped from the swing and ran past the front gate and up the north road.

Aunt Maria dried her hands on her apron as she called out after her.

"Pilar?"

The conversation on the porch ceased as all watched Pilar streak up the road, graceful, even at a run.

Matt smiled broadly as he saw Pilar running towards him. He held out his bouquet of blue and purple sage but she pushed right past it and into his arms. They hugged for a moment and she pulled back and smiled at him.

"You were right," Matt said. "I missed you more than I thought."

"Matthew," she sighed, and Matt pulled her towards him, kissed her gently, and then hugged her tightly.

"I don't want to lose you."

"You will not," said Pilar, tears of happiness flooding her eyes. "Not unless you choose to."

"Not likely," returned Matt, his heart pounding against hers.

Bigelow patted Jesus on the back as they watched the scene.

"I wonder if he's Catholic."

"Of course," said Jesus. "I asked him long ago."

Bigelow laughed heartily and was joined by Jesus and Santiago, while Aunt Maria dried her eyes with her apron.

****

Over a thousand miles to the northeast, a blonde, curly-haired little girl was visiting her grandfather on the edge of the Blackland Prairie in Alabama.

"Oh, this one here is so pretty, Grandpa. It has blue eyes!" The little girl held the young dog up as she inspected it, then hugged it, and laughed as he licked her.

"Yup. Sure enough, he does," said her grandfather as he lit his pipe. I can see well enough now to tell that."

"And he smells good, too," laughed the girl.

"Near as I can figure, he gets that from his daddy. Smells sweet as candy. Only one from the whole litter like that. Reckoned I'd keep him for myself, but he's a finicky eater, so y'all take him if ya see fit. Belle won't mind, now that they're old enough to be on their own. You can bring him back to visit her every time ya visit me."

"Oh, thank you, Grandpa."

She hugged the dog close again.

"I'm going to love you forever!"

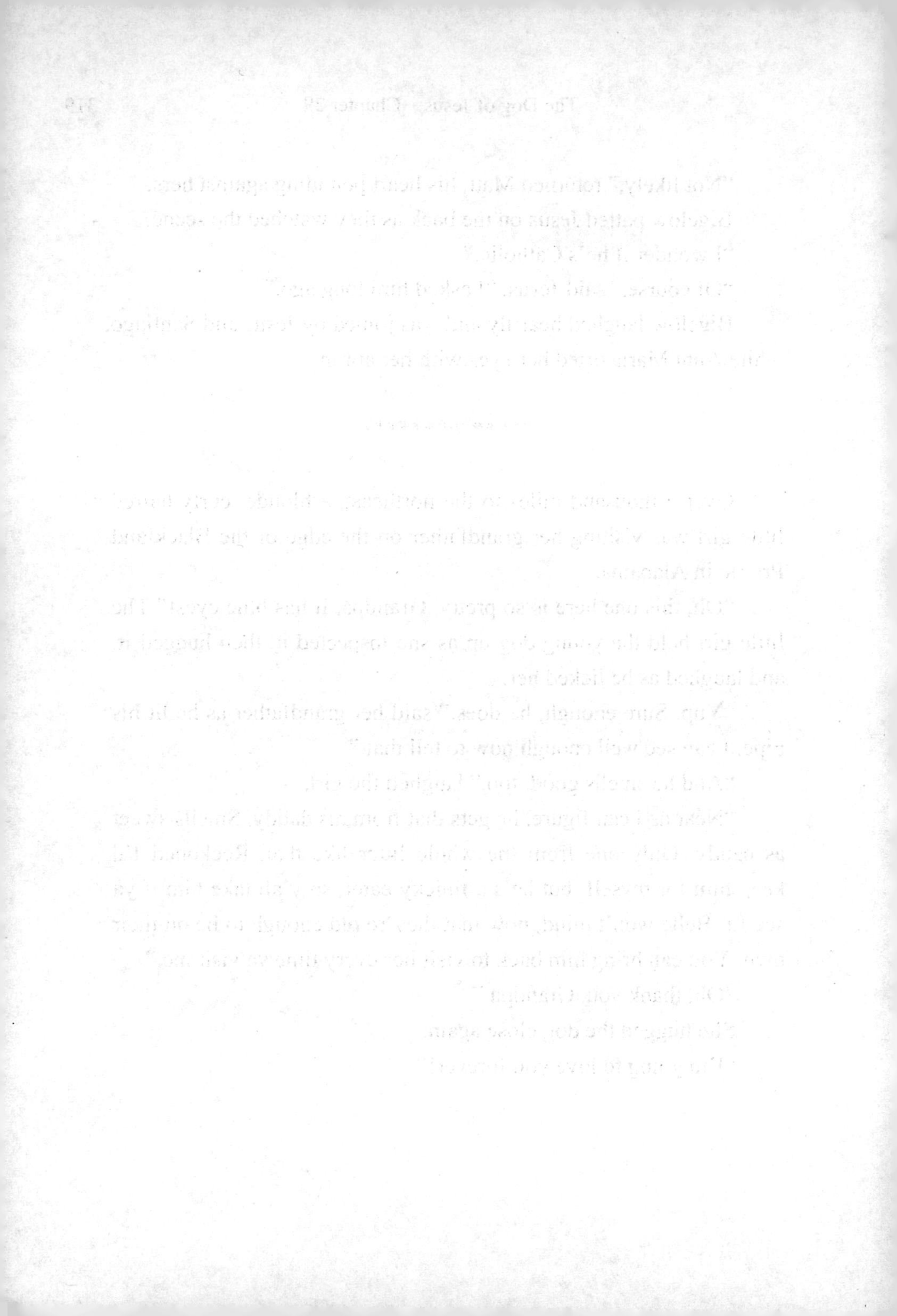

Afterword

This book was an accident. I was speaking with my son some years ago about how Hollywood screenwriters often smash loglines of popular movies together in an attempt to get new ideas. A logline, for those who don't know, is just a one-sentence synopsis of a movie. The process is to take any two hit movies and combine their loglines, (called smashing loglines together by screenwriters) to come up with a new hit movie idea. I explained that the same process could be done with movie titles or novels, and since I was writing novels, I chose two random hit book titles that were out at the time and smashed them together as an example.

"Suppose," I said, "you take 'The Da Vinci Code' and combine it with 'Marley and Me', what would you get? A book about Jesus and a dog…'*The Dog of Jesus.'* The title moved me. "Hey," I said, "that sounds really interesting. What would it be about?"

That was the inspiration for the title, but only God knows how the story actually formed in my head. The premise of an immortal dog with healing powers came first, and that was a story I wanted to think about. An old friend and mentor (who helped talk me out of pursuing screenwriting) John Hill, once explained succinctly to me that a story is a person with a problem. Owning an immortal dog with healing powers would present some very big problems. That was the accidental beginning of the story. Many of the details are based on actual facts, including the travels of Saint James, Gurwitsch radiation, bacteriaphages, the immortality of unicellular creatures, and the references to the "Three-One God" in ancient

Thracian texts.

The character Pilar was inspired by a photo I saw of a little girl with her Afghan dog.

While I was writing this story, I learned of a man named Jesus in Spain, whose wife was "snatched away" by the bombers in Madrid. His story moved me to tears, and I referenced the Madrid bombers as a tribute to the memory of his wife, who coincidentally, just happened to be named Pilar. The story of those many innocent lives stolen from the world by terrorists in the name of their god sickened me and inspired me to see a vision beyond their evil deeds.

Finally, the political aspects of this story were not planned. Our future is thrust upon us, and as individuals, we can only do the best we can to build a better world. I would like to thank my wife, for her constant belief in this story, and for her assistance in bringing this manuscript to completion and final publication.

Michael P. Sakowski
Baltimore, June 2012

A Few Notes about Carolina Dogs

The Carolina Dog, unlike most dogs, is a true primitive dog, and has existed independently in America for many thousands of years. Some theorize that they crossed the land bridge with Asians about 8,000 years ago, but those theories could be wrong, upended by new artifacts found in America that date men as being here 200,000 years ago. In fact, dog relatives predate man by many millions of years and Hesperocyon, a prehistoric canine, lived in North America 40 million years ago, long before man ever walked the earth (so far as we know). Therefore, dogs are our seniors in evolution, and we are relative babies next to them. Present theories date early man's ancestors, (Homo habilis), back a mere 2.3 million years.

The primitive dog evolved to perfection in its environment and was a smart social animal. Perhaps that social nature is why there seems to be a natural affinity between our two species. It is interesting to wonder how a bond of love and affection between men and dogs develops, but the loyalty of many dogs is unswerving, and some dogs would willingly sacrifice their own lives in defense of their owners. How can science measure such unselfish love and affection? It cannot, and such love between dogs and men makes it easy to understand how dogs were bestowed with the title of "man's best friend." How many of us are so lucky as to have a best human friend that we can trust as much as a dog?

It is an interesting fact that dogs left to breed unfettered as mongrels, soon return to the same general characteristics, and those are like the ancient Pariah, the Dingo, the Singing Dogs of New Zealand, the African Basenji, and here in the United States, our own native Carolina Dogs.

About the Author

Michael P. Sakowski, with complete candor, admits to being a very strange man, even down to his vegan diet of nearly thirty years duration. His temperance and avoidance of alcohol, (although he can consume great quantities if called upon to do so), his absence of vices, such as drugs, smoking, and chasing women, and the ascetic lifestyle of a monk that he led for over twenty-five years of his adult life, lend testimony to his claim that he was always a misfit in society.

He was thrown out of high school twice in his senior year just before graduation for having missed over sixty days, and he finally graduated third from the bottom, in a graduating class of 258. He then attended college for two years and received no credits, before reversing himself, taking an overload of twenty-three credits in one semester, and making the Dean's List while carrying that course load. He completed an associate degree program at a local community college (since it was the only place that would accept him with his dismal high school record), and then transferred to the University of Maryland where he took a dual degree program in physics and electrical engineering.

After leaving university, he started an electronics sales and service business which grew to a maximum of seventeen employees before going bankrupt. He spent two tumultuous years trading stocks, and later was employed as an electronics engineer, before starting a successful industrial electronics service company which he still owns today.

His first novel, “The Enterprise Zone,” was adapted as a screenplay, which achieved international recognition in The Chesterfield Writer’s Project, but his foray into screen-writing lasted only several years before he returned to writing novels.

The author feels his Taiwanese wife of the last six years, greatly broadened his world view, both through their shared travels in Asia, and his exposure to other cultures. Her selflessness and devotion to helping others might have been the inspiration for his more recent participation in several local community organizations that helped grow his thinking and social awareness. Before marrying Yinglee, he relates, “he was the maverick of all mavericks, a stubborn, hard-headed, individual who had existed outside the bubble of mainstream society for most of his life.”

The “Dog of Jesus” took eight years to finish, and was shaped by world events. It might have remained uncollected from the ether, if not for the inspiration and constant prodding of the author’s wife.